A CATERED
FOURTH OF JULY

Center Point
Large Print

Also by Isis Crawford and available from
Center Point Large Print:

A Catered St. Patrick's Day
A Catered Christmas Cookie Exchange

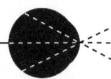

**This Large Print Book carries the
Seal of Approval of N.A.V.H.**

A CATERED FOURTH OF JULY

A Mystery with Recipes

Isis Crawford

CENTER POINT LARGE PRINT
THORNDIKE, MAINE

This Center Point Large Print edition
is published in the year 2014 by arrangement with
Kensington Publishing Corp.

The text of this Large Print edition is unabridged.
In other aspects, this book may vary
from the original edition.
Printed in the United States of America
on permanent paper.
Set in 16-point Times New Roman type.

ISBN: 978-1-62899-182-6

Library of Congress Cataloging-in-Publication Data

Crawford, Isis.
A Catered Fourth of July : a mystery with recipes / Isis Crawford. —
Center Point Large Print edition.
  pages ; cm
 Summary: "When a notorious playboy is killed during a Revolutionary
War battle reenactment, catering sisters Bernie and Libby have their
plates overloaded with suspects"—Provided by publisher.
 ISBN 978-1-62899-182-6 (library binding : alk. paper)
 1. Simmons, Bernie (Fictitious character : Crawford)—Fiction.
   2. Simmons, Libby (Fictitious character)—Fiction.
   3. Caterers and catering—Fiction.
   4. Historical reenactments—Fiction.
   5. Murder—Investigation—Fiction. 6. Large type books. I. Title.
PS3603.R396C367 2014
813′.54—dc23

                                                    2014018941

To my family, who makes it all worthwhile.

Acknowledgments

I'd like to thank Lexie Baker, Amber Lough, and Mike Ruffo for their help and encouragement.

A CATERED
FOURTH OF JULY

Prologue

The person looked at the musket and smiled. It was going to be easy . . . as easy as apple pie, to coin a metaphor. Of course, since it was the Fourth of July the saying should be as easy as blueberry pie. Who knew it was going to be so simple?

Vengeance is mine saith the Lord. Or something like that. But not in this case. In this case, it's mine.

It was ridiculous to assume that God had time to deal with such nonsense. But the person had time . . . lots of time.

The truth was that Devlin definitely had it coming.

The man sowed discord wherever he went. He was a cancer in the community and cancers had to be burned or cut out before they spread, otherwise the whole body was in danger. Everyone knew that. The person was doing the community a favor.

The person put a handful of powder in the musket, rammed it down with a rod, then put a generous amount of shot in and repeated the process twice more just to be on the safe side. Doctoring an old-fashioned musket, or flintlock as it used to be called, was easy to do. A modern weapon would not have lent itself to similar treatment. The person would have had to have found an alternative method to accomplish the goal.

As the last bit of shot was put in the barrel, the person wondered whether to feel a tiny bit of remorse . . . or not. After a moment, the decision was made not to. After all, the person had tried to show Jack Devlin the error of his ways by making suggestions, albeit subtle ones to be sure. If Jack Devlin's heart had been open he would have seen the light instead of wallowing in his fleshpots. But he had laughed at the suggestions. Laughed! Well, Jack Devlin wouldn't be laughing soon. No indeedy.

He should have listened. He should have paid attention. Heaven only knows the person had attempted to educate him about the dangers of what he was doing. There comes a point in anyone's attempts at betterment when trying simply doesn't work anymore. Especially if being laughed at.

The person didn't impose beliefs on others and was satisfied the best had been done. Everyone had their own choices to make and Jack Devlin had made his. Karma really was a bitch.

Jack Devlin. He represented everything that was unclean. Unsavory. He was a home wrecker. He ruined people's lives. He didn't care what he did and to whom he did it. He thought he was above punishment and that he could charm his way out of any and every situation.

But that was not so. Jack Devlin was about to learn his lesson and it was going to be an expensive one. For him. The most expensive kind there was.

The person bent down, took a handful of dirt, and jammed it down the barrel of the musket for added insurance. When Devlin pulled the trigger the musket was going to blow up in his face.

The person sat back and contemplated the work completed, feeling quite pleased. The spectacle of the reenactment should be quite entertaining, not to mention edifying.

Chapter 1

It was July fourth, twelve noon, and ninety-nine degrees in the shade at Highland Park in Longely. Bernie Simmons was wishing she was in the Arctic. Or the Antarctic. Or anyplace cold. Twenty straight days over ninety degrees was a little much even for a sun lover like herself.

If she had wanted to live in Dallas she would have moved there instead of living in Westchester. Never mind that she was wearing the coolest dress she owned—a pink voile sundress with spaghetti straps she'd gotten on sale at Barney's—that she was downing bottles of water as if she was in the Sahara, or that all she had to do was set up the picnic she and her sister were catering in the gazebo.

Even with all that, she was still sweating like a pig, though that expression was a misnomer. "Pigs don't sweat," she reminded herself as she looked at Hilda. That was the reason they were susceptible to heat stroke. Maybe it was good to sweat. In fact, she knew it was good to sweat. It was her body's way of cooling itself off. So what if it was? Why couldn't her body find a better way to cool itself down? Seriously. Her hair frizzed up. Her makeup ran. She looked like a mess. Of course, in Victorian times women never sweated. They glowed. Well, she was sure glowing.

It could be worse, Bernie told herself as she fixed her ponytail.

She and Libby could be slaving over a hot grill.

But then, it was axiomatic that things could always be worse.

All she could do was thank God she and her sister had settled on a room temperature buffet instead of the usual hamburger and hot dog Fourth of July bacchanal. Bernie told herself to think positively. It didn't help. Every time she moved, she felt rivulets of sweat running down her back.

At least she hadn't put on any mascara. Thank God for that. Waterproof or not, it would be streaking down her cheeks, which was not the kind of look you wanted in the person who was serving your food. All she wanted to do was get back to her air-conditioned flat and take a nice, long, cold shower, but that wasn't going to happen; at least not until four o'clock, it wasn't. Thanks to her big sister and her promises, she and Libby were stuck there until the reenactment was over.

Ah, the reenactment. What was it her mother used to say? Something along the lines of "no good deed goes unpunished."

Bernie looked at the banner proclaiming REENACTMENT OF THE BATTLE OF MEADOW CREEK tied between two oak trees and sighed. It wouldn't be so bad if it weren't so hot. Or if there was a breeze. Or if they were getting paid. *Especially that.* But they weren't and there wasn't. Not even a breath of air. Bernie felt as if she was in a sauna and she hated saunas. She just hoped that Hilda didn't die of heat stroke.

"It's okay, Hilda," Bernie reassured her, patting the pig's head. Her bristles tickled Bernie's palm.

Hilda didn't lift her snout.

Bernie figured it took too much effort. One thing was for sure, she definitely knew how Hilda felt.

"At least we're not out there." Bernie gestured toward the meadow where eight unfortunate residents of Longely were getting ready to recreate the Revolutionary War Battle of Meadow Creek.

Actually, the incident, as Rick Evans had taken to calling it, had taken place in a bar called The Pitcher, and it hadn't really been a battle. It was more like a drunken brawl. A brawl that had involved five British soldiers, fifteen Longely townsmen, a large, cranky pig—hence Hilda, who was really a mini potbellied pig, but nothing is ever perfect—and several growlers of beer, the ownership of which had come under dispute.

Bernie wasn't sure about the pig's role in the proceedings and she strongly suspected that Rick Evans wasn't clear about it, either.

She also strongly suspected that the newly elected Longely councilman and the person responsible for the event, didn't really care. Like most politicians he never let facts hinder him . . . especially if they stood in the way of what he wanted to accomplish. He was a say-it-and-they-will-believe-it kind of guy. He was on record as saying that Longely needed to stop being a sleepy bedroom community and become a tourist destination on the Hudson River trail.

Why anyone would want to put Longely on the tourist map was lost on Bernie. She liked the town just the way it was, thank-you-very-much. Even though it would be good for her business, she didn't want to see the quaintness factor upped. The thought of bunches of day-trippers traipsing through the town, taking up her customers' parking spaces didn't exactly thrill her. She turned her gaze on a group of nine women standing near the rose garden.

The Deitrich Rose Garden was up on a hill enclosed by old weeping willows, making it a little difficult to see what was going on. Not that anything much ever was. Usually it was just the odd wedding or members of the rose society watering and weeding. Bernie blinked a bead of sweat out of her right eye and took a closer look.

Was that Juno Grisham, Whitney Peters, and Holly Roget up there? Were those wings they were wearing? Wings with glitter? Not that the glitter really mattered. After all, if you were going to wear wings, what was a little glitter?

Bernie squinted. It certainly looked that way. Or maybe the heat was making her hallucinate. Wasn't that the first sign of heat stroke? Then she remembered she'd seen a notice tacked to the library bulletin board inviting Wiccans from the three towns to gather at the Deitrich Rose Garden at eleven o'clock on July fourth to invoke a blessing and help with a manifestation, whatever that was.

So Holly, Juno, and Whitney were New Age witches. Who woulda thunk? Bernie laughed at the thought. Longely was not a hippie-dippy, New-Agey kind of place. If anything, it erred on the conservative side of the ledger.

Maybe not anymore. It would seem that things

were just getting weirder and weirder in Longely. In a quiet, well-bred kind of way, of course. Pigs. Reenactments. Wicca. Her dad blamed the Internet, but she blamed the heat. Heat did strange things to people. She took some ice out of the ice chest the container of deviled eggs was sitting in and put the cubes on the floor for Hilda to eat. She didn't know if pigs were supposed to eat ice or not, but she figured it couldn't hurt on a day like this.

"At least there's some shade in the gazebo," Bernie told Hilda.

Hilda snuffled and oinked and chewed on the cubes. They seemed to be perking her up. Bernie was just about to offer her an apple when Rick Evans came running up. His face was bright red, which went nicely with the redcoat uniform he was wearing. Beads of sweat ran down his chin.

"Have you seen Marvin?" Rick sounded out of breath. "I've been looking all over for him."

Marvin was Libby's boyfriend and the reason they'd gotten involved in the little drama in the first place. Well, one of the reasons. As a small business owner, Bernie had found over the years that it was wise to be on good terms with the powers that be. Unfortunately Rick Evans was one of those.

"I think he's over by the tennis courts."

Rick frowned. "Doing what?"

Bernie explained. "Libby is helping him into

his costume. The coat is a little snug." *A little* being a massive understatement.

"He should have taken care of that before." Rick tapped his watch with a well-manicured fingernail. "We're supposed to start at twelve. It's five after. Everyone is waiting for him. No one knows what's going on. I should never have put him in charge."

Bernie was inclined to agree. Managing group activities was not Marvin's strong point. On the other hand, the surrounding hillside wasn't exactly dotted with people waiting with breathless anticipation for the reenactment to begin. There was a handful at most, which was unusual. Normally, the park was crowded with couples and families and dog walkers. Aside from the Wiccans and the people there for the reenactment, it was empty. She figured it must be the heat that was keeping everyone away.

Even her father had begged off, preferring the air-conditioned comfort of their flat above their store, A Little Taste of Heaven. She and Libby had made enough food for seventy-five people. So far, she'd counted twenty spectators. With the reenactors, that brought the total up to twenty-eight. Thirty-seven if one counted the Wiccans. Hopefully more people would show up. If they didn't, there sure were going to be lots of leftovers. Chicken salad was definitely going to be featured on tomorrow's menu.

"Maybe you should give people more time to get here," she suggested to Rick.

"Twelve o'clock is twelve o'clock," Rick grumped. "You'd think people would have more town spirit."

"Well, it *is* almost one hundred degrees," Bernie pointed out.

Rick didn't answer. He was too busy looking at the fairy circle up on the hill.

"Oh my God," he cried, pointing. "Are those who I think they are?"

Bernie fanned herself with her hand. "Yup. They sure are."

"What in heaven's name are they doing?"

"Some kind of Wiccan ritual." Rick wrinkled his nose. "Wiccan?"

"As in white witches."

"You're kidding me."

"Nope. I think they've been watching too much HBO." Bernie smiled. "Hey, I have an idea. If this doesn't work out, maybe next year we can stage the Salem Witch trials."

Rick glared at her. "Very funny. There was never anything like that here."

"Well strictly speaking, there was never a Revolutionary War battle in this park, either," Bernie said sweetly. "Let's face it. Witches are sexier. Maybe we'll get a bigger turnout."

Rick's face got redder, if that was possible. He pointed to Hilda who had half hidden herself behind the coolers holding the food. "What's she doing here?" he demanded, abruptly changing the subject and going on the offensive.

Bernie thought he looked like a plum tomato on the point of bursting. "Sitting in the coolest spot she can find, I would imagine."

"She shouldn't be here," Rick protested. "It's a health hazard."

"You've heard of a pig in a poke? This is a pig in a gazebo."

Rick folded his arms across his chest. His double chin wobbled. "She shouldn't be here," he repeated. "The Health Department would not approve."

Bernie spotted two half-moons of perspiration under his arms. "The food isn't out yet. Anyway, they won't know unless someone tells them."

Rick's voice rose. "And what if someone does?"

"I'll deny the whole thing."

Rick pointed to himself. "What if they come to me and ask? As an elected official, what am I supposed to do?"

"That's easy. Do what elected officials always do. Lie."

Rick clenched his fists. His eyes looked as if they were going to pop.

Bernie decided he actually resembled one of those fancy goldfish. "You do realize that Hilda could die if she's out in the sun for any length of time." She pointed to the meadow. "Not to mention get a sunburn."

"Pigs don't get sunburned."

"Do you know that for sure?" she demanded. When Rick didn't answer, she said, "Just as I thought."

"And you know this how?"

"Because I read it in a magazine," she lied.

"Which one?" Rick challenged.

"*Farmer's Way*. It was in the doctor's office," she added by way of explanation before he could ask. "Somehow I don't think you'd like to be known as The Man Who Caused The Pig To Get Sunburned."

Rick opened his mouth. Nothing came out. For a few seconds, he was rendered speechless. He finally growled, "Have it your way."

"Thanks. I usually do." *Except for today.*

Things weren't going her way at all. First, she hadn't been able to peel the hard-boiled eggs for the deviled eggs she and Libby were making because the eggs were too fresh. Then the watermelon for the feta and watermelon salad had been mushy and tasteless, so they'd run out to get another one. And last, Libby had burned the bottoms of half the batch of fried chicken she'd been making, forcing her to do it all over again. They couldn't find one of the coolers they'd needed to pack the food in, and as if that wasn't enough, Bernie was stuck in the park for the rest of the afternoon when she should be back at the shop making pies.

"If I see Marvin, I'll tell him you've been asking after him," Bernie told Rick.

"You do that," he said stiffly. Then he turned around and marched off.

As Bernie watched him go, she decided that like skinny jeans, breeches did not do men any favors, especially men who were fifty pounds overweight. Of course, they weren't so great on women, either.

As soon as Rick left, Hilda came out from behind the coolers and poked Bernie's leg with her snout. She gave Hilda the apple she'd been holding and started opening the cartons she and Libby had packed their supplies in.

Chapter 2

Bernie had just finished opening up all the cartons when Libby trudged up the steps. She decided her sister looked like a limp dishrag, to use one of her mother's expressions.

The outfit Libby was wearing didn't help matters. Bernie loved her sister but the truth of the matter was that Libby was sartorially challenged. Bernie had offered to lend her one of her light, silk sundresses, but Libby had insisted on wearing her kelly green polo shirt and green plaid Bermuda shorts. Those were both hot and made her look like a marcher in the Saint Patrick's Day parade. But try telling that to her older sister. Actually, Bernie had tried telling her several times, and her sister had told her to mind her own business. Bernie was just thinking that as a color, kelly green had absolutely nothing to recommend it when her sister started speaking.

"The jacket is so tight, Marvin can't even lift his arms up." Libby grabbed a bottle of water and began chugging it down.

"Must make it hard to aim a musket," Bernie observed.

"Poor guy. He's just miserable."

"So am I," Bernie said, not wanting to be left out of the pity party. After all, fair was fair.

"Yeah, but Marvin is going to be out there marching around in the heat shooting people. At least, we're in here where it's marginally cooler."

"*Marginally* being the operative word," Bernie told her as a bugle sounded.

"It looks as if we're about to begin soon," Libby observed.

Bernie put her hand to her breast. "Be still my heart."

"There's no need to be sarcastic."

"I'm not," Bernie protested. "I'm genuinely thrilled. The sooner we start, the sooner we can go home."

Libby was just about to reply when Jack Devlin,

Longely's modern day answer to Casanova, came bounding up the steps into the gazebo.

"Ladies"—he bowed low at the waist—"always a pleasure." He grabbed Hilda and tucked her under his arm. "Come my little chickadee," he cooed in Hilda's ear, "it is time for your performance."

Hilda oinked and stopped squirming.

"We are old friends," Devlin explained.

Bernie swore Hilda was batting her eyelashes at him.

"Don't worry," he told Bernie and Libby as he scratched Hilda's back. "I will bring her back unharmed. I treat all my ladies well." He winked in case they didn't get it.

"So I heard," Bernie replied.

He grinned. "I'll be happy to demonstrate anytime. Anytime, anyplace," he said over his shoulder as he went back down the stairs. "That offer goes for both of you. You name the site and I'll be there. Reliable Jack, that's me."

"Not bad," Bernie mused as she looked at Jack Devlin's retreating behind.

Libby sniffed. "If you like that kind of person."

Bernie rolled her eyes. "And what kind of person is that?"

"A sex addict. He's only interested in one thing."

"That's what I like about him. But for the record, I was talking about his ass, which you have to admit is pretty nice."

"Brandon wouldn't like to hear you say that."

"He looks. I can too." Bernie clasped her hands over her head and stretched. "I mean, it's not as if I'm going to sleep with the guy."

Libby smiled. "God knows everyone else has."

Bernie brought her arms down and stretched out her calves. "Not everyone, just half the female population of Longely, including Juno."

"Why do you say that?" Libby asked.

"Devlin's comment about he and Hilda being old friends."

"So?"

"So Juno owns Hilda."

"She does?" Libby asked.

"Yup. All I'm saying is connect the dots."

Libby shook her head. "I just don't get Devlin's appeal. I mean he's good-looking, but not movie star good-looking."

"It's easy," Bernie replied. "He likes women and he's available. Maybe it's as simple as that. Young. Old. Rich. Poor. Fat. Thin. Married. Single. You can't say he isn't democratic."

Libby rubbed her bottle of water over her face to cool herself off then took another drink. "I'm surprised some enraged boyfriend or husband hasn't shot him yet."

"That's so nineteen hundreds. Anyway, if we were talking about that kind of stuff, my money would be on a discarded lover, the female being the deadlier of the species when it comes to

26

matters of the heart, in addition to having a longer memory." Bernie paused for a moment. "At least in my experience."

"True." Libby harked back to the homicide cases she and her sister had been involved in, not to mention her lingering homicidal thoughts concerning her old boyfriend, Orion.

Bernie laughed. "Good thing for Jack, he's pretty nimble. Not to mention energetic."

"He has to be. Otherwise he'd have died of exhaustion a long time ago." Libby pointed to the meadow where Longely's citizen reenactors were beginning to congregate. "They're starting."

Bernie brushed a strand of hair out of her face and repositioned her bobby pin. "I guess we'd better finish setting up. The ravening hordes will be here soon."

Libby scanned the area. "Certainly not a horde. Hardly even a group. And it's definitely too hot to raven anything. We should have served a shrub like I wanted to."

"Libby, no one knows what a shrub is."

"We could have written a sign and explained."

"That it's a drink made with vinegar?"

"As well as blueberries and sugar, and that the colonists used to drink it back in the day in the summer, and that it's supposed to be not only cooling but healthful."

"I don't think anyone would have touched it," Bernie said.

"Well, we won't know now, will we?"

"It certainly would have been a conversation piece," Bernie said, rethinking her stand.

"Exactly." Libby swatted away a mosquito. "Maybe we can do it next year."

"Hopefully there won't be a next year. Or at least if there is, we'll get paid."

Libby thought of their balance sheet. "I certainly wouldn't say no if the council offered." She paused for a moment then said, "Remind me. Why did we make so much food?"

Bernie answered promptly. "Easy. We were going on the head count Rick Evans gave us."

Libby surveyed the group of spectators one more time. "I would say he was a little optimistic."

"Just a tad. Not that I blame anyone for not coming. I mean, I wouldn't be here if I didn't have to. It's too hot. Would you?"

"Unfortunately, yes," Libby promptly replied.

"I mean if Marvin wasn't in it."

"Then no. Absolutely not."

"My point exactly." Bernie stifled a yawn. "I'm not sure that I would be here even if Brandon was."

"Harsh," Libby commented.

"No. Tough love. Although, it might be worth it to see him in breeches."

Both sisters stopped talking as they contemplated the spectacle that was taking place on the hill. Nine adult wing-wearing women were dancing around in a circle, twirling as they went.

"I don't think I could do that," Libby observed.

"The wing part?" Bernie asked.

"The twirling part."

"So you could do the wing part?" Bernie asked her sister.

"Ha-ha."

"How about if the wings were black?"

Libby grimaced. "Even if they were purple."

"You know, I didn't think Wiccans wore wings in their ceremonies. I thought they ran around naked in the forest under the full moon."

"Obviously, not these. Maybe they're inspired by Tinker Bell." Libby changed the subject. "Given the temperature, I think the deviled eggs should go on a bed of ice when we serve them."

"Definitely. Giving everyone food poisoning would not be a good thing," Bernie noted.

"Not if we want to stay in business."

The sisters spent the next fifteen minutes setting up the tables, putting tablecloths on them, and laying out the decorations and condiments. While they worked, the redcoats and the colonists began their skirmish. Three of the redcoats snatched growlers of beer away from the colonists. The colonists grabbed them back. Something, Bernie presumed it was water with caramel coloring, sloshed over the sides.

"You have no business doing this," one of the

colonists (vacuum cleaner salesman Tony Gerard) declaimed.

"I have every reason," Marvin replied.

"State it," another colonist (Samuel Cotton, a third grade teacher) demanded.

Marvin drew himself up to his full height and sucked in his stomach. "I do it by the authority the Crown invests in me."

"Thou shalt not trample on our liberties," Elise Montague, the only female colonist in the reenactment, proclaimed.

"Thou speakest treason," Marvin roared.

Libby smiled. "He's not bad."

"Not at all." Bernie watched a fourth colonist (Sanford Aiken, plumbing supply store owner), who was holding Hilda under his arm, tell Marvin to "bugger off."

Jack Devlin stepped up to Marvin's side. "For your misdeeds, we take the pig in the name of the Crown," Devlin pronounced.

"By God, you shall not," Aiken thundered.

"We shall, sir." Marvin tried to lift his arms up in a menacing gesture, but his jacket was so tight he couldn't.

"You did say the jacket was a tad snug," Bernie noted.

"I'm afraid we might have to cut him out of it," Libby replied as David Nancy, redcoat and industrial designer, stepped up and pretended to wrest the wriggling Hilda away from her owner.

"Give me that sow," Nancy ordered.

"I shall not, good sir," the putative owner replied.

The two men began circling each other while Marvin made suitably menacing noises. Libby clapped. Marvin stopped and took a small bow before reentering the action.

At that point, Aiken put Hilda on the ground. "Go. Seek safety."

Hilda sat down.

Aiken lifted up his arm and pointed to a willow tree twenty feet away. "Moveth."

Hilda lay down.

It was an impasse.

After a minute, Elise Montague lifted her up and put her under the tree Aiken had indicated.

"Thou art a traitor to the king," Marvin said once Hilda had left the area. "And thou shall be punished accordingly."

Libby clapped again and Marvin paused to take another bow.

"He's really enjoying this," Bernie said.

Libby shook her head. "Who would have thought he was such a ham?"

"It's comforting to know that if Marvin's father's business fails maybe Marvin can find an acting job. Not that it's going to," Bernie added hastily. "Funeral homes never do."

"True. They just get taken over," Libby replied.

"I refuse to pay taxation without representation," Aiken announced.

Marvin looked temporarily confounded.

"I don't think that was part of the script," Libby observed.

"Me either," Bernie agreed.

After a moment, Marvin rallied. "By God, you shall for the sake of king and country."

Aiken put his hand on his chest. "We shall be quit of you before the year is out. This I do swear."

Marvin raised his arm as far as he was able and cried, "Let's go get them, boys."

"Somehow I don't think 'Let's go get them, boys' is a Revolutionary War phrase," Bernie noted as the four redcoats and four colonists joined in a full scale altercation.

There were lots of "forsooths" and "by the power of the Crown" and "by God, thou shall not trample on our rights" flying around, not to mention the occurrence of a modest amount of judicious pushing and general threatening, with an occasional pause in the action for a swig from plastic water bottles.

Bernie found the water bottles somewhat jarring seeing as how people weren't drinking Evian and Dasani back in the Revolutionary War days. Aside from that, she thought that, given the circumstances, everyone was doing a spot-on job. In any case, everyone was definitely having a good time—especially Rick Evans, who seemed to be pushing people around with abandon.

She and Libby watched the drama unfold as

they worked. They had just finished arranging the paper plates, napkins, and plastic eating utensils at one end of the table and were putting the paper cups out on a second, smaller table when the redcoats and the colonists ran in front of the gazebo. The redcoats stopped and turned on their pursuers. The colonists advanced. The redcoats raised their muskets.

"By the power of the Crown, I command you to stop," Marvin intoned.

Colonist Number One, aka Tony Gerard, pounded his chest. "Kill me if you must, but I shall never betray my country."

Jack Devlin said, "So that's the way of it?"

"Indeed it is," Gerard said. "Shoot me if you must . . . excuse me . . . if you will."

"Is this your final decision?" Devlin asked.

"It is," Gerard said.

"Give 'em hell, Dad," Gerard's son yelled from the bleachers.

"Then what is done, must be done," Rick Evans intoned.

Libby turned to Bernie. "What does that mean?"

"Not a clue. Sounds like a cross between Dickens and Shakespeare to me."

"I hope we're reaching the end of this. Marvin looks as if he's going to faint."

"Yeah. Bright red is not a becoming facial color. Actually, Rick Evans doesn't look much better," Bernie observed. "In fact, they all look

33

as if they're going to collapse from heat stroke."

Libby leaned over. "Speaking of heat stroke, where's the pig?"

"Good question." Bernie began scanning the area for her. She wasn't a big animal person, but she'd become rather fond of Hilda in the short time she'd made her acquaintance and she didn't want to see anything bad happen to her. Who would have thought?

She had just located her lying in the grass under the Rose of Sharon bush when Marvin yelled, "Ready."

"Ready," Devlin echoed.

"Aim," Marvin called.

"Aim," Devlin repeated.

"Fire," Marvin ordered.

"Fire, lads," Devlin yelled. "Into the breech," he added for good measure.

"What is a breech?" Bernie asked Libby.

Her sister shrugged. "I'm guessing some kind of opening, but if you really want to know you'll have to ask Marvin."

The redcoats fired their weapons. A thick cloud of smoke and the acrid smell of gunpowder filled the air. It was difficult to see anything for the moment.

Then Bernie and Libby heard Jack Devlin scream.

The smoke cleared. They saw Devlin's musket fall as he let go of it and clutched his face. Then he fell to the ground and began to writhe.

"Bravo," someone on the hill yelled. "Great dying. Can you do it again?"

Devlin didn't answer.

Libby leaned over and confided to Bernie, "This is a little too realistic for me."

Marvin began speaking. "I will avenge you in this life or the next." Then he got a good look at Jack Devlin and stopped talking.

Libby could see blood seeping through Devlin's fingers.

For a nanosecond, Libby and Bernie thought *wow, great special effects, great acting!* Then they realized that everyone had turned quiet. No one was making a sound. No one was moving. Everyone was frozen in place.

They looked at each other. Along with everyone else standing there, they had the same thought at the same time. *This isn't an act. This is real.*

That's when all hell broke loose.

Chapter 3

"Oh my God," Libby cried as she ran down the steps and plunged into the crowd of people below.

Bernie was right behind her.

The scene was pandemonium. The reenactors, plus the spectators and the Wiccans, were gathered around Jack Devlin. Marvin was yelling,

"Someone call 911, someone call a doctor," while Rick Evans was repeating, "I don't understand," over and over again. Three colonists and four Wiccans had whipped out their cell phones and were talking on them.

Libby and Bernie heard snippets of their conversation as they made their way through the crowd. Phrases like, "You're not going to believe this," "You should come down and take a look, seriously," and "I'm surprised it took this long," peppered the air as they elbowed their way to where Jack Devlin lay. By the time they reached him, Elise Montague, former commodities trader and putative EMT, was kneeling down next to Devlin and feeling for his pulse.

"So?" Bernie asked her. But she knew the answer before Elise shook her head.

It was obvious to her as well as to Libby that Jack Devlin was going to be needing Marvin's services instead of a doctor's. ·

Rick Evans pointed to Devlin's musket, which was lying on the ground beside him. The barrel had melted from the heat. He bent over and touched it, then drew his hand back quickly. "Hot," he cried, waving his finger in the air.

Bernie squatted down to get a better look. The musket barrel wasn't glowing, but the top part of the barrel was peeled back. The metal reminded her of the skin of a half eaten banana. Obviously, the thing had misfired.

"I wonder what would cause that," she murmured to herself as she straightened up and took a quick look at the other muskets the men were holding. They all seemed fine.

Rick ignored Bernie and turned to Marvin. "Didn't you have charge of the guns?" he loudly demanded.

Libby snorted. She'd always thought that Rick lived by the principle assign blame early and often. This just proved it.

Marvin nodded and blinked. "Y-You know I did," he stammered. He looked as if he was going to cry.

Libby wished there was something she could say that could make things better as Rick pointed to the musket.

"So what happened?" he asked. "Why did it do that?"

"I-I don't know." Marvin's lower lip began to tremble.

Rick put his hands on his hips and jutted his jaw out. "How can you not know? You must have done something to it."

"I didn't do anything," Marvin protested.

"You had to have," Rick insisted. "Something like this doesn't just happen by itself."

Everyone stopped talking and crowded in closer so that they could hear Marvin's answer.

Marvin waved his hands around. A bead of sweat dripped down his face and fell on his shoulder. He didn't like being the center of attention in the best of times and this situation certainly didn't qualify as that.

He started to speak. "It's . . . I . . . the guns . . . sorry. It's just . . ."

Libby leaned over and patted him on his shoulder. "It's okay. Take your time." Of course, what she really wanted to do was tell Rick to go to hell, but that would just make things worse, so she didn't.

Marvin stopped, gave Libby a grateful smile, and took a big breath. After a moment, he started over again. "The guns—"

"Muskets," Rick corrected.

"Let him talk," Libby snapped. She could feel herself losing control.

Rick threw up his hands. "Just clarifying."

Libby turned back to Marvin. "Go on."

Marvin took his hat off and wiped the sweat off his forehead before he answered Rick's question. "I did what you told me to. I picked the muskets up from Costumers To The Stars two days ago and put them, the powder, and the costumes in the shed next to the rose garden. As far as I know, that's where they stayed until today. When I came out of the shed with the muskets, people started grabbing them out of my hands, so I put them on the bench and everyone took theirs."

Rick looked at the assembled reenactors for verification. "People?"

38

"We were running late," Tony Gerard said. "We just wanted to get out there."

"It was nuts," Dave Nancy agreed.

Sanford Aiken shook his head. "Sorry. I was trying to remember my lines."

Rick turned his gaze back on Marvin. "We can sort that out later, but one thing I know. Muskets don't explode on their own." His voice was accusatory. "Especially something that is nothing more than a prop."

"Don't blame him," Libby cried, leaping to Marvin's defense.

"I'm not blaming him. I'm stating the obvious," Rick said.

"Actually, they do . . . did," Bernie said, interrupting the conversation.

Everyone turned to her.

"Muskets did explode on their own," she explained. "I remember reading it was a big problem in the Revolutionary and Civil Wars."

"But that was when they were using live ammo," Cotton objected. "We weren't using live ammo. We were using fake stuff."

"True," Bernie said. "But if one of the barrels was plugged, the result might be the same."

"I very much doubt that," David Nancy, the last of the redcoats, replied in an antagonistic tone. "Even if what you're saying is true, I don't see how that happened here."

Bernie shrugged. "The same way it did back

then, I imagine. People leaned the muzzle's barrel on the ground and got a rock, or a branch, or some mud in it. Maybe one of you guys did the same thing."

Rick snorted. "Talk about far-fetched."

"Not so far-fetched at all," Bernie told him. "That kind of thing happened a lot back in the day."

"But not now." Rick bared his teeth in a smile. "What makes you such an expert anyway?" he challenged. "I thought pie dough was your specialty. Maybe you should stick to that."

"And maybe you should listen to what I was saying," Bernie retorted. "I never said I was an expert. I was just telling you about what I've read."

"I thought you just read cooking magazines," Rick snipped.

Elise stepped between them before Bernie could reply, which was probably a good thing. Bernie noticed a small spot of blood on the underside of Elise's sleeve from when she'd knelt by Jack Devlin. She didn't get why Elise was playing a male colonist in the first place, but who knew? Maybe there had been cross-dressers back then.

"So exactly what is it that you are saying?" Elise asked Bernie.

"It's pretty obvious, isn't it?" In truth, Bernie hadn't liked Elise when she was younger and she didn't like her now, although everyone else except Libby seemed to.

"Not to me," Elise replied as she pulled up her breeches.

Libby answered for Bernie. "It's simple. My sister is saying that we should wait and see what the police have to say."

Rick pointed at Marvin. "The police should talk to *him*. He was the one who put the powder in the guns to begin with. He was the one who handed Jack Devlin the musket."

"I'm sure they will," Bernie said, trying to calm the situation down. "In fact, they're going to want to get all of our statements."

Everyone continued talking as if she hadn't spoken.

Marvin turned to Rick. "I don't know why you just said that. I already told you I put all the muskets down on the bench next to the shed and Devlin came up and took one just like everyone else. I didn't hand it to him. For all I know, someone else did. I was too busy doing other stuff to notice."

"Like what?" Rick demanded.

"Like making sure the rest of the supplies were where they should be."

"So you say," Rick sneered.

Marvin crossed his arms over his chest. "Yes, I do."

"And who would this other person be that

handed Jack Devlin his musket?" Rick demanded.

"How would I know?" Marvin admitted. "I just know that it wasn't me. In fact, how do you know anyone handed him the musket?"

"Because you just said so."

"I was using a figure of speech," Marvin explained.

"Then you should be more careful," Rick said. "Are you always this careless? Maybe that's why the musket exploded. Maybe you did something you weren't supposed to."

A murmur ran through the crowd. Several people nodded in agreement.

"Listen," Marvin said, his eyes pleading with everyone. "The powder in the muskets was just supposed to make noise and smoke. The muskets were props. That's all."

"Maybe you put too much of that powder in," Samuel Cotton said.

"It wouldn't have made any difference if I had," Marvin retorted.

"So you're the expert now," Sanford Aiken said.

"No," Marvin said. "I never meant—"

"Exactly," Aiken said, cutting him off. "And that's where the problem lies."

"Why don't you leave him alone," Libby cried. "Can't you see how upset he is?"

"You're right," Aiken said, holding up his hands, palms outward. "I apologize. I shouldn't have said that. I'm upset, too. It's just this day. I mean who would have thought when I got up this morning . . ." Aiken's voice trailed off.

Tony Gerard jumped in, uttering his first words since Jack Devlin's death. "We're all upset. Of course we are. My God, we could have been killed." He pointed to Jack Devlin lying on the ground. "That could have been any one of us."

"Yeah," David Nancy echoed. "We could all be dead."

"There m-must have been a m-malfunction of some s-sort," Marvin stuttered.

"Or a careless error." Elise shuddered theatrically.

"Isn't that manslaughter?" Rick asked the crowd. "I think it is."

"He's right," someone murmured. Heads bobbed as another ripple of agreement moved through the group.

This is how lynch mobs are formed, Bernie thought. She put her fingers in her mouth and let out a loud whistle. Everyone turned toward her. "Let's not get ahead of ourselves here." She could hear police sirens in the background. For once, she was glad they were coming. "The police will be here any minute. Let's let them take care of this. Let's let them do their job."

"Fine with me," Rick said.

Is it? Libby asked herself as the sirens got closer. After all, he was the one inciting people. She wondered why as she whispered, "It'll be fine," in Marvin's ear.

Marvin shook his head and bit his lower lip. "I don't think so."

"No. It will be," she reassured him. "Trust me on this."

"I do," Marvin said even though Libby could tell he really didn't.

Heads turned in the direction of the police siren's wail and the crowd waited for the constabulary to arrive.

"Can I see the muskets?" Bernie asked. She'd suddenly realized it would probably be the only time she'd get to look at the weapons before the police arrived and confiscated them all. If it wasn't an accident—and it looked as if it wasn't—she should take a look.

"Why?" Samuel Cotton asked.

Bernie hedged. Somehow saying *I want to see if they've been tampered with* didn't seem like the best reply, so she said, "I'm just curious."

"About what?" Rick demanded.

"About the muskets," Bernie said, improvising. "I've never seen guns like that."

"Since when have you become so interested in munitions?" David Nancy asked.

"Can't a girl expand her horizons?" Bernie answered, doing her best Mae West imitation.

"You want to expand your horizons, go to a museum," Rick snapped at her. "And can the act. It's not working on me."

"What act?" Bernie asked.

"The one you're doing now. Do you think I'm an idiot?"

"Pretty darn close," Bernie retorted.

"One day, your smart mouth is going to get you in a lot of trouble," Rick warned her.

Bernie was just coming up with an answer when she felt Libby's hand around her arm.

"Leave it. You're not helping the situation."

Rick grinned. "How bad is it when your own sister has to tell you to shut up?"

Bernie could have answered. She wanted to answer. But she didn't. She let herself be dragged away by her sister because Libby was right in her assessment of the situation. This was about Marvin. It wasn't about her. A minute later, the police arrived, along with the Longely Fire Department.

"Good," Rick said as people made way to let them through. He puffed his chest out. "Now maybe we can get this thing sorted out."

Chapter 4

Everyone—the reenactors, the Wiccans, and the spectators—was gathered around the police and fire vehicles in a ragged circle with Marvin and Jack Devlin at the epicenter. Everyone that is, except Elise Montague. She was stumbling in the direction of the rose garden.

Bernie noticed her out of the corner of her eye and nudged Libby. "You stay here. I'm going to see what's up with Elise."

Libby nodded then turned her attention back to Marvin. At the moment, he was her most important priority.

Bernie pushed her way through the crowd of people, and caught up with Elise at the base of the hill. "Are you all right?" she asked.

Elise nodded, but her breath was shallow and she looked as if she was going to pass out, a fact that surprised Bernie. Of all the people, she would have picked Elise as the last one to get the willies.

"Maybe you should sit down," Bernie suggested.

Elise shook her head. "I just needed some air." She pointed to the police. "I have to go back. They're going to want to speak to me."

"They're going to want to speak to everyone. There's a long line in front of you."

Elise didn't reply. She just stood there, swaying slightly, a fine sheen of sweat on her face.

"Let's go," Bernie said.

When Elise didn't move, Bernie put her hand under one of Elise's elbows, guided her to a bench under an aspen tree, and sat her down. Then she went back to the gazebo, got two bottles of water out of the cooler, returned, and handed one to Elise. "Drink," she ordered.

When Elise raised the bottle to her lips, Bernie noticed that her hands were shaking.

Elise took a long drink. "Thanks. I know you and I aren't exactly friends."

"Not a problem." Bernie wondered if she looked as shook up as Elise did.

"I just never expected . . ." Elise said.

"Expected what?" Bernie asked, opening her bottle and taking a gulp then another. She hadn't realized how thirsty she was.

"This." Elise touched the spot of blood on her sleeve.

"I don't think anyone did."

Elise ran her finger over the spot again. "That's Devi's."

"I know."

Elise's eyes began to mist up. "I suppose all good things must come to an end," she murmured.

"Are you talking about Jack Devlin?"

Elise gave a sharp little laugh. "I suppose I am." She took another gulp of water. "People said bad things about him, you know."

"Indeed, I do," Bernie replied.

"Very bad. But he was really a very nice man. Very sweet." Elise looked up at Bernie. It's true," she cried.

"I'm not disagreeing," Bernie told her.

"Do you know that he was religious?"

"Now I find that surprising, given his conduct and all."

"He believed in the creative principle."

"Of course he did." Bernie stifled her desire to laugh.

"It's true," Elise insisted again.

Bernie made a calming gesture. "Hey. I believe you."

"I should get back." Elise started to stand up then abruptly sat back down. "Everything is spinning."

"You're probably in shock. Try putting your head between your knees."

Elise did. A moment later, she lifted it back up. "You know, I passed my test to be an EMT."

"So I heard," Bernie told her.

"But I don't think I'm going to do that. Seeing Devi like that . . . his face . . . his face all mashed up, I don't think I can do this kind of thing after all. Maybe I should go back to bond trading."

"Maybe you should," Bernie agreed.

"Or find something altogether different. Could you do it?"

"Do what?"

"You know. Be an EMT."

Bernie didn't have to think about the answer to that one. "Absolutely not."

Elise stood up. Some of the color had come back into her face. "Thanks. I think it's time to go back and face the music."

She passed Libby on the way down and they nodded at each other. Bernie walked over and Libby took the bottle of water out of Bernie's hand and drank. "The police want to speak to us," she said as she handed the bottle back.

"Immediately?" Bernie asked.

"In a little while. They want to know if we saw anything."

"Nothing that everyone else didn't see, I suspect."

Libby nodded in Elise's direction. "What was that all about?"

"She felt faint."

Libby snorted.

"She did," Bernie insisted. "She was very upset."

"That's a new one," Libby noted.

"She said she didn't expect . . ."

"Devlin to look so bad," Libby said, finishing the sentence for her.

Bernie shrugged. "I thought she was going to say she didn't think the sight of blood would upset her so much, but I could be wrong."

"And frequently are," Libby couldn't resist saying. "Do you believe her?"

"That she was so upset?"

"Yes."

"Well, she certainly acted that way."

Libby took the water bottle back from Bernie and took another sip. "I'm not sure I do."

"Why?"

Libby shrugged. "No reason really. Just a feeling."

"Maybe it's because you don't like her," Bernie suggested.

"Me, allow my personal prejudices to cloud my judgment? Never."

Bernie smiled.

Libby was about to follow up on her comment when she spotted Marvin waving to her. "Come on. Marvin wants us."

"I'll be there in a minute. I just want to stay here, poke around a little, and see if I can find anything."

"Like what?" Libby asked.

"Don't know. But I don't like the way this thing is heading."

Libby frowned. "Me either."

Chapter 5

Gossip is a terrible thing," Sean Simmons observed as he studied his daughters' faces. They both looked exhausted. It had been six hours since Jack Devlin had been shot and the family was finally sitting down to a light evening repast—leftovers from the picnic that had never happened—in the Simmons's flat. "Especially in a town this size." He raised his voice so he could be heard over the clanking of the air-conditioner.

"Yes, it is," Clyde agreed. A frequent visitor to the Simmons household, he was Sean's oldest friend. Unlike Sean, Clyde was still a member of the Longely police force, although he was thinking of retiring next year. He reached over and cut himself another sliver of blueberry tart, his third, and carefully conveyed it to his plate. "Remember the Clemson case?"

"Sure do," Sean replied, nodding vigorously. "That was so sad." Before his daughters could ask what had happened, he explained it to them. "I'd just been made police chief and there was a peeping Tom going around this neighborhood."

"It created quite the uproar," Clyde interjected.

"It certainly did," Sean agreed. "This guy had been running around for a couple months when everyone, and I *do* mean *everyone,* settled on Bob Clemson as the culprit—probably because he was a little weird. There was no proof. In fact there was the contrary, but it didn't matter. Bob Clemson was the guy. I kept on getting calls asking me what I was going to do about the situation and I kept telling everyone I wasn't going to do anything because Clemson hadn't done anything to do anything about."

Sean paused for a moment to take a sip of his lemonade. "In retrospect, I should have been more forceful. If I had been, maybe I could have headed off what happened next."

"Which was?" Bernie asked after a minute had gone by.

Her father didn't answer. He seemed lost in thought.

Clyde took up the narrative. "A group of our 'upstanding' citizens," he bracketed the word *upstanding* with his fingers, "took it upon themselves to teach Clemson a lesson. Fortunately, your daddy got there before the beating had gone too far."

Bernie ate another deviled egg. She'd used a little tarragon in them and decided the herb was a good fit. "So what happened?"

Sean straightened up. His expression was grim. "What happened was that I took everyone into custody and charged them, but the judge let them go. The DA wouldn't prosecute. The case never even went before the grand jury."

"After he got out of the hospital, Clemson moved out of town," Clyde said.

"Understandable," Libby commented.

"Very. Last I heard he was out in Southern California. I don't think he ever got over what happened to him." Sean took another sip of lemonade and carefully put the glass down on the table. "Three months later we caught the culprit, one Pete Morrelli, by accident. I think he served a year in jail. At most. And that as they say, is that."

The room was silent for a moment as Libby and Bernie thought about the story their dad and Clyde had just told them.

"I think Marvin is going to be tarred with this forever," Libby said, breaking the silence.

She helped herself to a second helping of watermelon and feta salad. Somehow, given the events of the day she hadn't expected to be hungry. But she was. She was starving. Embarrassingly so. She'd already had two servings of fried chicken and a couple glasses of freshly squeezed lemonade.

"Not if we find the person who did it," Sean said.

"Yeah," Clyde agreed. "You're going to need a name to hang this on."

"And we'll get one," Bernie said, trying to buck up her sister. "You can count on that."

"How's he doing?" Sean knew in Marvin's situation he wouldn't be doing well.

Libby put her fork down. Suddenly she felt guilty about eating. "He's distraught. When I picked him up at the police station, he didn't even want to come over and have anything to eat. He wanted to go straight home."

"He didn't even want any fruit tart?" Sean asked.

Libby shook her head. "Nothing. He said he couldn't eat a bite. He'd throw up if he did."

Sean downed another piece of the blueberry and strawberry tart his girls had made. The flaky crust, almond cream, blueberries, and strawberries lightly dusted with cardamom and sugar were an especially good combination. "He's worse off than I thought." Marvin would do anything for a piece of Libby's fruit tarts. "Do you think I should call him? Reassure him a little?"

"It couldn't hurt," Libby told him.

Clyde put his fork down and frowned. "I have a feeling things might be getting a whole lot worse for Marvin."

Libby paled. "What do you mean?"

"I mean the DA is talking about charging Marvin with manslaughter."

"That's ridiculous," Libby cried out.

Clyde looked grave. "But true."

"How can they do that?" Libby demanded.

Instead of answering, Clyde moved a small piece of pastry around on his plate with his fork.

Libby crossed her arms, tucked her hands underneath her armpits, and leaned forward. "Well? Tell me."

"You're not going to like it," Clyde said.

"Probably not," Sean said quietly. "But we need to hear it, anyway."

Clyde rubbed his hands together and cleared his throat. "Okay then. Here goes. Someone put real shot into the musket, overloaded it, and then plugged the barrel up with mud."

"So I was right," Bernie muttered.

Clyde nodded toward her. "Indeed you were. That's why the thing exploded the way it did."

"Meaning," Sean said, "that this was no accident."

"That's definitely the thinking at this point." Clyde rubbed his hands together again. "Unfortunately for Marvin, he was the person in charge of the weapons. *He* got them from the costume store. *He* put them in the shed. *He* put the powder in them. *He* could have handed the musket to Jack Devlin."

"But he didn't," Libby cried. "He already said he didn't, right Bernie?"

Bernie nodded.

"Why did anyone have to hand Jack Devlin that musket, anyway?" Libby demanded. "Why couldn't he have just taken it himself?"

"Okay. Let's assume you're right," Clyde allowed. Libby started to speak but Clyde put up a hand to forestall her. "You're saying that this was just bad luck? That no one was the target?"

"Yes," Libby said defiantly. "That's exactly what I'm saying."

"And Marvin didn't want to kill or cause grievous bodily harm to Devlin."

Libby looked at Clyde as if he'd lost his mind. "Why would he possibly want to do that?"

"Because of the argument he had with Devlin."

"What are you talking about?" Libby asked.

Clyde leaned forward. "He didn't tell you?"

"Obviously not," Bernie put in.

"What was the argument about?" Libby asked.

"Evidently, Marvin backed into Devlin's car at Trader Joe's and Devlin called him a moron and a menace and said he shouldn't be on the road."

Libby's eyes widened. "That's it? That's all the fight was about?"

Clyde shrugged. "Allegedly."

"That's absurd," Libby said.

"I agree," Clyde replied. "But that seems to be enough for the DA. According to him, Marvin has the motive, means, and the opportunity. The golden threesome of law enforcement."

"Jeez," Bernie said. "Talk about lame."

"Marvin said the shed wasn't locked," Libby protested. "Anyone could have come in and fooled around with one of the guns."

"I know," Clyde agreed.

"Jack Devlin had lots of enemies and most of them had lots better reasons to dislike Devlin than an argument over a fender bender. Who would kill someone over something like that?" Libby protested. "You'd have to be psychotic and Marvin certainly isn't."

"I'm right with you," Clyde said. "However, the problem is that Rick Evans is bringing lots of pressure on the DA. He wants a quick closure on this and Marvin is the easy candidate. Why go out and look for a new bird when you already have one in your hand?"

"Why is the DA listening to him?" Sean asked.

"Glad you asked that." Clyde leaned back in his

seat. "Word is that Rick Evans is going to be the next mayor of Longely."

"Great," Bernie muttered. "Just what this town needs. A moron for a mayor."

"Always a good thing to be on the right side of the powers that be," Sean commented.

"A lesson you never learned," Clyde said.

Sean smiled. "Nope. Never did."

"Otherwise you would still be the chief of police."

Sean leaned over and took a brownie off the plate in the center of the table. "The price wasn't worth it."

"No, it wasn't," Libby agreed. "At least from what you tell me."

"It wasn't," Sean assured her.

Libby nodded and went back to talking about Marvin's situation. "Does the DA know that Rick Evans has a much better motive for wanting Jack Devlin out of the way? After all, he did find Devlin fooling around with his wife Gail two months ago. Or was it three?"

"Three," Bernie promptly answered. "Bree Nottingham came in and told me."

Clyde downed the rest of his lemonade. "In answer to your question, yes the DA does know. As a matter of fact, Evans went out of his way to tell the DA he didn't care about his wife screwing around. It was fine with him. He and Gail have an open marriage. Or so he says."

Sean snorted. "I wonder what Rose would have said if I had suggested that to her?"

"About the same thing as my darling Clara. I'd definitely be sleeping on the sofa," Clyde said.

"But they haven't charged Marvin yet, have they?" Libby asked, interrupting.

Clyde shook his head. "No, they haven't. But like I said they're definitely thinking about it."

"Thank God for small favors," Libby replied. "At least that gives us some time to find out who the responsible party is."

"But not a lot," Clyde warned.

"We're not going to need a lot," Bernie said.

"I wouldn't be so sure," Sean said.

"Why are you saying that?" Libby asked him.

"Because there are a lot of people, male and female, who didn't like Jack Devlin," Sean replied.

"You can say that again," Clyde said as he leaned over and snagged himself a mint chocolate chip brownie. "I'd say you've got at least half a town's worth."

Sean grinned. "I think maybe we can narrow that down a bit."

Chapter 6

As Libby and Bernie pulled into RJ's parking lot they could hear the sound of fireworks going off in Cedar Bay Park.

"Nice night for it," Bernie commented wistfully as a rocket exploded in the dark, sending down showers of white lights. She loved fireworks and was sorry they were missing them, unlike Libby who couldn't have cared less. Bernie looked around for Marvin's vehicle and didn't see it. In fact, aside from Brandon's truck, they were the only other vehicle in the place. *Strange.*

Libby bit her lip. "I wonder where Marvin is?"

"He'll be along soon," Bernie said as she got out of the van.

"I'm not so sure," Libby replied, shutting the van door behind her. "We should have picked him up."

"You worry too much, Libby. He'll be here." Bernie looked at her watch. "We're five minutes early."

Libby shook her head and walked inside. It was all very well for her sister to tell her not to worry, but it had taken all her powers of persuasion to get Marvin to come to RJ's. She just hoped he hadn't changed his mind.

When he arrived five minutes later, Libby heaved a sigh of relief.

"See," Bernie said. "Told ya."

He's moving like an old man, Libby thought as she watched Marvin walk across the floor. She patted the stool between her and Bernie. "Sit here."

"Yeah. We saved you a place, seeing as it's so crowded and all," Bernie cracked.

Despite himself, Marvin smiled. "I've never seen the place this empty." They were the only people in the place.

"I think the word is *dead,*" Brandon replied. "Everyone's probably watching the fireworks display."

"And talking about what happened this afternoon," Marvin reflected gloomily.

Brandon reached under the counter, came up with a bag of pretzels, and refilled the bowl sitting between Libby and Marvin. "Nothing like a murder to inspire communal bonding."

Marvin flinched. "We don't know that it was a murder," he protested. "It could have been an accident."

Brandon turned and got a bottle of McClelland's off the shelf. "If you say so."

"I do."

Brandon got a glass out. "Glad I missed it."

"I wished I had," Marvin said.

"I bet you do."

"A good time was definitely not had by all," Bernie said.

"Certainly not by Jack Devlin." Brandon poured Marvin a shot of the single malt Scotch and put it down in front of him.

"His face . . ." Marvin's voice trailed off. He shuddered at the memory.

Brandon indicated the glass in front of Marvin. "On the house." When Marvin didn't pick up the glass, Brandon ordered, "Drink it."

"No thanks," Marvin said. "I don't do hard liquor."

"Yes, you do. You drink vodka," Bernie pointed out. "That's the same thing."

"No. It's different," Marvin said.

Brandon pushed the glass closer to Marvin. "Seriously, take it. You look like crap."

Marvin raised an eyebrow. "And this is going to help?"

"Well, it's certainly not going to hurt," Brandon retorted.

Marvin sat there for a moment deciding. "What the hell," he finally said. "You're right. It can't hurt." He took a sip and then he took another. "Not bad," he allowed.

"Not bad?" Brandon squawked. "This stuff is top of the line."

"How come you never give anything like that to me?" Bernie asked.

Brandon laughed. "Because I give you me instead."

Bernie rolled her eyes. "Jeez. Talk about overwhelming ego."

"Then how about because you don't like Scotch. How's that for a reason?"

"That would work," Bernie acknowledged.

"Anyway, Marvin has had a tough afternoon. He deserves something good," Brandon said as he watched Marvin drain the glass.

Marvin hiccupped twice.

"That stuff is meant to be sipped," Brandon told him.

Marvin hiccupped again. "Sorry. Very rude of me. I promise I'll sip the next one." He slapped the palm of his hand on the bar. "Give me another, my good man."

Brandon shot Libby a questioning look.

"Only if I'm driving," she told him.

"If you insist," Marvin said, putting on a sorrowful face. "Drive if you want. I don't care." He let out a theatrical sigh. "Never mind that this might be the last time I get to drive my car. I don't think you can drive if you're in jail."

Bernie laughed. "Marvin the drama queen. Who would have thought?"

Marvin's mouth turned down. He crossed his arms over his chest. "I can't believe you're saying something like that at a time like this."

"That's precisely my point," Bernie told him.

Marvin shook his head. "Which is what?"

"That you're exaggerating."

Marvin uncrossed his arms, turned, and faced her. "Me, exaggerate?" His voice rose a notch. "*Exaggerate?* Are you kidding me? They're going to arrest me. I've never even gotten a traffic ticket. Nothing my whole life and now *this*. I can't believe this is happening. It's like a nightmare. No. It *is* a nightmare."

"Calm down," Libby told him. "They're not going to arrest you."

"They might. In fact, they probably will. My horoscope said this was going to be a bad day. I should never have gotten out of bed."

"You read your horoscope?" Brandon asked incredulously.

Marvin gave him a defiant stare. "So what if I do?"

Bernie gave Brandon a dirty look.

His eyes widened. "Did I say something wrong?"

Bernie ignored him and turned back to Marvin. "Don't worry. We're not going to let anything happen to you," she said in the best soothing voice she could manage.

Marvin looked anything but reassured.

"No. We're not," Libby echoed. "You can count on that."

Brandon leaned over and refilled Marvin's glass. He then pulled two Blue Moons, took two orange slices, put them on the glass rims, and handed the drinks to Bernie and Libby. "My treat. You look as if you can use these, too."

"Well, I know I can," Bernie said as she took a sip. She liked wheat beer, especially in the summer. It was light and cold and had a pleasant flavor. She liked the golden color and the small bubbles that worked their way up the glass, too. "It's been a bad day."

"But not as bad as mine," Marvin replied.

"True enough," Bernie said. "You win the My Day Sucketh prize."

Marvin took another sip of his Scotch. Libby put the plastic bowl of pretzels in front of him. He fished a couple out of the bowl. As he ate them, he realized that they were the first things he had eaten since breakfast.

"Did Clyde say anything to your dad about what the DA is thinking?" Marvin asked Libby.

"No," she lied.

"You're a lousy liar," Marvin said, looking at her face. She'd developed a tic under her left eye, a sure sign she wasn't telling the truth. "Tell me," he insisted when she didn't answer. "I really want to know."

"You don't," Libby replied.

"I do," Marvin said even though what she'd said was 100 percent correct.

Libby ate a pretzel and had another sip of beer before answering. She noted the pretzels were the saltless kind. Not a good choice in her opinion.

Marvin leaned forward. "Well?"

"Well, what?" Libby asked.

He took a deep breath and exhaled. "What did Clyde say?"

Libby sighed. She hated to be the bearer of bad news.

"Spit it out," he ordered.

"Okay." Libby looked him in the eye and told him. "Clyde said the DA was thinking of charging you. But that's different from saying he's *going* to charge you," she added hastily, trying for upbeat and failing. "We have to remain positive here."

Marvin snorted.

"Seriously," Libby said.

"It's marginally different. A hairsbreadth different." He shook his head. "God, I wish I'd told my dad no."

Chapter 7

Bernie raised an eyebrow.

Libby leaned forward. "What do you mean?"

"I told you. Being in the reenactment was his idea. He wanted me to do it. Said it would be good for community relations. You know, giving back to the town and all the rest of that—" Marvin almost said *crap,* but stopped himself—"stuff" instead.

"Well, you can't say it didn't get you noticed,"

Bernie said, trying to be funny and failing. "Your dad was right about that."

Marvin glared at her.

Bernie backtracked. "But not in the way he had in mind, unfortunately." She picked up her orange slice and ate it. "Sorry." She put the rind down on her napkin. "That was out of line. I was just trying to lighten things up. Obviously, I didn't succeed."

"Obviously," Libby said.

Marvin gulped. Loudly. Bernie, Libby, and Brandon looked at him.

"I can't do jail time," Marvin wailed as pictures of prison movies he'd seen in his youth flashed through his head. "I just *can't*. I wouldn't last a day in there! Not even an hour!"

"Can we go for five minutes?" Bernie asked.

Libby glared at Bernie and she shut up. Libby leaned over and patted Marvin's arm. "You're not going to. I repeat, don't worry. We're going to find out who did this and have them arrested."

"Yeah," Bernie added. "We've done it before and we can do it again."

"And Dad will help," Libby said. "So you've got all three of us in your corner."

Brandon poured himself a ginger ale. He didn't drink on duty. "Make that four of us." He took a sip of his soda. "Maybe Marvin's right. Maybe it was an accident."

Libby turned to Bernie. "Back in the park you

said that in the days of the Revolutionary and Civil War guns discharging accidentally were a common occurrence."

"See." Brandon gave Marvin an encouraging smile.

Bernie nodded. "True. Soldiers got scared in the heat of battle and loaded their guns a second, third, and even fourth time, at which point the barrels exploded."

"Maybe that's what happened at the reenactment," Brandon suggested as he began washing glasses.

"I don't think so, Brandon," Bernie said.

"Why not?"

"Because, no matter how much powder you put in one of those muskets, it never would have shredded Jack Devlin's face like that. The musket was loaded with shot."

Brandon put the glass down and looked up. "Shot?"

"That's what I just said," Bernie replied.

"You can get that at any sporting goods store," Brandon noted. "Hell, you can even make it yourself."

"They did during the Revolutionary War."

"Some guys do it now. You know, for kicks. Are you sure it's shot?"

Bernie nodded again. "I saw some scattered on the ground around Jack Devlin's body. The shot . . . shots?"

"Shot," Brandon told her.

"Okay then. The shot looked black and they were about this big." She made a small circle with her thumb and forefinger to show the size.

Brandon turned off the water. "There goes the musket as a prop theory. However, that still wouldn't be enough to make the musket explode the way they said it did on television."

Jack Devlin's story had been featured on the six o'clock news, much to the dismay of Marvin and his dad.

"No, it wouldn't," Bernie agreed. "Clyde said the muzzle was also stuffed with mud and sticks, which means that once Devlin pulled the trigger, the thingie—"

"The thingie?" Brandon said. "What's the thingie?"

"The thing that ignites everything."

"You mean the percussion cap."

Bernie waved her hand. "Whatever. The percussion cap then. It caught, the shot had nowhere to go, and blammo! Instant Jack Devlin hamburger."

Marvin turned white. He'd already seen Jack Devlin's face. He didn't need reminding.

"That's disgusting," Libby informed her sister.

"But true," Bernie said.

Brandon cleared his throat. Everyone turned toward him. "That wouldn't necessarily have killed Devlin. It could have just maimed him pretty badly."

"Maybe that was the intention," Bernie noted after thinking for a moment about what Brandon had said. "Maybe someone wanted to take away Devlin's looks. He certainly would have needed extensive plastic surgery if he'd survived."

"I could see this being a punishment," Libby added.

"Like the guy who throws acid in a woman's face because she'd rejected him," Brandon said.

"Exactly," Libby said. "Or maybe in this case, a woman getting her own back."

"Or a guy," Bernie said.

"Then the motive would be different," Brandon said. "I can't see a guy doing something like that. I can see him killing Devlin, but maiming him? Not so much."

"We really don't know a lot, do we?" Libby observed.

Bernie ate a pretzel. "We do know a couple things. We know that screwing around was Devlin's favorite occupation and we also know that someone had to hand Devlin the musket. Those two facts we are sure of."

"Are we?" Brandon asked.

"Yes, we are," Bernie answered. "That is, if we're proceeding under the assumption that the purpose of this little exercise was to kill or maim Devlin."

"And we know I didn't do it," Marvin said. "We're sure of that. That's a third fact."

"But we don't know who did," Brandon stated.

"Correct. If we did, we wouldn't be having this conversation," Bernie pointed out.

Everyone was quiet for a moment.

Bernie ate another pretzel. The crunch echoed through the room. "We have eight people, seven excluding Marvin, who were directly involved in the reenactment. That's another thing we're sure of."

Everyone was quiet again. They could hear a freight train tooting its horn in the distance.

Brandon poured the last of the ginger ale from the bottle into his glass. "Let's go over this one last time."

Marvin groaned. "I've already repeated this at least a hundred times."

"Then one more time won't make any difference," Brandon told him. "So who was responsible for the muskets?"

Marvin raised his hand. "I was."

"How did you get them?"

"I picked them up at the costume place along with the rest of the garb."

"Did they seem all right?" Brandon asked.

Marvin shrugged. "Sure. I guess."

Brandon took a sip of his ginger ale and put the glass down. "What do you mean *I guess?*" he demanded. "Did you look at them? Inspect them, look in the barrels to see if they were clean?"

Marvin looked miserable. "No," he whispered. "I didn't."

"Why not?" Brandon asked.

"They weren't real. Even if they were, it wouldn't have made a difference. I don't know one end of a barrel from another. I've never shot a gun in my life. I've never been near them."

"So it would seem," Brandon said. "So what did you do with the muskets then?"

"I stored everything in the shed by the rose garden just like Rick Evans told me to. It was the easiest thing to do. I figured I'd give everyone their costumes before the reenactment and they could change in the Longely Historical Society bathrooms. Inez said it would be all right. That way no one would lose anything." Marvin bit his bottom lip. "I thought I was being smart."

"That's when I make my worst mistakes," Libby volunteered, trying to make Marvin feel better. "Why is that, I wonder?"

"What kind of lock did you use on the shed door?" Bernie asked Marvin, declining to go through the door her sister had opened.

Marvin shook his head. "I didn't."

Brandon frowned. "You didn't? Why not?"

Marvin slunk lower in his seat. "Because Rick told me the shed had a padlock. He even gave me the key for it. But when I got there the lock was already open. It was hanging on the hasp. After I was done putting things inside, I tried closing it, but I couldn't. The padlock was broken. I knew I should have gone to the hardware store and gotten a new one, but I was running late. I figured everything would be fine. As it turned out, I was wrong."

Bernie almost said *I'll say,* but stifled the comment. Instead, she asked if anyone had seen Marvin storing the clothes and the props.

"Maybe."

"Maybe?" Bernie repeated. "What do you mean *maybe?*"

"Well, there were people around. I mean, there are always people around so I'm sure someone saw me."

"Like who?" Bernie asked.

"I don't know," Marvin said angrily. He was suddenly tired of defending himself. "I wasn't paying attention, okay? I was thinking about other stuff."

Libby lifted her hands then brought them down in a calming gesture. "Maybe we should try another tack."

Marvin gulped down the last of his Scotch. "I'm listening."

"Let's start off with who besides Rick Evans knew that the reenactment stuff was in the shed," Libby said.

"That is *the* question, isn't it?" Bernie said.

"One of them," Brandon said. "I can think of several others."

Bernie shot him a look and he shut up.

"Everyone knew," Marvin said, answering Libby's question. "I sent out an e-mail to everyone who was involved in the production."

"Then the second part of the question is, who knew that the shed's lock was broken?" Brandon asked.

Marvin shook his head again. "You got me, but I can't believe it was a secret."

"What else is the shed used for?" Libby asked.

"Nothing," Marvin replied. "It's empty. The Longely Rose Society used to store their gardening tools in there, but they moved them to the outbuilding on the other side of the garden."

"How long has the shed been empty?" asked Brandon.

Marvin shrugged. "I'm not sure. Maybe a year. Maybe six months."

Everyone was silent for another minute as the weather announcer forecast the weather for the rest of the week. It was going to be in the nineties for the next three days.

"I never thought I'd say this," Brandon said, "but I'm actually looking forward to winter."

"Well, I for one, refuse to complain about the heat," Bernie said.

"Ha!" said Brandon.

Bernie lifted an eyebrow. "Ha?"

73

"Yes, ha. You've been complaining about the heat nonstop."

"Have not," Bernie protested.

"Have so." Brandon turned to Libby. "Isn't that right?"

She threw her hands up in the air. "I'm staying out of this."

"You know your sister does." He shook a finger at Bernie. "You complain about the winter, you complain about the summer. What does that leave you?"

"Spring and fall, of course," Bernie replied.

Marvin waved a pretzel in the air. "Could you two stop bickering and get back to me?"

"I suppose that's only fair," Brandon said.

"I think so," Marvin replied. "Especially since I'm the one who's going to be indicted for murder."

"Manslaughter," Libby corrected.

"I'm still going to jail," Marvin said.

Libby reached over and patted him on the back again. "You won't. Okay. So let's go over this one last time."

Marvin groaned. "You're worse than the police."

"Please," Libby said. "We're just trying to help."

Marvin hung his head. "I know," he said in a contrite voice.

"Okay." Brandon took a sip of his drink. "One more time. Did anyone hand Jack Devlin his musket?"

"How many times do I have to tell you I don't remember?" Marvin demanded.

"You're sure?" Brandon asked.

"Of course I'm sure," Marvin cried. He took a pretzel out of the bowl and crumbled it into little bits. "If I knew, don't you think I'd tell you? I've tried remembering, but I can't. Things were so hectic and I was so hot. All I was thinking of was how long it would take before it was over." Marvin shook his head. "I've tried picturing what happened, but I can't. My mind is a blank."

"Someone had to have handed the damn thing to him," Brandon observed.

"Why?" Bernie said. "Devlin could have picked it up by himself."

"But then how could whoever wanted him dead make sure that the musket reached its intended target?" Brandon asked her.

"I don't know," Bernie told him.

"How about Rick Evans?" Libby asked Marvin. "What about him?"

Marvin pounded the bar. "How many times do I have to tell everyone I didn't see anything?"

Brandon leaned forward. "So tell me what you did see."

Marvin frowned. "I put the guns in a pile on the bench and everyone took one."

"Where were you when this happened?"

"I already told you, Brandon. I was there, but I wasn't watching."

"What were you watching?"

"I was watching Libby walking toward the gazebo. I was thinking how nice she looked."

"That's so sweet, Marvin," Libby said.

Marvin blushed.

"And then?" Brandon prompted.

"And then I turned back and all the muskets except the one I was going to use were gone."

"And none of them looked any different from any of the others?" Brandon asked.

Marvin shook his head. "Not that I noticed." He buried his hands in his face again. "I am so screwed. So, so screwed."

"Don't say that," Bernie told him.

"But we're not getting anywhere," Marvin told her. "We're just going around in circles."

Bernie drummed her fingernails on the bar. "You're right. This tack is getting us nowhere. We might be better off figuring out who among the people at the reenactment had a motive to kill Devlin."

Brandon laughed. "That would be everyone."

"I think we need to be a tad more selective," Bernie said.

"Give him the list," Libby told Bernie.

"I am giving him the list," Bernie shot back. "Jeez." She took out the list that she, her sister, her dad, and Clyde had compiled earlier in the evening and handed it to Brandon. "We're concentrating on these people. We're convinced that

76

somewhere in here is the person who wanted Jack Devlin dead."

"Or maimed," Libby said.

"What difference does it make? No matter what the intention was, the result was the same," Bernie snapped. "A dead Jack Devlin."

Libby put up both her hands. "So-r-ry."

"What do you want me to do with this?" Brandon asked, waving the paper in the air.

"I want you to tell me who you think the most likely candidates are," Bernie told him.

"You want me to rank them or something?" Brandon inquired.

Bernie nodded. "That's exactly what I want you to do."

"What if these people don't pan out?" Marvin asked.

"Then we'll broaden our search," Libby informed him.

Marvin drummed his fingers on the bar. "To whom?"

Libby noticed that he was beginning to slur his words. "To the other people who were there."

Brandon drank the rest of his soda. "Why are you asking *me* to do this?"

Bernie laughed. "Simple. Because you know everything that goes on in this town."

Brandon sniffed. "You're saying that I'm the gossip king?"

"No, Brandon. I'm saying you're a bartender

and bartenders, like hairdressers, know every-thing."

"It's true. I do." He took a pen from the side of the register and began putting numbers next to names. "This is kind of fun," he told Bernie and Libby when he was through.

Marvin looked woeful. He hiccupped again. "I don't feel so well," he mumbled.

"Somehow, I'm not surprised," Libby told him. "What did you have to eat today besides the pretzels?"

Marvin looked at her. "Not much," he managed to get out before he did a face plant onto the bar.

Brandon looked at Marvin and shook his head. "I haven't seen one of those for quite a while."

"Me either," Bernie said.

Brandon pointed to Marvin who was lying there with his mouth open. "I guess he doesn't have much of a tolerance for alcohol."

"Obviously," Libby said.

Marvin began to snore. Loudly.

"I'll tell you one thing," Brandon said. "He's not going to be a happy camper when he wakes up tomorrow morning."

"On that," Bernie said, "I think we all can agree."

"And," Brandon added, stating the obvious, "he's not going to be fun to carry out and get into his car."

Chapter 8

By five o'clock the next morning the temperature had already climbed to seventy degrees. The air-conditioning was going full bore in the kitchen of A Little Taste of Heaven, but it was no match for the heat the ovens were throwing off. Even the fans Bernie had set up weren't having much of an effect. They were just moving the hot air around. Both Libby and Bernie were dressed in shorts, tank tops, and flip-flops, but that wasn't helping, either.

"I'm going to get heat stroke and die," Libby moaned as she rolled out the pie crusts for the lemon meringue pies she was making.

"You can do that after you finish the pies," Bernie informed her while she measured out ingredients for the red velvet cupcakes they were featuring that day.

"Thanks." Libby took a sip of the iced coffee she'd made the night before.

Bernie paused to pin a stray lock of hair off her neck. "That's me, compassionate to a fault. By the way, have you thought of getting a pedicure? It *is* the summer and you *are* wearing sandals."

Libby frowned. "I thought we agreed that my feet were not up for discussion. I don't like nail polish on them."

"But they look so naked."

"And yours look so . . . so . . ."

"Good." At the moment, Bernie was wearing green nail polish with blue tips.

"Not the word I was going to use." Libby totally changed the topic, going off on a food tangent because it was just too early in the morning to argue. "I've been thinking. Maybe we should sell ice cream or frozen yogurt."

"Frozen yogurt is the new big deal," Bernie reflected. "It would give us another income stream. Especially if weather like this becomes the new norm."

Libby looked up as she finished her first pie crust and went on to her second. *Only ten more to go,* she thought. For some reason, lemon meringue and chiffon pies of various kinds were turning out to be their best sellers this summer. Maybe it was a retro thing, since those kind of pies were particularly popular in the fifties. Or a comfort food thing. The dessert equivalent of meatloaf, so to speak. Or perhaps they were a hot weather thing, because they were light and refreshing.

In any case, Libby wasn't complaining because the chiffon pies were easy to make, their ingredients were cheap, and their profit margins were large. The pie crusts were baked blind, cooled, and then filled with a variety of flavors.

She rolled the portion of pie dough she'd been

working on into a circle. "We could always rent one of those frozen yogurt machines with an option to buy," she suggested as she transferred the dough to the waiting pie pan, patted it down, and began to crimp the edges. She loved the way the pie dough felt like velvet underneath her fingers.

"Then we'd have to break it down and clean it every night." Bernie added a stream of cocoa powder to the contents of the mixer bowl. Red velvet cake was a Southern thing that had suddenly become popular in the northern states. "Remember. All those little tubes have to be cleaned with brushes. Or have you forgotten?"

Libby wrinkled her nose. "God, what was I thinking? How could I forget?"

"Probably because you repressed it."

"I think you're right."

Libby's memories of working at the frozen custard stand in the Catskills were not good. Aside from having two sex-crazed coworkers who insisted on indulging in that activity every time they got a break—unsettling since she never knew where she was going to come across them—it had taken her the better part of two hours every evening to disassemble, clean, and reassemble the custard machine. Eventually, she'd broken one of the little tubes and gotten herself fired—which had been fine with her.

"Ice cream would be better," Bernie continued,

thinking out loud. "We'd just need a larger freezer and cooler." Her voice gathered enthusiasm as she went on. "We could do all local fruit and maybe a few exotics like vanilla with black pepper or lavender and cardamom or avocado ice cream."

Libby smiled. She liked the idea. "I heard the pizza place in the strip mall near town is selling their freezer. Someone said they'd be willing to take two hundred for it."

Bernie nodded. "Not bad. We could sell ice cream for—" She stopped. Price point calculations had never been her thing.

"Give me a sec to figure it out," Libby said, being the better of the two at that particular task. Her lips started moving, but no sound came out as she did the arithmetic in her head. "Ballpark, I think we could sell the ice cream for two-fifty for a single scoop, three dollars for a double."

"Including the cones?"

"They can't be more than a nickel each. And I'm being generous."

Bernie nodded. "That would work. We'd be undercutting Schneider's by a nickel a scoop." Schneider's was the only place in town at the moment that sold homemade ice cream.

"Always a good thing. We could do sorbets as well."

"We should talk to Stonewall Dairies," Bernie

suggested, "and see if they can give us a deal on milk and cream."

"I'll call them later today," Libby promised.

The sisters worked in silence for the next couple minutes. When Libby was done with the last of the pies and had them all safely secured in the oven, she poured herself a second cup of coffee and perched on one of the kitchen stools. "I've been thinking," she began as she stirred a lump of raw sugar into her coffee.

Bernie looked up from putting frilly cupcake papers into muffin tins. "Always a dangerous occupation," she cracked.

Libby ignored her and continued on with what she'd been about to say. "Do you believe that Rick Evans really didn't care that his wife was sleeping with Jack Devlin?"

"No," Bernie promptly replied. "I've never met a guy who didn't care about something like that. Even the ones who don't like having sex, care. It's a control thing."

Libby raised an eyebrow. "Is there such a thing as a man who doesn't like sex?"

Bernie laughed. "I think there might be one or two out there. Not our men of course, but I know that Brandon would leave me if I fooled around."

Libby reached over, snatched one of the strawberries that was about to become part of a strawberry chiffon pie, and ate it. "So would Marvin."

"Rick Evans is a Type A control freak. If Gail did something like that, he'd be livid." Bernie began pouring the batter into the paper cups. On three occasions, she had placed the paper cups on baking sheets instead of in muffin tins and the batter had ended up spilling over the sheets and onto the counters. Definitely not worth the cleanup. Using the muffin tins was a little slower, but definitely safer. And faster in the end. It was a tortoise and hare kind of thing.

"Maybe they really do have an open marriage," Libby suggested while she handed Bernie a strawberry. "Maybe Rick was telling the truth down at the station. Or maybe he just likes to watch. Maybe he's a voyeur."

"Maybe," Bernie said, plucking the stem out with her fingernails and plopping the berry into her mouth. "But this is Longely, gossip capital of the world. If he and his wife were doing that, we would have heard. But I haven't heard a hint of anything like that. A whisper. Anything at all. Have you?"

"Nope."

Bernie ate another strawberry. "Neither has Brandon. So there you go."

"It doesn't mean it's not happening," Libby objected.

"True. But it makes it more likely that it isn't."

"Okay then," Libby continued. "We come to Gail. Do you believe that she wasn't furious when she found out that Jack Devlin was stepping out on her with Juno Grisham, her arch nemesis?"

"Who also happened to conveniently be there when Devlin was killed," Bernie pointed out.

"Except she was on the hill, which is nowhere near where the reenactment took place. We saw her there, remember?"

"Of course I remember," Bernie replied. "She was quite the spectacle with those wings."

"She had a good motive, but the husbands of those two women had better ones. And what about David Nancy? His wife—" Libby paused because she couldn't remember her name.

Bernie supplied the name. "Cora. I'm sure he wasn't too pleased either."

"If he knew."

"True." Bernie went over to the refrigerator and poured herself a cup of iced coffee. "The husbands are usually the last to know, although given the level of gossip in this town that's probably not true." She shook her head. "Just thinking about who did what with whom is giving me a headache. I think we're going to need a flowchart."

"I think you may be right. I'll tell you one thing. These people have way too much free time."

Bernie poured some heavy cream into her coffee and watched the swirls the cream made as it turned the black liquid a pleasing shade of tan.

It was so much better than adding skimmed milk to coffee. The skimmed milk turned the coffee an unappetizing shade of gray. Really. In the scheme of things what did fifty calories matter? It was worth it for the taste it imparted.

"So what about Gail?" Libby asked, getting back to her original question. "Do we like her for Devlin's murder?"

"Are we calling it murder now?"

"Yes, we are."

"Last night you said you weren't sure."

"I didn't say that."

Bernie snorted. "You most certainly did."

"I was just exploring possibilities," Libby retorted. "But the more I think about it the more I think that, for once, the DA is right."

"Me, too." Bernie tapped her nails on the counter. "So let's talk about Gail, Rick Evans' charming wife." She took another sip of her coffee, put the cup down, finished pouring the batter into the cups, and put the muffin tins in the oven. She carried the empty bowl over to the sink and rinsed it out so she could make the bitter-sweet chocolate frosting she was going to top the cupcakes with.

"Yeah, she is a piece of work." Libby remembered the time she'd seen Gail lash out at the checkout girl in the local hardware store when the store didn't have what she'd needed.

"She does not take losing well," Bernie said

slowly. "Not well at all. Remember when she lost the school election for class president and put a snake in Patti Jensen's locker and Patti fainted? Gail claimed it was an accident. Like that snake just *happened* to find its way in there. Like the musket just *happened* to explode."

"I'll never forget that one," Libby exclaimed. "I had the locker two doors down."

Bernie smiled. "That was all you talked about for weeks. Somehow I don't think Gail's changed. I think she's just gotten better at hiding it."

"As do we all. One thing is for sure. She can't have taken it well. Losing Devlin to Juno, I mean."

Bernie snorted. "Now that's an understatement if I ever heard one. Gail has hated Juno ever since she was crowned Miss Apple Queen at the Longely Apple Festival."

Libby wrinkled her nose. "But Gail had to know Devlin was a well–known philanderer."

"Maybe that was part of Devlin's appeal. Philanderer." Bernie rolled the word around in her mouth. "The word reminds me of the word *philatelist*. Stamp collector," she explained, seeing Libby's puzzled expression. "One collects women while the other collects stamps. One has a black book and the other has an album."

Libby shook her head. Sometimes she didn't understand her sister. "Surely, given his reputation, Gail couldn't have been surprised when Devlin went off with someone else."

Bernie dried the mixing bowl, set it on its stand, and started measuring out the ingredients for the frosting. "You know what they say about denial being a river in Egypt. Anyway, knowing Gail, she would have thought she was so wonderful that Jack would stay with her forever. Or at least until *she* threw him out."

"Yes. She'd definitely want to be the one doing the leaving," Libby agreed.

"Don't we all." Bernie took the butter out of the cooler so it would have time to soften then got out the sugar, vanilla, dark chocolate, and coffee extract.

"Yes, we do. But some of us feel more of a need than others."

Bernie put her hands on her lower back and stretched. She'd slept wrong the night before and her lower back was killing her. "Maybe Rick and Gail Evans worked together to kill Jack. Each of them does have a motive."

Libby raised an eyebrow. "Interesting theory. The family that kills together, stays together? An exercise in family bonding?"

"Well, it is possible. It has been known to happen. Look at Bonnie and Clyde."

"I don't think they were married."

"The Macbeths?"

Libby groaned. "Just stop."

"All I'm saying is that what I suggested is within the realm of possibility."

"Agreed. However there is one small glitch. Gail wasn't there."

"A mere detail," Bernie said.

"However, Rick Evans was there, putting on quite the performance, accusing Marvin the way he did."

"Indeed he did. It's like he wanted people to forget that *he* was the person who developed the idea for the reenactment. *He* was the person who knew all about the arrangements."

"And he was the person who arranged for the costumes," Libby said.

Bernie went over to the counter and turned on the radio. Music helped her focus. "We should talk to Rick and Gail."

"Why both of them?" Libby asked as the timer went off for the pies.

"Because maybe Gail knows something."

Libby snorted. "She's not going to tell us."

"She might if she's approached in a low-key informal way."

Libby got up, turned the oven off, took the pie crusts out of the oven, and lined them up on the cooling racks. "Perfect," she said, looking at the golden, flaky crusts.

"Yes, they are." Bernie inhaled their aroma. "And they smell wonderful. You know, I have an idea."

"Don't tell me."

"You'll like this. Okay you won't like it, but I think I have a way to get Gail to talk. She has a standing appointment for a mani-pedi at La Dolce Vita at eleven every Tuesday . . . and today is Tuesday."

"You're telling me this, why?" Libby asked.

Bernie grinned. "Because I think you should go. It would be the perfect opportunity to chat her up."

"Why can't you go?" Libby demanded. "Excessive grooming is your specialty."

Bernie raised an eyebrow. "Excessive grooming? I think I'm going to ignore that."

"Seriously, why do I have to go?"

"Because while you're talking to Gail, I'm going to be poking around in the Evans's house."

"Why?" Libby asked.

"You said it yourself. Rick seems way too anxious to point a finger at Marvin. I want to find out why."

"What are you looking for?"

"Evidence."

Libby rolled her eyes. "Could you be a little more specific?"

"No."

Libby sniffed. "That's because you don't know what you're looking for."

"Untrue," Bernie shot back.

"Here's what I think. I think *I* should search the place and *you* should get the mani-pedi." Libby stared at her sister. "How's that?"

Bernie shook her head. "Sorry, but that won't work."

"Why in heavens not?" Libby protested.

"Because, Libby, for openers, you're Marvin's girlfriend and I am not."

"So what?"

"So Gail will be more likely to talk to you."

"How do you come up with that? I'd think it would be just the opposite."

Bernie flicked a speck of flour off of her tank top. "And you would be wrong. It's called bonding."

"Bonding?" Libby repeated.

"Yeah. In a manner of speaking. You're going to tell Gail how upset you are that Marvin did what he did and how upset he is about the incident. You're going to talk about what a terrible accident it was and how you're going to miss Jack Devlin. Poke in the ribs. Wink. Wink."

"But I'm not going to miss him," Libby objected. "Not one single bit."

"I know that. You know that. But Gail doesn't. It'll be interesting to see the expression on her face when you mention his name."

Libby started dissolving gelatin in orange juice, after which she got eggs out of the cooler. She slammed the door shut. "If it's going to be that interesting, you go," she said ungraciously.

"It won't be the same. Really. Otherwise, I would." Bernie put her hand up. "Swear."

"No, you won't. You just want me to get my nails done even though you know how much I hate having someone touch my hands and feet."

"Tsk-tsk." Bernie shook her head slowly. "Such a lack of trust."

Libby put her hands on her hips. "It's true, Bernie."

"No, it isn't," Bernie answered in as sorrowful a tone as she could manage.

Libby decided her sister looked as if butter would melt in her mouth. She wished she had her sister's ability to play the innocent.

Bernie turned serious. "I really do think you have the best chance of getting something out of Gail. If I didn't, I wouldn't ask you to go."

Libby crossed her arms over her chest and frowned. She felt herself begin to weaken. "I don't know."

"Well, I do. Even if you don't want to, do it anyway. Do it for Marvin," Bernie urged. "After all, that's what this is all about."

"That's a low blow. Even for you."

Aware that she had scored the winning goal, Bernie smiled sweetly. She was always magnanimous in victory. "But an accurate one." She went over and planted a kiss on Libby's cheek. "Thank you. And who knows? You might actually like it. The mani-pedi, that is."

"I won't," Libby said, getting the last word in.

Bernie let her. Given the circumstances, she figured it was the least she could do.

Chapter 9

W hat are you going to do if the garage door isn't open? " Libby asked her sister as they drove toward the Evans's house.

Bernie had confided that she planned on entering the Evans's house through their garage. That would give her a chance to try and open the door with the picks she'd "borrowed" from her dad's desk drawer without anyone seeing her.

"Then I'll find another way, but it always is," Bernie replied.

"And you know this how?" Libby asked.

"Because I usually go by their house when I go to Eli's to get the flour." Bernie fiddled with the air-conditioning in the van, trying to get a little more cool air out of it.

Libby fanned herself with the side of her hand. "You go this way?"

"It's shorter."

"Not by much."

"By enough." Bernie gave up on the air-conditioner and leaned back. *If I don't move, I'll be fine,* she told herself. Maybe she should buy a fan. One of the old-fashioned paper variety. She remembered seeing a lovely one in an antique store in the city.

She ate the last of her slightly stale raspberry chocolate muffin and brushed the crumbs out of the smocking on the front of her dress. Raspberry and chocolate were a no-fail combination, even if she did say so herself.

It was ten forty-five in the morning and almost ninety degrees. Rain was predicted in the early afternoon from a storm moving up the East Coast. Given the grayness of the sky, it looked as if the rain was going to be coming a lot sooner than that.

"Good luck," Libby said as she dropped Bernie off three blocks from the Evans household.

Since they only had one vehicle, a vehicle with the name of their business emblazoned on the side, they'd decided it would be smarter if they met up again at the salon. Parking the van in front of the Evans's house was out of the question. Bernie's walk from the house to the nail salon was a mile at most, which wasn't terrible.

Ordinarily, Bernie wouldn't have thought anything of it, but it was like a steam bath outside. Even though she had her bottle of water and was wearing a light silk dress that was as close to wearing nothing as she could manage, her walking flip-flops, and a hat, it was still going to be a schlep. In fact, she was a little sorry—no very sorry—that she wasn't the one having her nails done and that Libby was the one snooping around the garage.

Obviously, she had grossly underestimated the humidity. *There's a lesson to be learned here,* Bernie told herself. *Don't believe the weather forecaster.*

Oh well. What was done was done, as her mother used to say. Anyway she was better at this kind of thing—criminal activity of the lite variety—than Libby was. It wasn't something to brag about, but it was true. For one thing, she didn't get as easily flustered as her sister did.

"Tell them to shave your calluses," Bernie told her sister as she got out of the van. "It's ten dollars more, but it's worth it."

"Shave my calluses?" Libby repeated. "How do they do that?"

"With a razor."

"No one is getting near my feet with a razor."

Bernie shrugged. "Okay, but your heels are cracking."

Libby sniffed. "They're fine, thank-you-very-much."

"Don't you want soft feet?"

"I really don't care. My feet take me where I want to go and that's good enough for me."

"You're just a tad grumpy this morning."

"That's because I'm about to do something I don't want to do."

"You need chocolate," Bernie observed. "You're going into chocolate withdrawal."

"There is no such thing," Libby said.

"Yeah, there is and I think you're the poster child for it."

"Maybe you're right," Libby conceded as she pulled away and headed toward her putative rendezvous with Gail at the nail salon, leaving Bernie on the side of Maple Tree Lane.

The Evanses lived in a middle-class homogeneous development. That was Homogeneous with a capital *H*. The buildings had gone up in the seventies and mostly consisted of two-story colonials, which appeared to have been designed by someone using a Xerox machine. The fact that almost all of the houses were painted white, with a few light blue and beige ones sprinkled about, didn't help. Bernie had always thought the people who lived in the blue and beige houses had to be the rebels in the development. It was the kind of place where it would be easy to go out, get slightly tipsy, and wander into the wrong residence.

Built by the same developer who had built several other developments in and around Longely, the area featured the same touches. They included but were not limited to tree names for the main streets, black and gold decorative street lamps, houses with entrances that faced the street, attached garages, and gold eagles perched on the eaves over the front doors.

Although the landscaping had not been mandated, each house featured evergreen foundation plantings in front of the houses, as well as petunias and impatiens in the summer, mums in the fall, and tulips in the spring.

In addition, ninety percent of the houses had American flags flying out front. The only difference between the residences was that some of the houses had children's toys strewn on the front lawn and some didn't. Rick and Gail's house was one of those that didn't, a fact Bernie was reminded of as she neared their residence.

She noted another fact and her spirits plummeted. Despite what she'd said to Libby, the garage door to the Evans's house was closed. Shut tight like a drum, although why a drum should be shut tight she didn't know. Bottom line, that sucked. She couldn't even look inside. The garage door was one of those cheapo models that didn't have any windows.

Bernie slowed her pace as she thought about what to do next. Of course, she could always leave, but that would mean admitting to Libby she was wrong and she wasn't prepared to do that. Also, most important, was the fact that, given the circumstances, Marvin did need as much help as he could get. A fact she shouldn't lose sight of.

Bernie nibbled on one of her fingernails as she considered what to do next. She guessed it would have to be the picks she'd brought along. After all, she couldn't climb in through the second-story. She wasn't wearing the right shoes for that sort of endeavor. Flip-flops just didn't cut it when it came to second-story work. Besides, the windows were probably sealed, anyway. That left the first floor. She thought about breaking a window in the back, but discarded the idea. She didn't want to alert Gail or Rick to the fact that someone had been inside.

Of course, she could make it seem like a robbery had been committed . . . but that was a lot of work. Too much work and it increased the danger of being caught. If listening to her father's stories over the years had taught her anything, it was that the more complicated things were, the more clues were left behind, which meant the greater the chance of being apprehended.

The only problem with using the picks, as she now remembered was that she wasn't very good with them. She sighed. Oh well. She guessed she was going to have to give it a try anyway.

On the bright side, the neighbors were at work and no one would see her.

Bernie stuffed her water bottle in her bag and walked quickly to the back. She spent the next twenty minutes trying to open the door . . . and failing. Finally, she gave up. She was just about to leave when she looked at the wreath full of herbs that was tied on the door and laughed. She couldn't believe it! All this time struggling, and there was a key tied to the wreath. She hadn't seen it because the black nylon cord had blended in with the willow branches intertwined with the herbs, which of course was the whole idea.

She carefully took the wreath off its hook, unfastened the key, and wound the tie around her finger so she wouldn't lose it. She put the wreath back, inserted the key in the lock, and turned it. The door swung open. Elated, she did the happy dance, then got control of herself and went inside, carefully closing the door behind her.

She found herself in the kitchen. She took a quick look around, noting the time on the clock. She figured that to be on the safe side she should be out of the house by twelve o'clock at the latest. Bearing that in mind, she continued on through the living room and dining room, pausing on the way to look at the mail and the bank statement that had been left out on the dining room table. Nothing in it raised any alarm bells. From what she could see, Rick and Gail Evans looked like the average carrying-too-much-credit-card-debt couple.

She headed upstairs and did a quick run-through of the second floor. She found nothing noticeable so she returned to the first floor, went into the kitchen, and opened the door that led to the basement.

She switched on the light and slowly walked down the ten steps into something that wasn't quite as bad as the pictures of hoarders' houses on TV . . . but it was pretty darn close. Furniture was piled on top of furniture without much space to walk through. *How odd,* Bernie thought. The upstairs was immaculate. The downstairs was an incredible mess. It was as if the house was schizoid.

Looking around, it was obvious the basement was the repository of twenty years worth of stuff. At least. Probably more. In fact, there was so much stuff that it took her a minute to break what she was seeing into individual components.

She identified a washer and dryer sitting on top of a chest of drawers, two old refrigerators and an upright freezer piled together, a pool table with a tear in the felt, a foosball table with one leg propped up on a load of books, four file cabinets, a kitchen table, shelving of various sizes, old aquariums, stacks of old newspapers, innumerable cartons filled with who-knew what, piles of empty laundry detergent and Clorox bottles, not to mention a scattering of tools, some with their price tags still attached.

Bernie sighed. Looking through the mess would take weeks and all she had was half an hour, maybe three-quarters of an hour at most, if she pushed it.

"Of course it would help if I knew what I was looking for," she muttered as she skirted a dining room table. She took another step, jamming her little toe against an old generator that had been lurking under the table. She cursed as she hopped on one foot. *Serves you right for wearing sandals,* she could hear Libby say as she bent down and rubbed it.

When the pain subsided, she opened the top drawer of the filing cabinet nearest her and began looking through the papers jammed into it. From what she could see, they were a potpourri of bills, receipts, recipes, newspaper articles, and tax returns, some of which dated back thirty years or more.

She looked closely at a few of the papers then stopped and closed the drawer, certain that nothing in there had anything to do with Jack Devlin's death. She quickly looked through the second and third drawers, but they contained the same materials as the first one. She thought about looking in some of the other file cabinets and changed her mind. She was positive it would be more of the same. Turning, she scanned the basement again and shook her head. The chaos made her think about the state of A Little Taste of Heaven's office. It wasn't nearly as bad as the basement, but it wasn't good.

Truth was, she'd be lucky if she could lay her hands on the shop's tax returns for the last year. Well, that wasn't exactly true. She knew they were in a pile in the office; she just didn't know which pile, and that was true of their expense sheets, as well. It was one of the reasons tax season was always such a nightmare. One of these days, she and Libby were going to have to go through their papers, keep what should be kept, and throw out what needed to be thrown out before their office ended up looking like this basement. Fortunately, their office was smaller, which kept the mess down.

Bernie shook her head again as she contemplated the task in front of her. Herculean was a fairly accurate term, she decided as she cruised up and down the basement randomly opening cardboard cartons. Most contained clothes, some contained books and magazines, while others contained dishes, glasses, and sundry pots and pans. One thing was for sure. None of them contained anything that indicated Rick or Gail . . . or both . . . had anything to do with Jack Devlin's death.

If she ever wanted to hide something, this would be the place to do it, Bernie reflected.

For a moment, she weighed the idea of giving up the search and getting out of the Evans's house, but she remembered what Cheech had said about not being able to catch the wave if you weren't in the ocean and she made the decision to keep going. She spotted a door across the basement and made her way to it. Opening it, she clicked the switch, and went inside.

Chapter 10

The room was eight feet by ten feet wide. It was cooler than the rest of the basement and smelled of oil and metal. The walls were painted a high gloss white and lined with shelves. A recliner and a small TV sat in the left corner of the room. A large metal table with two stools stood in the middle. A collection of coffee cups, take-out containers, and rags smelling vaguely of oil were strewn over the top.

As Bernie looked around, she saw lots of guns, lots of gun paraphernalia, and realized she was in the room of a serious gun collector. *This is it,* she thought. *Rick Evans is responsible for what happened at the reenactment.* Then she took another look around and thought, *maybe not.* What she didn't see was anything resembling the muskets that the reenactors had used. She stepped up and studied a pair of mother-of-pearl handled dueling pistols displayed in a red velvet-lined case. Next to that were a Walther PPK, a German Luger, a Lancaster Oval Bore, a Browning, a Beretta, and a Glock. All of them were in their cases. All of them were neatly labeled.

She was especially taken with a tiny pearl-handled revolver that was simply labeled LADIES GUN. 1875. WYOMING. *The trouble with owning something like that,* she thought, *is I'd never be able to find the damned thing among all the junk I carry in my bag.* Of course, she'd certainly be able to find the AK-47 on the next shelf, or the Sterling submachine gun, the Colt carbine, or the Uzi, not to mention the Remington rifle, the Winchester, or something called the Needle gun. Again, all were neatly labeled.

As Bernie studied the guns, it occurred to her that they must be worth quite a bit of money. She moved around the room, spotting boxes of ammo, rods for cleaning the rifles, bags of rags, bottles of oil, and a machine she thought Rick Evans used to refill his bullets. A couple targets were tucked in one corner. She didn't see anything that looked like the muskets used in the reenactment. Of course, they could be hidden somewhere, but that seemed unlikely. Why hide something from yourself? Nevertheless, she took another look through the room just to make sure.

She was still looking when she got a call from her dad. The moment she picked up, she knew that she shouldn't have.

"Where are my picks?" Sean asked.

"No hellos? No hi, how ya doing?" Bernie replied.

"Don't start with me, Bernie. What are you doing?"

She told him.

She heard a sharp intake of breath, then silence. That meant that her dad was really mad.

"Don't you want to know what I found?"

"No. I want you to stay out of my desk."

"Would it help if I told you I was looking for some Scotch tape?"

Silence.

"I'll snap some pics and send them to you. You don't have to look at them if you don't want to."

More silence.

"Come on, Dad," she wheedled. "I need your opinion."

There was another moment of silence, then Sean said, "I'll see," and hung up.

"Okay," Bernie said to herself as she took out her cell and began snapping pics of the gun collection. Then she sent them off to her dad with a text. What do you think?

Her dad didn't reply. Not that she had expected him to. It would take him a little while to cool off.

Bernie dawdled for a couple minutes, looking around a bit more. Something was bothering her, but she couldn't figure out what it was. Then she had it. Rick Evans had never mentioned anything about guns. He'd never given the impression that he knew anything about them.

But so what? Bernie thought as she eyed the items in the room. That really didn't mean anything. There was no reason why he had to say anything. On the other hand, he had given the clear impression that he knew as much about muskets as Marvin did, which was to say that he didn't know anything at all. Hence, Rick Evans was lying by omission.

Maybe *lying* was an inaccurate word. Maybe the word she wanted was *dissembling*. Whatever term one applied, the truth was that he had the capability of loading up his musket with shot, swapping it out with one of those Marvin had gotten from the costume store, and handing it to Jack Devlin.

After all, Rick Evans had come up with the idea for the reenactment. Maybe the whole thing was just a way to help him get to Devlin. Maybe Marvin was just collateral damage, a convenient scapegoat. Maybe Devlin wasn't supposed to die. Despite what Brandon had said, maybe Rick had wanted to just hurt Devlin. Maybe he wanted to teach him a lesson he'd never forget, especially when he looked in the mirror every morning.

Bernie thought about how Devlin's face had looked and shuddered. Devlin would have been seriously maimed or blinded if he had survived. Was it possible to calibrate the misfiring of a musket so that whoever was holding it would be hurt, but not killed? Was that even possible? Bernie would have to ask her dad and Brandon, but she was pretty sure she knew the answer already. It wasn't.

She took a deep breath and blew it out. She had no proof of anything. The entire case she was building in her mind was strictly circumstantial. It was even less than that, really. She was stretching the facts to fit her hypothesis. She could see no muskets in the basement and nothing to indicate that Rick even had any. Bernie wondered how many people involved in the reenactment had muskets in their houses. She wondered how many were gun collectors. How many were hunters?

Good questions.

Bernie's cell rang. She looked down. It was her dad. Not answering it wasn't an option.

"Are you out yet?" he asked when she picked up.

"On my way." Well, she was. Almost.

"Hurry up. If you get caught, I'm not bailing you out of jail." He hung up before she could ask him if he'd had a chance to look at the pics.

Bernie took a final look around, put her cell phone back in her bag, and walked out of the room, taking care to close the door behind her. She threaded her way through the basement, went up the stairs, and through the house. At the back entrance, she let herself out, locked the door, carefully reattached the key to the wreath, and left the Evans house.

The heat hit her full force. She stood for a moment, wiping the sweat off her neck and regretting the fact that she was going to have to walk to the nail salon. Unfortunately, she couldn't think of another option.

Bernie pulled the water bottle from her bag and took a sip as she walked to the front of the house. She put on her sunglasses to block the sun's glare and looked around. It was still. Nothing was moving. No one was outside on the front lawns. No one was on the road.

The only sounds she could hear were the droning of the air-conditioners and the buzz of a lawn mower off in the distance. Even the birds were quiet in the noonday sun, lulled into a torpor by the heat.

She walked to the corner, made a right, and continued until she was on one of the smaller, secondary roads in the development. A quarter mile later, she made a sharp left. The last thing she wanted was Gail passing her on the way home from the salon in the event that she'd finished early. It wasn't likely to happen, but Bernie decided it paid to be careful. She'd pushed her luck far enough for one day.

If Gail saw Bernie, she'd stop and offer her a lift. Then she'd want to know what Bernie was doing in that part of town and why she was on foot. Frankly, Bernie couldn't come up with a good answer. Call her crazy, but somehow a reply like, *Oh, I'm just walking back to meet my sister after breaking into your house,* probably wouldn't be well received. Nor would, *And by the way, is there anything you want to tell me about your husband's gun collection?*

Bernie took another drink of water, found a tissue, and blotted the sweat off her face. She didn't want her eyeliner and mascara getting into her eyes. The stuff was supposed to be water-proof, but she had her doubts. She'd gotten her cell phone back out to call Marvin and tell him what she'd found, when he called her. She punched the ANSWER button. "Hello."

"I think someone took a shot at me."

"Ha-ha. So not funny," Bernie told him.

"I'm not kidding," Marvin said.

Chapter 11

Bernie came to a dead halt in the road. She figured maybe she'd heard wrong. "Excuse me?"

"I said someone shot at me," Marvin repeated.

Bernie could hear the panic in his voice. She leaned against an oak tree. The heat was making her light-headed. "What makes you think that?"

"There's a bullet hole in my windshield," he said, his tone turning sharp, "that's why I think that."

"Were you in the car at the time?" Bernie asked.

"No. I'd just gotten out."

"Did you see who did it?"

Marvin coughed. "No."

"Maybe it was an accident," Bernie said, straining to find a credible explanation for what had just occurred.

"How could it be an accident?" Marvin demanded.

"Someone might have been firing at a target and missed. Bullets can travel a long way." She couldn't fathom why someone would want to shoot at Marvin. She could understand Jack Devlin being killed, but Marvin? To her knowledge, he had no enemies. "Where were you when this happened?"

"Where I am now. At the funeral home."

"Very efficient of whoever it was," Bernie noted.

"I thought so."

Bernie was silent for a moment as she pictured the place. The odds of a bullet accidentally finding its way into Marvin's windshield from the surrounding area seemed unlikely, to say the very least. The area was mostly private housing with retail establishments running down a main road. Although there was a gun range in Longely, it was nowhere near the funeral home. She took another sip of water. Could someone have fired from the road? From the parking lot? Maybe whoever took the shot was aiming at someone else. She would like to believe that.

"What car were you driving?" Bernie asked.

"The Taurus. Why?"

"That car is extremely common. Maybe someone mistook you for someone else."

"I hope so." But Marvin didn't sound convinced. She switched her cell phone to her other ear. "When did this happen?"

"Not that long ago."

Bernie fought an impulse to sit down under the tree. She should have had something more than a blueberry tart to eat before she left the shop. She should have had the Parma ham, caramelized onion, Fontina cheese, and arugula sandwich that she had wanted. She couldn't go without eating actual food anymore. If she did, she'd get the shakes.

"How long is not that long ago?"

"About an hour," he answered.

"An hour?" Bernie fanned herself with her hand.

"That's what I just said."

"Why did you wait to call?"

"Because I was tied up with the police. They're finishing up now."

"When did they get there?"

"Almost immediately. Our tax dollars at work."

"That was fast," Bernie observed.

"They said they were in the neighborhood."

"Interesting," Bernie muttered.

"What did you say? I didn't get that."

"I just said they responded really fast." She wondered if the Longely PD was keeping an eye on Marvin.

"They said they were investigating a shoplifting complaint at Target," Marvin explained. The store was just down the road from the funeral home.

"So what did the police conclude?" Bernie prompted when Marvin didn't say anything more.

"About Target?"

"No. About your getting shot at."

"Oh. They think that I did it," Marvin said after another moment of silence.

Bernie couldn't believe what she was hearing. "You're kidding me, right?"

Marvin's voice quavered. "I wish I was. They told me they think I did it to deflect suspicion away from myself."

"That's absurd," Bernie huffed.

"That's what I told them, but I'm pretty sure they didn't believe me."

"You don't even have a gun!" Bernie exclaimed.

"I guess they think I do."

"You don't know one end of a gun from

112

another," Bernie continued. This thing was just getting sillier and sillier. Well, one thing was for certain. The Longely PD hadn't been following Marvin after all. A fact that was good and bad.

"You should tell them that," Marvin said.

"I intend to." Not that it would make a difference.

"I think I should call a lawyer," Marvin opined.

"I thought you'd done that, Marvin. You said you were going to."

"Well, I haven't."

"Why the hell not?"

"I guess I was waiting for this to go away, but it's not going to, is it?"

"Most definitely not."

"I can see that now. Things are just getting worse. They . . ."

"They who?" Bernie asked.

"The police," Marvin clarified. "They said something about getting a warrant to search the house. My father will have a coronary if that happens. How's he going to explain that to our clients? Hell, how am I going to explain it to our clients?"

"Don't worry."

"Don't worry?" Marvin yelled into the phone. "Are you insane?"

Bernie held the phone away from her ear until he stopped shouting. "Maybe a little bit."

"I don't even know who to call." Marvin's

voice was plaintive. "The lawyer my dad uses does stuff like real estate."

"My dad will know. Come over to the flat and have some coffee and cake and we'll discuss strategy."

"I don't want to discuss strategy."

"Then what do you want to do?"

"Sleep. I want to wake up and find that this whole thing is a bad dream." There was a short pause then Marvin said, "I'm tired. I want to go to bed."

"Marvin, you can't go to bed and pull the covers over your head."

"I didn't say anything about covers, Bernie."

"You have to fight this, Marvin," she told him as a car went by. The Miata slowed down, and for a moment, she thought the driver was going to stop and ask for directions. Then it sped up and turned the corner, leaving a vague smell of exhaust in its wake.

"But I don't want to fight," Marvin wailed, responding to Bernie's last comment. "I just want this thing to disappear."

"Libby and I are trying to make that happen." Bernie watched a butterfly land on a daisy growing by her left foot. "We really are. But we can't do it without your help."

"All right," Marvin said grudgingly after a minute had gone by.

Bernie shifted her cell to her other ear. Her face

was slick with perspiration. She was positive that the suntan lotion she'd applied earlier was now on the face of her cell phone. "So you'll come to the flat?"

"Yes, I'll come. I don't want to, but I will."

"And drive over in the Taurus. I want to look at the windshield."

"I can't. The cops are impounding the car."

"That's absurd."

"Tell me something I don't know," Marvin said. "But what can I do?"

"Stall them until Libby and I get there," Bernie told him.

"How am I supposed to do that?"

"I don't know, Marvin. Figure something out." Bernie hung up and called Libby. The phone rang and on the seventh ring went to voice mail. "Come on, Libby, pick up the phone," Bernie urged as she called again.

But Libby didn't answer. Then Bernie's phone went black.

"Arrrgh," Bernie cried. She'd run out of juice.

She slipped her cell back in her bag and started walking. She didn't think it was a good omen for how the rest of the day was going to go.

Chapter 12

Libby was sitting at the nail drying station trying to keep from scratching an itch that she'd suddenly developed when her cell started playing *Bernadette*. It was her sister's ring. *Drats and double drats,* she thought, wondering what Bernie had found or if she'd found anything at all in Rick and Gail's house. For a moment, Libby considered digging her cell out of her purse and finding out, but then she decided she going to have to wait to hear the news until after her nails dried.

The phone rang again. She had second thoughts about not answering it, but quashed them. She was sure that whatever Bernie wanted to tell her could wait another fifteen minutes. She was always given to the dramatic. Libby knew if she got her phone out, she'd ruin her nails and she wasn't about to do that given the time and the money the mani-pedi had cost. Also, she was loath to admit it, especially to Bernie, but she kind of liked the way her nails looked. Pink was not such a bad color after all! Libby groaned to herself. She'd always made fun of women who couldn't do anything that would ruin their nails and now she was becoming one of them. Go figure.

She glanced at the clock hanging on the wall. Bernie would be there shortly. More to the point, Gail Evans was sitting right next to her. She'd finally started talking about something other than how hot it was and Libby wasn't going to do anything to stem the conversational flow. Otherwise, the torture she'd put herself through for Marvin's sake for the last three-quarters of an hour would all be in vain. One thing was for certain. She was never ever going to do it again, even though she did like the way her hands looked.

For openers, she didn't like someone she didn't know touching her feet. For some reason, getting a manicure wasn't as bad, but that was balanced by the fact that she couldn't stand the idea of not being able to reach into her bag and get a piece of chocolate out if she wanted to. Or answer the phone. The process made her feel claustrophobic. She was wondering why that should be when she realized Gail was talking again.

"You know," Gail confided in her chirpy voice, a voice that always made Libby want to put on a pair of noise canceling headphones, "I envy your talent."

Libby turned and looked at her. "For what?"

"For cooking, of course. I'm a complete klutz in the kitchen."

"I'm sure you're not that bad," Libby told her, although she thought that maybe Gail was.

It had been her experience that really skinny people, people who were that way not by nature but because they didn't like to eat, generally sucked in the kitchen. They were always in a hurry to get in and out. Understandable if one didn't like what one was doing. Cooking and baking took time and patience. Each step, no matter how trivial, contributed to the final result. If you didn't like to eat, you didn't want to be bothered.

Gail's cell began to ring. She ignored it. "I am a klutz," she insisted. "Every time I'm in the kitchen I either cut or burn myself." She gestured toward her left arm with her chin. "Look at those."

Libby squinted. She couldn't see anything. "What?"

"The scars, of course."

Libby studied Gail's arm again. It was suntanned and muscled and looked as if Gail hit the gym frequently.

"See them? I'm thinking of having plastic surgery."

It took Libby a moment, but she finally made out three thin raised lines radiating up from Gail's wrist. "But they're tiny," she objected.

"Not to me. I see them in the mirror every time I put on a short-sleeved shirt, which I'm doing a lot this summer."

Libby wanted to say *it must be hard being*

perfect, but she didn't. Instead, she asked Gail how she'd gotten the scars.

Gail put on a rueful expression. "I got too close to a roasting pan that was coming out of the oven."

"Ouch. That must have hurt."

"Oh. Believe me, it did." Gail was quiet for a moment.

Her phone rang again. "My husband," she explained. "I guess he forgot where I am." She was quiet for another moment then she said, "I still can't believe what happened at the reenactment." Her voice got shaky. "I just can't get that picture out of my mind."

"Neither can I," Libby said. It was true. She still couldn't.

"I keep dreaming about it," Gail confided.

"Me too," Libby said, which was also true. Her glance fell on Gail's toes. They were painted a dark shade of purple. Almost black. So were her fingernails. In Libby's opinion, Goth was not a good look on teenage girls, let alone on middle-aged ladies, especially middle-aged ladies who wore thigh-high skirts because they were trying to look like teenage girls.

Libby shook her head to clear it. Where had that come from? She was getting as hypercritical as Bernie. Maybe being in the nail salon had infected her in some way with Bernie-itis. Who knew where something like that would lead?

Libby might have to get her hair colored and styled or go clothes shopping or even, God help her, go to the gym and take spin classes. She felt a frisson of fear as visions of hours spent on self-improvement wafted through her head. *Get a grip,* she told herself. *Deal with the matter at hand.*

Gail leaned over. "You must feel so bad." She lowered her voice so none of the other patrons could hear her, not that there were many people in the place. It was why she always went to the nail salon at that particular time of the day.

Libby frowned. "Why should I feel bad?"

Gail's eyes widened. "Well . . . you know . . . being . . . with Marvin. It must be terrible."

Libby cocked her head. "Why?"

Gail gave her a pitying look and pointedly changed the subject. "Is this really your first time getting a mani-pedi?"

Libby nodded. She'd unwisely confided that fact to Gail when she'd sat down next to her.

"That's so sweet," Gail cooed. "Rick had his first pedicure last week. He found it very relaxing."

"That's wonderful," Libby said. She couldn't imagine Marvin doing something like that. "What did you mean about Marvin?" she asked, getting back to the topic at hand.

Gail tittered. "Oh, you know."

"No. I don't. I don't know at all."

Gail ducked her head, but not fast enough to hide the smirk on her face. "His being . . . involved . . . in what happened . . . and you seeing it. Being there. It just must be very upsetting. I know how upset I am. I can't imagine what I would be feeling if I were you. I mean, I'd be on Prozac or something like that."

"Seeing what?" Libby demanded even though she knew exactly what Gail was referring to.

Gail shifted in her seat and faced Libby. "What happened to Devi, of course."

Libby raised an eyebrow. "Devi? Who is Devi?"

"I'm sorry." Two red spots appeared on Gail's cheeks. She clicked her tongue against her teeth. "I meant Jack Devlin. Devi is, excuse me, *was* his nickname. It's what everyone who knew him called him."

"I knew him and I didn't call him that. No one else I know did, either."

"Well, his good friends did."

"Which you number yourself among?" Libby asked politely.

Gail sniffed. "He had a lot of good friends and yes, I was among them."

"It must have been interesting."

"What?" Gail asked.

"Being friends with him."

"It was, but why do you care?"

Libby gave an elaborate shrug. "I don't. I'm just trying to make conversation."

"I see." Gail looked at Libby, sussing her out. "I get it," she said after a moment. "You're here investigating." She gave the word *investigating* an ironic twist by stretching it out to three syllables. "You're investigating me! I find that hilarious. Well, investigate away. Not that it's going to help your boyfriend any. To use a current phrase, he's going down. At least according to Rick, he is. And Rick should know. After all, he does have the ear of the mayor and the chief of police."

"He's not going down if I have anything to do with it," Libby said grimly.

"Good luck."

"I'm not the one who's going to need it," Libby replied.

"Really." Gail smiled unpleasantly. "Then who is?"

"Whoever did it."

Gail shrugged and studied the board propped up next to the cash register that announced the salon's prices.

Libby continued. "I heard you were one of Devi's . . . ahem . . . closer friends."

Gail sniffed again then she smiled. "It's not a secret. Devi and I were close, as long as we're using euphemisms here."

"Should I have said *screwing?*"

"You can say whatever you want. It doesn't bother me. Anyway, as I was saying we were friends for a while and then we weren't."

"That must have been tough," Libby said, trying to sound sympathetic and failing.

Gail shrugged. "Not really. It's all a matter of expectations. When you take in a tomcat, you feed him, and play with him, and then you let him go. It's the nature of the beast, so to speak."

"What if he gallivants next door and gets more food?" Libby mused out loud. "Maybe even better food—"

"That I highly doubt." Gail cut Libby off.

"Fine then." *I've struck a nerve,* Libby noted.

"It's true." Gail's voice rose.

"If you say so," Libby answered, sticking the needle in a little deeper.

"I do," Gail said in a superior tone of voice.

"All I know is that I would find that chain of events upsetting."

"You probably would. But then, you're not me." Gail chortled at the idea. "If you must know, I was the one that told Devi to go."

"Oh." Libby gave Gail her sweetest smile. "How stupid of me. I thought it would have been your husband who did that. Shows you what I know."

"Not much," Gail said coldly. "No one tells me what to do. Anyway, Rick understands. I love my husband. Devi was merely a . . . diversion. Something to pass the time. Diversions are nice while they last, but then it's time to give them up and get back to the real world."

She looked at the TV screen on the other side of the salon. The sound was off, but the weather-girl was pointing to the weather map. It looked as if a storm was still on its way. That would be a good thing since they could use the rain.

"I hear Devi found"—Libby paused for a moment as if searching for the right word—"a more . . . youthful friend."

"Really. Is that what you heard?"

"Yes. It really is," Libby replied.

Gail bit her lip and narrowed her eyes. "Well, that didn't last for long. Devi wanted to come back. In fact, he was begging me to take him back. I guess he knew where the good stuff was."

"Do tell," Libby said.

Gail turned back and faced her. "Do tell yourself. In some things, experience does matter. It matters a lot."

"I guess you'd know," Libby sniped.

"Yes, I would." Gail's tone of voice was nothing if not smug. "I'm lucky to have found a man who understands . . . my needs. Some wouldn't."

"I take it you're referring to your husband?"

Gail didn't say anything.

"So Rick really didn't care?" Libby persisted.

"No. He didn't. We're soul mates. When you're soul mates, there are more important things than the merely physical."

Libby couldn't help it. She rolled her eyes. "He wasn't jealous?"

Gail gave a dismissive sigh. "Jealousy is a childish emotion. Adults have learned to overcome it. Nonattachment is the key."

"I didn't know Rick was a Buddhist," Libby said. If anyone was the antithesis of being a Buddhist, Rick was it. He was one big ball of *I wants*.

Gail smiled thinly. "He's not. He's an evolved human being."

"Well, so is Marvin, but that doesn't mean that he wouldn't be jealous if I was going around with someone else," Libby blurted out.

"I guess that's not going to be an issue for you," Gail told her sweetly.

Libby stared at her. She didn't understand. "What do you mean?"

"I mean, my dear, he's going to be in jail soon, so he'll hardly be in a position to object to whatever you decided to do. Jail does tend to put a damper on one's love life, though I do hear they allow conjugal visits . . . but maybe that's just in Mexico. I'm not sure. Oh. Excuse me. That's in the minimum security places."

Libby's eyes narrowed. "Marvin had nothing to do with what happened at the reenactment. Absolutely nothing and you know it."

Gail tossed her head and sat up a little straighter. "No, dear. I know nothing of the kind," she huffed. "Don't be ridiculous. Of course Marvin is responsible. Everyone knows that."

"That's not true," Libby protested.

"Just because you want something to be true, doesn't mean that it's going to be," Gail shot back.

"In this case, it is."

"The police don't think so," Gail retorted. "I know that for a fact."

"They've gotten things wrong before," Libby replied.

"Not in this case. You and your sister were both there. You saw what happened."

"Yes, we were—which is why I'm saying what I'm saying. Marvin had nothing to do with that musket misfiring. Someone else did. It could have been anyone."

Gail raised her carefully tweezed eyebrows. "Anyone?"

"Yes, anyone," Libby replied.

"That, my dear, is a triumph of wishful thinking. I feel badly for you. I know this is hard, but you have to learn to face reality."

"I think I'm doing a pretty good job of that."

Gail snorted as she tilted back her head and looked at the ceiling. "You're not. I'm only saying this to you because I like you."

"That's news."

"It's true. I do," Gail protested. "It pains me to say this, but you're acting like a fool. You have to get your head out of the clouds. You're a good baker, but a fool. The rest of the town agrees that

126

Marvin did it. Just read your Facebook postings. He did it because he was angry at Devi."

"Because of a fender bender? Don't be ridiculous," Libby snapped. "People don't kill people over things like that."

Gail shrugged. "Some people do."

"But not Marvin."

"Bad things have been known to happen for far less reason," Gail pointed out. "Perhaps Marvin just wanted to teach Devi a lesson and things got out of hand. Perhaps something else was going on. Maybe Marvin was doing something bad and Devi found out and threatened to go to the police."

"Like what?" Libby demanded.

Gail shrugged again. "I don't know. Something."

Libby took a deep breath to keep herself from yelling. "He didn't do anything. Absolutely nothing."

"I know it's painful, but you have to accept the fact that Marvin is the most likely suspect. There's no arguing with that."

"Nonsense. Total nonsense. Everyone had the opportunity," Libby countered. "Anyone could have gone into the storeroom. The lock was broken."

"So Marvin says. We only have his word for that."

"I believe him."

Gail sighed. "Then you and your sister are the only ones who do."

"He's being railroaded."

"By whom?"

"By your husband, for one."

Gail gave Libby a more sorrowful than angry look. "The truth of the matter is that your boyfriend is going to be arrested soon. It's just a matter of time. And I have to say I don't think it's going to be good for your business to be associated with him." Gail leaned over in Libby's direction. "I'm just offering a friendly piece of advice, for what it's worth," she confided. "You girls have good food. I'd hate to see you close."

"Is that a threat?" Libby asked.

Gail tittered. "Oh dear me, no. It's an observation."

"And you're saying that, why?"

"Well, you know how people are. Especially in small towns like this one."

"No, I really don't. Why don't you explain it to me?"

"They're always so suspicious. So anxious to affix blame."

"What are you saying, Gail? Exactly."

Gail gave Libby a brittle smile. "It should be apparent. I'm trying to do you a favor and give you a few words of wisdom," she informed Libby in a patronizing tone. "But evidently you're too . . . too . . . blind to listen to them."

Libby didn't answer because anything she had to say would have been beyond rude. She closed her eyes and took three deep breaths. How had the conversation shifted from Rick to Marvin? Somewhere along the way Gail had gained the upper hand. How it had happened Libby had no idea. What she did know was that it was all Bernie's fault.

If it hadn't been for Bernie, she wouldn't be there. She wouldn't be angry and frustrated. She wouldn't want to strangle Gail or eat a piece of chocolate. Both activities would be equally satisfying. Unfortunately, she couldn't engage in either at the present moment since her nails weren't dry . . . which was probably a good thing.

Another minute went by. And another. Libby couldn't stand it. She felt as if she was going to scream. She had to have a piece of chocolate to calm herself down. Surely her nails were done. She reached into her bag and took out a chocolate kiss. She was just about to unwrap it when Bernie burst into the salon.

She looked hot and disheveled and extremely cranky. "Why the hell don't you answer your phone?" she snarled as she advanced on the nail drying station.

Libby held up her hands and wiggled her fingers back and forth. "I didn't want to ruin these."

Bernie pointed to a ridge on Libby's thumb

where the nail polish had come off when she'd stuck her hand in her bag. "You already have."

Libby groaned. All that work for nothing.

"Come on," Bernie told her. "We have to go."

"Why? What's up?"

Bernie noticed that Gail's ears had perked up— metaphorically speaking.

"My, my," Gail purred. "What new and exciting developments are happening?"

"Nothing that need concern you," Bernie told her, which was a big fat lie. If it didn't concern Gail, she didn't know whom it did concern. "Absolutely nothing," she reiterated then turned to Libby. "We gotta go. Our cooler is on the fritz."

"That's terrible." Gail's face was a mask of fake concern.

Bernie didn't reply. She was too busy hustling her sister out of the salon door.

Chapter 13

As soon as Libby stepped outside she could feel her shirt sticking to her back. "What's wrong with our cooler?" she asked as they headed toward the van. She didn't want to think about how fast everything was going to spoil in the heat.

"Nothing's wrong with it." Bernie held out her hand. "Give me the keys. I'm driving."

"Then why did you say it was broken?" Libby asked her sister as she handed them over.

"Because I had to say something in front of Gail." Bernie opened the van door and rolled down the window to let some of the heat out. It had to be over a hundred degrees inside the vehicle. Unfortunately, there wasn't time to let it air out. She touched the seat. It was hot. "You should have parked in the shade."

"I would have if there had been any shady spots available." Libby took a rubber band out of her bag, lifted her hair off the nape of her neck, and formed a ponytail. There. That was better. "Are you going to tell me what's going on?" She hopped into the van and rolled down the window.

"In a sec." Bernie got in on the other side. The moment she sat down she could feel the heat radiating from the seat. It burned the back of her legs. "We need to get one of those reflective folding things for the windshield."

"The sooner the better," Libby agreed, wishing she had taken Bernie up on her offer and worn one of her long silk sundresses instead of what she had on. "So tell me. Is this about what you found at the Evans house?"

Bernie started the van up and turned on the air-conditioning. "Nope. It's about Marvin."

Libby put her hand to her mouth. "What about Marvin? Did they arrest him? Is he in jail?"

Bernie fanned herself. "Someone shot at him."

"Shot?" Libby echoed.

"That's what I said." Bernie started backing out of the parking lot. "But he's fine," she quickly added. "He didn't get hit."

"At least there's that." Libby blinked the perspira-tion out of her eyes.

Bernie put her foot down on the pedal and the van lurched forward.

"What happened?" Libby asked.

"From what Marvin said, he'd just parked the Taurus near the back door of the funeral home and was getting out of the car when someone shot at him. He didn't even realize what was happening until he saw the hole in the wind-shield."

"Then what did he do?"

"He ran inside and called the police."

"So he didn't get a look at the shooter?"

Bernie shook her head. "I don't think so."

"When did this occur?"

"As near as I could tell about an hour ago."

"And he called you? That's how you know?"

Bernie nodded.

"Why didn't he call me?" Libby asked.

"Maybe because you weren't answering your phone."

"Good point." Libby reached into her bag, pulled out her cell, and checked it. Her sister was right. Marvin had called. Twice. She felt embarrassed at the stab of jealousy she'd felt.

"Happy now?" Bernie asked, interrupting her thoughts.

Libby nodded. She was quiet for a moment as she thought about the implications of what Bernie had just told her. Then she said, "Do you think the shooter, whoever he—"

"Or she," Bernie interrupted.

"Or she . . . was aiming for Marvin? Or do you think this could have been an accident of some sort?" Libby asked, repeating Bernie's idea as the air-conditioner wheezed into life and began sending a tepid stream of air into the van's cab.

"I wish it was, but I don't think so. It happened in the back parking lot of Marvin's dad's funeral home."

"Okay. I'm not getting your point."

"Think about it. It's not as if there are any shooting ranges around there."

"True. Or places to hunt," Libby reflected, thinking of the last case they'd solved. "The area around the funeral home is all commercial retail and private homes."

"Exactly," Bernie said, blowing through a stop sign.

"We're not doing traffic signals anymore?"

"It's not as if anyone was at the intersection." Bernie gestured toward the road. No one was on it. "It's empty and we're in a hurry."

133

"Good excuse. I can hear you saying that to a cop."

"Do the words *backseat driver* mean anything to you?"

"Do the words *safe driver* mean anything to you?" Libby replied.

"Do you want to drive?" Bernie asked Libby.

"No."

"Okay then."

"Fine." Libby brooded for a couple minutes then she went back to thinking about what had happened to Marvin. "Maybe someone was shooting at a target in their backyard and missed," she suggested.

"That's possible," Bernie agreed.

"But you don't think that's what happened?" Libby asked, reading the expression on her sister's face.

"No, Libby. Honestly, I don't. It's too much of a long shot."

"What kind of bullet was it?" Libby asked.

Bernie shrugged. "Marvin mentioned a cartridge so it was from a modern weapon."

"Not a musket?"

"No, not a musket."

"So Devlin's death and this shooting might not even be related," Libby said.

"Maybe not, but it's hard to think they wouldn't be."

"Yeah. It is, isn't it," Libby conceded.

"At least Marvin's okay," Bernie reflected after another moment of silence had gone by.

"That's the important thing." Libby began tapping her fingers on the van's dashboard.

"Can you please stop that?" Bernie told her after a minute of *rat-tat-tatting* had gone by. "It's making me crazy."

"I'm thinking, Bernie."

"Well, could you think a little quieter?"

"I don't think that's a sentence."

Bernie didn't answer. She refused to be drawn into another quibble with her sister. She leaned over and turned on the radio. The sounds of early Madonna washed through the van.

"There might even be an upside to Marvin's being shot at," Libby said after they'd driven a couple more blocks.

"I know where you're going with this," Bernie replied, anticipating what her sister was going to say next as she cut off Libby and a bus at the same time.

Libby gasped and closed her eyes.

"We had room to spare," Bernie said defensively when Libby opened her eyes again.

"I didn't say anything," Libby countered.

"You didn't have to say anything. Your expression did it for you. God, you have no appetite for risk."

"That's not true. I'm just more prudent . . ."

"Wussy."

"Careful than you are," Libby said.

"Admit it. You're a backseat driver. You're even worse than Dad."

"I am not," Libby protested.

"You most certainly are," Bernie disputed. "No wonder Marvin lets you do all the driving."

Libby waved her hand in the air. "Can we just end this conversation?"

"With pleasure."

The sisters were quiet for another couple minutes.

Libby waved to a man walking down the street with his Jack Russell. "Ted Swanson. A large coffee, double sugar, no cream, and a blueberry scone." She recited his daily order. "He just got laid off last week."

"There's a lot of that going around," Bernie noted.

"Unfortunately. As I was saying . . ."

"It's not true."

"What?"

"That someone shooting at Marvin proves that Marvin had nothing to do with what happened to Devlin."

"How can you say that?" Libby protested. "Of course it does. If anything, the shot is a game changer. It shows that Marvin was the intended target, not Devlin."

"One would think."

"Yes, one would," Libby replied.

"Unfortunately, the police, in their infinite wisdom are not taking that view. According to Marvin, the police think he did it himself and then made up a story to explain it."

"But why would he do something like that?" Libby asked. "What would be the point?"

"Duh. Obviously, to take attention away from himself," Bernie replied in a sarcastic tone of voice. "At least, that's what the police are thinking."

"But that's ridiculous," Libby objected.

"No kidding. I know that and you know that, but the police don't know that."

"I bet this is Lucy's doing," Libby said bitterly. Lucy, aka Lucas Broadbent, was the present Longely Chief of Police.

"I wouldn't be surprised," Bernie agreed. "It's nice to know he hasn't strayed from his usual modus operandi—pick the most obvious solution and stay with it no matter what. He really is a jerk."

"An ambitious jerk." Libby slumped in her seat. She felt like a wet dishrag. Or was it a cloth? She didn't remember. "Can't we crank the air-conditioning up any higher?" she complained.

"I wish."

"I think I'm going to faint."

"It's not that bad."

"Yes, it is," Libby insisted.

"Okay, I won't argue. It is that bad."

"If it weren't, we wouldn't be selling four iced coffees to every hot one," Libby replied.

"Maybe we should get that iced-coffee maker," Bernie mused, going off on a tangent for a moment. "The glass one that looks like a piece of sculpture." She'd first seen the machine in a restaurant supply place down on the Bowery a couple months ago, then in a café in Dumbo and had been lusting for it ever since.

"For four thousand dollars? I don't think so."

"But it is so cool in a techno-Japanese kind of way."

"I didn't say it wasn't, but that's four thousand dollars we should be spending on other things like fixing up this van or getting another cooler before the one we have really does die."

"I suppose you're right," Bernie said sadly.

"I know I'm right."

No doubt about it. A Little Taste of Heaven's business had suffered in the heat. No one seemed to have an appetite, although to be fair, their picnic basket business was doing well. Libby turned around and looked out the window. The sunlight was blinding. Cars baked in the sun. Flowers wilted in the yards. The lawns, usually emerald, had taken on a drab olive color. They were at Acre Avenue. In another few minutes, they'd be at the funeral home.

Bernie cleared her throat. Libby turned and looked at her.

"One more thing. The police are about to impound Marvin's Taurus."

"Oh no," Libby cried.

"Oh yes. Evidently, they're treating it like a crime scene."

"Wonderful. Poor Marvin. Not only does he get shot at and called a liar, he gets his vehicle taken away. I'd say he's had a really sucky day."

"To say the least." Bernie turned onto Maiden Lane. "I want to see Marvin's Taurus before they tow it away."

"Why?"

"Maybe it will tell me—us—something."

Libby looked at her sister. "Like what? That it needs to have its windshield replaced?"

"Among other things," Bernie replied.

"So now you're a forensic expert."

"Listen, it can't hurt."

Libby looked out the window again. Even the crows had settled down for a nap. "I suppose you're right. It can't. So what did you find in the Evans's house?" Libby asked, changing the subject.

"Which do you want first? The good news or the bad?"

"The good news."

"Rick Evans is a gun collector."

"And the bad news?"

"He doesn't collect muskets."

Chapter 14

Bernie and Libby arrived at the funeral home ten minutes later. As Bernie followed the road around to the rear parking lot, they could see that Marvin's Taurus was already on the tow truck. Then they caught sight of Marvin standing next to the truck.

Hangdog was the word that came to Bernie's mind as she looked at him. "Damn and double damn," she cursed, pulling in next to the tow truck. She slammed on the brakes and rolled down her window. "I knew we should have gone faster," she muttered.

"I think we were going as fast as the van could go," Libby told her.

Bernie was about to reply when Marvin walked over. "I asked the driver to wait, but he wouldn't listen."

"Do you mind if I give it a try?" Bernie asked as she got out of the van.

Marvin shrugged. "Be my guest, but I don't think it'll do any good."

Bernie smiled. "Oh, I'm not so sure about that."

Marvin frowned. "Why? What do you have that I don't."

Bernie's grin grew wider. "Girl power." With that she advanced on her prey.

While Bernie sashayed over to the tow truck driver, Libby got out of the van and walked over to Marvin. It had only been a day since she'd seen him, but he looked as if he'd aged a couple years since then. His complexion had grown grayer, he'd developed black circles under his eyes and a stoop to his shoulders.

"Hey. How ya doin'?"

"Not too well," Marvin responded.

"I can tell." As Libby hugged him, she could feel the stubble on his cheek and the rapid beat of his heart. They stayed like that for a minute.

"You smell nice," he told her when they separated.

"Thanks. Bernie told me what happened."

"I figured she would."

"So you didn't see anything?"

Marvin shook his head.

"Are you sure?" Libby pressed. "Sometimes people see things and they don't realize that they have."

"I'm positive." Marvin flicked a gnat off his polo shirt. "I was busy thinking about the Jack Devlin thing. I wasn't paying any attention to my surroundings."

"Okay," Libby replied.

"I mean"—his voice rose—"it's not as if I expected to get shot at."

"Of course not." She put her hand on his arm and gave it a reassuring squeeze.

Marvin smiled weakly.

"Why don't you tell me what happened from the beginning. Maybe we can make sense of it."

Marvin shrugged. "I don't see what difference it's going to make."

"Humor me on this."

"If you think so . . . although I really think this is just going to be a waste of time." He closed his eyes for a moment, trying to remember the sequence of events. When he was done he opened them again. "What do you want to know?"

Libby took two steps back so she was partially in the shade—which helped a little, but not as much as she would have liked. "You can start by telling me where you were coming from."

"Spenser's," Marvin answered promptly. "I was picking up Dad's dry cleaning."

"And then?"

"And then I paid for the suit and came back here."

"You didn't stop anyplace else?"

"Nope."

"Did you notice anyone following you after you left the store?"

Marvin shook his head. "No. Scratch that. I'm not sure. I mean, it's not as if I was checking in my rearview mirror or anything."

"What roads were you using?"

Marvin thought for a moment. "Ashcroft, Beech, then Main."

Those are local roads that don't have much traffic on them. If someone had been following Marvin, he would have noticed, Libby thought. She was beginning to understand why the police had taken the view they had. "Then what happened?"

"Nothing. Nothing unusual. I got here and drove around to the back entrance the way I always do. I remember I was reminding myself to check with the florist about the floral arrangements for Mrs. Fields's funeral. Her family wanted all white gladioli around her casket. Weird. Like it was a wedding instead of a funeral."

"Maybe it is to them," Libby commented.

"Maybe," Marvin said before returning to his monologue. "Anyway, I turned off the engine and pocketed the keys. I stepped out of the Taurus and that's when I heard this humming sound. I thought it was a bee or a wasp or maybe some kind of bird so I looked around, but I didn't see anything. Then I saw the hole in my windshield." Marvin stopped for a moment. "I didn't know what it was at first. It just didn't compute. Then I realized someone was shooting at me."

"Whoever it was shot at you after you got out of your car?" Libby asked, wanting to make sure she got the sequence of events correct.

Marvin nodded.

"He missed and hit the windshield instead?"

"Yes." Marvin swallowed.

Libby reflected that he still looked unsettled and his voice was still a little on the shaky side. Of course, given the circumstances she'd be pretty shaken up, too.

"Thank God. If I'd still been sitting there . . ." His voice trailed off. He shivered at the thought.

"But you weren't," Libby said firmly.

"No. I wasn't. Two more minutes . . ." His voice trailed off again.

"The shooter probably wasn't even aiming at you, Marvin. It was probably an accident."

Marvin visibly brightened. "You think so?"

"Absolutely," Libby lied. "Now, tell me what happened afterward."

Marvin took a deep breath and answered. "When I realized what it was I just . . . I . . . I panicked."

"Understandable. It's not every day a person gets shot at. At least not in Longely."

The corners of Marvin's mouth edged up into a small smile. "At that point, I ran inside and called the police. Now I wish I hadn't," he said bitterly. "I should have stayed and looked around. Maybe I would have seen something."

"No no, you did the right thing," Libby reassured him.

Marvin scowled. "No, I didn't. Calling the police has made things worse. Now they think I did it, and on top of everything else, they're impounding my car. Heaven only knows when I'm going to get it back."

"That should be the least of your problems," Libby told him as she watched the interaction between Bernie and the tow truck driver.

Bernie was listening intently to what the man had to say. Her head was cocked to one side and her eyes were locked onto the driver's eyes. You would have thought he was revealing the secrets of the universe. From what Libby could see, the only thing Bernie wasn't doing was batting her eyelashes at the driver. Libby wouldn't be surprised if that wasn't coming next.

He, on the other hand, was busy gawking at Bernie's ample tatas. In the couple feet between the van and the tow truck, Bernie had managed to unbutton the top two buttons of her blouse. Something told Libby it wouldn't be long before the driver winched Marvin's car down so Bernie could take a look at the windshield.

"So," Libby said to Marvin, wrenching her gaze away from Bernie and returning to the matter they'd been discussing, "where were you parked when this happened?"

He pointed to a space a foot away from the door. "There. Next to the hearses."

"That's your usual spot?"

Marvin nodded. "We like to leave the spot next to the door free for deliveries."

Libby didn't ask what deliveries he meant. She

didn't want to know. She studied the area. "I don't get it. How did the bullet hit the windshield instead of going through the rear window first?"

"Because I backed in, obviously. The front of the car was facing out," Marvin explained.

Libby nodded. That made more sense.

They heard a *clunk* as the Taurus came down. Score one for Bernie.

Libby felt a quick pang of envy at Bernie's prowess with the opposite sex and suppressed it.

"Don't tell anyone," Libby heard the tow truck driver saying to Bernie.

Bernie grinned. "Cross my heart and hope to die."

"Are you going to go over and look, too?" Marvin asked Libby.

She shook her head. Privately, she thought that what Bernie was doing was a waste of time, but she wasn't going to say that to Marvin. "I'm sure she's got it covered." Instead, she walked into the middle of the parking lot and looked around her.

The funeral home was surrounded on three sides by expensive housing developments situated on gently rising hills covered in grass with an occasional bunch of wildflowers thrown in. There were no trees, no tall grasses, nothing, as far as Libby could see, for a sniper to hide behind. *A sniper in Longely?* She shook her head. There might as well be hippos parading down the main square.

Maybe there were. She brought her palms

146

together and touched her fingers to her lips. Could Marvin have been the intended victim? Could Jack Devlin's death be an accident? It seemed so unlikely, but unlikely didn't mean it wasn't possible. She supposed she'd just have to wait and see.

She dropped her hands to her sides and turned toward the funeral home. A busy main road filled with retail establishments of one kind or another ran in front of it. No one could have taken a shot from the front of the building. They would have had to have driven up the narrow road to the back. If that had happened, Marvin would have heard them coming. If by some remote chance he didn't, he certainly would have seen them leaving.

"What are you doing?" Marvin asked as he joined her.

"Just thinking." She stepped back to where Marvin's car had been. As far as she could see, the only place the shot could have come from was the backyard of one of the houses in the development and that seemed highly unlikely. Unless of course, some kid was shooting his BB gun out in the backyard.

She went over and joined Bernie and the tow truck driver. They were staring at the Taurus's windshield. Maybe Bernie was right after all. Maybe looking at the windshield was going to help.

Libby pointed to the hole. "Do you think a BB pellet could have done that?" she asked Bernie.

The tow truck driver answered instead. "Not likely. It would've had to have been very close. Otherwise, it would have just cracked the windshield."

"How about a musket shot?" Bernie asked him.

"A musket is a rifle and that scatters shot. It would have peppered the windshield." He pointed to the hole. "I'm pretty sure a twenty-two made that."

"How come?" Bernie asked.

"Because I hunt and because I was an armorer and that makes me an expert on weapons."

"Armorer?" Bernie repeated. "Doesn't that have to do with knights and swords and stuff like that?"

The tow truck driver laughed. "Maybe back in the day, but now it has to do with the U.S. Army. I took care of weapons in Iraq," he explained.

"So you know about bullets and all the rest of that stuff," Bernie said, fluttering her eyelashes.

The tow truck driver grinned and leaned forward. "Yes ma'am. You could say I have it down cold."

Libby left Bernie and the tow truck driver to their flirtation and drifted away. *So much for my theory,* she thought. She went back to staring at the housing developments on the hills above the funeral home.

"What are you looking at?" Marvin asked as he came up beside her.

"Nothing really. Just trying to figure things out." She began chewing on the inside of her cheek, realized what she was doing and stopped. She would have loved a piece of chocolate—it helped her think—but that wasn't an option at the moment. It was simply too hot. The chocolate would melt in the heat.

She made a face. Okay. Shooting at Marvin was one of two things—an accident or on purpose. If it was an accident, it was a no harm no foul kind of situation and she didn't have to worry about it. However, if it was an on purpose deal, she did. If it was on purpose, the question was who had done it and why? *Good questions.* Of the seven reenactors, Rick Evans was the first one that came to mind given his conduct toward Marvin and the fact that he was a gun collector. But the other reenactors might have guns, too.

Why would Rick do something like that? What would he have to gain? Nothing, as far as Libby could see. He would gain no advantage whatsoever, especially since the police had already tagged Marvin for Devlin's death.

Then there was the how. Rick and Gail Evans's house was a solid twenty-minute drive away from the funeral home. In order to have executed this particular maneuver, Rick would have had to have driven over there, run through someone's backyard, and taken the shot from there. No other possibility that Libby could see. But that was taking an awful risk. If he were caught, it would be a difficult thing to explain. What would he say? That he was hunting turkeys? That he'd been seized by a sudden inexplicable desire to rid the area of crows?

Libby clicked her tongue against her teeth and studied the houses in the developments again. They all faced toward the road. She was looking at the rear of the houses and their backyards. All of them had large windows. She wondered if the windows were sealed. If they weren't, someone could have taken a shot at Marvin through one of the windows. No need to even go outside.

She stared at the houses again. There was something else. She just couldn't figure out what. She watched a cardinal fly by and land on a tall, white fluffy weed. It reminded her of a ball of cotton.

Cotton. That was it! She'd been thinking of cotton weed, which made her think of Samuel Cotton. The third grade teacher. His house was up there. He'd been a colonist in the reenactment, although he was supposed to have been a redcoat. Speaking of redcoats, David Nancy lived in the next development over and he had been a redcoat, too. Either one could have handed the musket to Devlin or taken a shot at Marvin or both.

Libby thought for another moment. Where was everybody? That was the question. Rick Evans was presumably at his office in the city. He went in every morning. It was a little after twelve so Samuel Cotton should be at school overseeing the summer camp the town was running, which left David Nancy, who worked at home, as the most likely suspect.

Libby smiled. At least it was a start. She always felt better when she had a plan.

Chapter 15

The moment Bernie parked the van in David Nancy's driveway, Libby hopped out, walked behind the garage, and contemplated the view from there. She could see two hearses parked out back of Marvin's father's funeral home. They shimmered in the heat. A dragonfly buzzed by her cheek as she watched a linen supply truck pull up to the funeral home entranceway. A moment later, the driver got out. He carried one large laundry bag under each arm. Libby noted that she had no problem reading the truck's logo.

"Dave Nancy has a clear shot at Marvin from here," she said as Bernie came up behind her. She waved her hand in the air to indicate the area that she meant. "It would certainly be easy enough to do."

"If he's a halfway decent shot," Bernie pointed out.

"Hopefully, that's one of things we'll find out."

"Even if he is, I don't see why he would do that." Bernie was less than enthusiastic about her sister's theory.

"Well, there is that minor point," Libby admitted. Offhand, she couldn't think of any reason why David Nancy would take a shot at Marvin.

Marvin hadn't been able to come up with a reason, either, but that didn't mean there wasn't one. After all, that's what investigations were all about. When she'd asked Marvin if he knew why, he'd just looked at her and said, "I have to move the sprinklers and then I'm going to go inside and lie down."

"He's shutting down," Bernie had said as Marvin had walked away.

"I should go after him." Libby had been about to take a step toward him when Bernie had put a hand on her shoulder and stopped her.

"Don't," she'd advised. "He needs some time alone."

Libby had acquiesced. In truth, she didn't have the energy to argue with him or with anyone else, for that matter.

They returned to the front yard. Standing out on the driveway, she felt as if the heat had soaked into her head and was turning her brain to mush. She was thinking that maybe she was getting sunstroke when Bernie nudged her in the ribs.

"What?"

Bernie handed her a water bottle. "Here. Have some of this."

Libby took a couple deep swallows and instantly felt better. "Come on," she said after she'd taken a few more. "Let's find out what David Nancy has to say for himself." With that, she turned on her heels, walked up to the house, and rang the bell.

A moment later, his wife Cora opened the door. She was a statuesque lady who was a good four inches taller and twenty pounds heavier than her husband, but there was nothing flabby about her, a fact that was immediately apparent because she was wearing the smallest bathing suit possible.

Really, it isn't a bathing suit at all, Bernie thought. *Just a G-string with a couple pasties on top.* "Nice outfit," she couldn't resist saying.

"Isn't it, though?" Cora favored her with a glittering smile. Her teeth were white enough to blind. "My husband says it's wrong to hide God's bounty under a bushel."

"I thought it was God's light," Libby said.

Cora shrugged. "Whatever. Now, what can I do for you ladies?"

"We'd like to speak to your husband," Libby said.

"Sorry," Cora replied promptly. "He isn't home. He's down in the city seeing a client."

"Funny. I thought I saw his car in the garage," Bernie said.

Cora crossed her arms over her chest. "That's because I drove him to the train station."

"He's an industrial designer, isn't he?" Libby asked.

Cora nodded. "Not an easy thing to be these days, especially when everything's being jobbed out to China."

"What does he design?" Libby asked, more to be polite than for any other reason. She didn't know a lot about Nancy and his wife, they being relative newcomers to the area.

Cora tittered and put her hand up to her mouth. "Sex toys."

"Interesting line of work," Bernie observed.

"He used to design perfume bottles, but his company got taken over." Cora shrugged. "Now he does this." She formed her lips into another smile. Her eyes didn't follow along. "You'd be surprised how much money is in this kind of stuff, and, hey, money is always nice."

"Yes, it is." Bernie agreed. She knew where some of that money was going, too. Plastic surgery was not cheap and from the looks of her, Cora had indulged in more than her share. She was one of those women who was never going to grow old, at least not if she could help it. From what Bernie could see, no part of Cora's body had escaped the surgeon's knife. She'd been nipped and tucked and Botoxed to within an inch of her life. Looking at her, Bernie thought maybe she'd wait to get some work done. Not that, given her financial situation, she was contemplating it any time soon.

"Can I tell David what this is about?" Cora asked.

"It's about the shooting," Bernie told her.

Cora put a hand to her bee stung lips. "I was there."

"Were you?" Bernie decided Cora had to be talking about the shooting that had happened during the reenactment, not the shooting at Marvin.

Cora shook her head. "I was late. It was terrible." Her voice rose. "Frankly, I wish I hadn't gone at all."

Bernie detected a sob or maybe a catch in Cora's voice, but whether it was one or another, it was certainly more of a reaction than she had anticipated. *Maybe too much of one,* she thought as she looked into Cora's eyes. They, unlike her voice, didn't seem at all troubled. In fact, they seemed positively serene.

Cora glanced from one woman to another. "Why would Marvin do something like that to Jacko?"

"Jacko?" Bernie asked, keeping her voice neutral.

"Yes. Jacko. Jacko Devlin. Jacko was his nickname," Cora explained when neither Bernie nor Libby said anything.

"I thought it was Devi," Bernie said.

Cora gave her a puzzled look. "Why would you think that?"

"No reason." Bernie took care not to look at Libby. "So he was a friend of yours?"

"Yes, he was," Cora replied.

"A good friend?"

Cora looked Bernie square in the eye. "Yes. A good friend. Why? Is that a problem?"

Bernie shook her head. "Not at all."

"He certainly was a man who knew how to share himself," Libby observed.

Cora put her hands on her hips and her face an inch away from Libby's. "Meaning?"

"Meaning nothing." Libby took a step back. "I was just making an observation."

"He was a wonderful man," Cora said, "and it's a shame that your boyfriend had to go and kill him. The world will be a less . . . exciting . . . place . . . with Jacko gone."

"That's one way of putting it," Bernie said.

"Marvin didn't do anything to him," Libby said at the same time.

"Everyone is saying Marvin did it," Cora retorted.

"Well, they're wrong," Libby told her.

"People were there. They saw what happened."

Libby was just about to trot out the bromide about not always believing what you see, when her sister started speaking.

"If you don't mind my saying so, you sound pretty mad at Marvin," Bernie told Cora.

"Of course I'm mad at him," Cora replied. "Like I said, Jacko was my friend."

Libby opened her mouth to say something, but Bernie shot her a look and she closed it again.

"Were you angry enough to shoot at him?"

"Marvin?" Cora asked.

Bernie leaned forward. "Yes."

"Someone shot at Marvin?" Cora asked.

"About an hour ago," Libby said.

"And you think that I did it?" Cora demanded.

"It crossed our minds," Libby told her.

Cora snorted. "That's stupid."

"So people say." Bernie nodded. "However, that doesn't change the question."

Cora pointed at herself and scoffed. "Do I look like someone who knows how to shoot a gun?"

"Why not? Lots of women do these days," Bernie noted.

"Maybe they do," Cora answered. "But I'm not one of them."

"So you've never shot a gun?" Libby asked.

"I've never even shot a BB gun," Cora replied.

"How about a cap pistol?" Bernie asked.

Cora gave her an incredulous stare. "I think you've been out in the sun too long."

"Or a water gun?" Bernie asked. "Have you ever used one of those?"

Cora shook her head in disbelief.

157

"I'll take that as a no," Bernie said.

"How about your husband? Would he have shot at Marvin?" Libby demanded.

"That's just beyond moronic. Why would he do something like that?"

"I don't know. That's why I'm asking you."

"I don't know, either," Cora told her.

"Well, someone does, because someone did take the shot," Libby pointed out.

Bernie chimed in next. "Maybe your husband rigged Jacko's musket, too," she suggested.

"David didn't shoot anyone." Cora's voice rose. "He didn't rig the musket. He didn't do anything. Nothing. Nothing at all. What is it going to take to get it through your thick heads?"

Bernie smiled. "He didn't do anything? Not even when he found out that you were having an affair with Jack Devlin?" she threw at Cora.

Nothing like a good guess to keep things moving, Bernie thought as she watched Cora freeze for a moment, then recover. From the reaction she got, Bernie guessed she'd hit the mark.

"That's simply not true," Cora protested. However, her voice lacked conviction.

Bernie laughed. "Please. You know my sister and I are going to find out. Secrets are hard to hide in a small town like Longely."

Cora reached down and readjusted her thong. "Let's say, hypothetically, I did have an affair with Jacko and my husband did find out."

158

"Hypothetically speaking," Bernie said.

"Yes. Hypothetically speaking. He wouldn't have done anything."

Bernie decided Cora sounded rather sad about that fact.

"For one thing, my husband doesn't know one end of a gun from another. I don't think he's ever handled a gun in his life. He's scared of them. Something about some childhood accident."

"He handled a musket at the reenactment," Libby reminded her.

"That was a prop," Cora snapped back. "It was supposed to be strictly for show. You know, like in amateur theater."

"Evidently it wasn't," Bernie said.

"No. It wasn't," Cora agreed.

"You must have been upset when your affair, excuse me, your hypothetical affair, with Devlin was over," Bernie said.

Cora sniffed and pointed a perfectly groomed finger at herself. "So now you're suggesting I did something with the muskets to make Devlin's musket explode? Unbelievable."

"My sister didn't say that," Libby told her.

"No. But she damn well implied it," Cora shot back. "Both of you should make up your minds about who killed whom. I'm getting really confused here. First, it was Dave shooting Marvin and Jacko, and then it was me. Well, for your information, we don't have any guns in the house."

"Can we come in and look?" Bernie asked.

Cora would have raised her eyebrows if she could have. "Are you kidding me?"

"Actually," Libby said, "I think my sister is quite serious."

"I am," Bernie said.

"No. You may not. Absolutely not."

"No need to get upset. I was only asking."

Cora shook a finger at Bernie and Libby. "You have some nerve coming here like this, interrupting my sunbathing. You want to talk to someone about guns? Talk to Samuel Cotton. He goes hunting all the time. He and Rick Evans. They're a real pair."

"Rick Evans hunts?" Libby was not surprised, given what Bernie had seen in the Evans's basement.

Cora flung her hands in the air. "How can you not know this? Duh. Of course he does. He belongs to the Musket and Flintlock Club out past Hudson Valley. That's where he got the idea for the reenactment. Muskets and Flintlocks puts one on every September. In fact, he tried to get my David to go."

"To the reenactment?"

"To the meetings." She sniffed. "As if."

"Why as if?" Bernie asked.

"Because he's . . . he's . . . he doesn't do things like that."

"Like what?"

160

Cora shrugged. "Like guy things. Now, if you wouldn't mind leaving, I'd like to get back to working on my tan."

"Libby, do you have a problem with that?" Bernie asked.

"No Bernie, do you?"

"You guys think you're funny, don't you?" Cora said.

"Well, I do, but Bernie doesn't."

"No, Libby. It's the opposite way around."

Cora snorted, turned on her heel, and walked inside her house, slamming the door after her.

"Oh well," Libby said.

"I guess we should work on a new routine."

"Guess so, Bernie."

They were heading for the van when they heard a man talking. The sound seemed to be coming from the back of the house.

"No can do," the man was saying.

The sisters exchanged glances. As one, they followed the narrow gravel path around the side of the house to the back.

David Nancy was sitting on a lounge chair talking on the phone. If his wife looked as if she spent every spare minute in the gym, Nancy looked as if he'd never set foot in one. His belly swelled over the band of his plaid bathing suit.

"You were supposed to be down in the city," Bernie said to him when she was a couple feet away.

David Nancy snapped his head around, saw who it was, and groaned. "I'll call you back later." He clicked off and put the phone down on the side table next to his chair. "Obviously I didn't make it."

Chapter 16

David Nancy bared his teeth in a semblance of a smile. "Charmed as always, I'm sure."

"Your wife told us you were in New York," Libby repeated.

He shrugged. "So you said."

With her middle finger, Libby pushed her sunglasses back up the bridge of her nose. "Evidently, she lied."

"*Lied* is a harsh word," Nancy noted as he reached over and took a sip from the glass that was sitting on the table.

"But an accurate one," Libby answered.

"It's not lying if it's in the service of a good cause." He plucked an ice cube out of his glass and began sucking on it.

"That's a new one," Bernie commented. "Tell me you don't really believe that?"

Nancy waved his hand in the air. "Okay. Bad sentence. She was protecting me."

Bernie batted her eyelashes. "From us two poor helpless females?"

His smile was for real. "Helpless?" He chuckled. "That would hardly be the word I would use to describe either one of you."

Bernie was going to ask him what word he would use, but Libby cut her off before she could. "Why did your wife cover for you?" she asked again.

"Because she is my wife, and that's one of the things wives do."

"I wouldn't do it," Libby told him.

"Maybe that's why you're not married," Nancy retorted.

Libby scowled and pushed her glasses up the bridge of her nose again. She really had to get another pair. These didn't fit right. But as Bernie had pointed out, what did she want from drug store sunglasses?

"Are you going to answer me or not?" she demanded.

"You want the truth?" he asked, parodying Jack Nicholson in *A Few Good Men*.

"I want the truth," Libby said, playing along.

Nancy sat forward and pointed at Bernie. "You want the truth?"

"I want the truth," Bernie answered.

"You can't handle the truth," he said then laughed. "Okay. Kidding aside. Like I just said, Cora lied to you because I asked her to run interference for me. My office is in the back of the house. I could hear your van pull into the driveway then you two talking when you got out, and I didn't want to be disturbed. I'm on an extremely tight deadline and I needed to get my work done."

"You don't look as if you're on a tight deadline," Bernie observed.

"That's because I just e-mailed my renderings off to LA and am waiting for approval before I continue. Not that it's any of your business."

"So you have time to talk to us now," Libby observed.

Nancy's affect changed. "No, I don't. I'm tired and I don't have the time or the energy to have a little chat with you. Have you guys not heard of calling ahead and making an appointment? And no," he said before Libby could continue, "I didn't shoot at Marvin or kill Jack Devlin."

"How do you know that's what we want to talk to you about?" Bernie asked.

Nancy snorted. "Well, I don't think you're selling Girl Scout cookies. Anyway, like I said, I could hear your entire conversation with my wife. One thing Cora was right about—you should talk to Samuel Cotton. He's the one you want."

"Because he owns guns?" Bernie asked.

"That and because he and Elise Montague had a thing going and it ended badly."

"I take it the ending badly thing had to do with Jack Devlin?" Libby inquired.

"As so many things around here seem to do," Nancy noted. "Go ahead. Talk to Cotton."

"Since we're here, I think I'd like to talk to you," Libby said.

"One can't always have what one wants, can one, dear?" he asked in a smarmy tone of voice.

"Actually, one can," Bernie told him.

"What's your heart's desire? Perhaps I can help." He looked Bernie up and down.

Bernie played dumb. "Maybe you can. Maybe you can tell us who you were standing next to when you picked out your musket."

Nancy chuckled. "I don't remember. The muskets were in a pile and I picked one up. If I remember correctly, I was busy trying to remember my lines."

Just as Bernie was about to reply, he sprang out of his chair. "Do you hear that?" he cried.

"Hear what?" Bernie asked.

"My fax is coming through. Now go." He made a shooing motion with his hand. "I don't have any more time to spare for you two." At that point his cell rang. He picked it up and started talking as he made his way to his office.

They watched him step inside and shut the sliding glass door behind him.

"Come on," Bernie said when Libby didn't move.

"Do you think there'd be a shell casing around if he took a shot at Marvin?"

Bernie considered the question. "No, I don't. I think he would have picked it up. I think he's too OCD not to. Now let's go. We've learned everything we can here."

"And that is?" Libby demanded.

"Not much," Bernie admitted. "Not much at all." She put her hand on Libby's elbow.

After a moment, Libby allowed Bernie to lead her away.

Bernie had just finished backing out of the driveway when a green Miata roared past them and parked. As they watched, a skinny woman in a tank top, shorts, and flip-flops got out of the car and hurried toward the house. She rang the bell. A moment later, the door opened and she went inside.

"I wonder who that was?" Libby said.

Bernie shook her head. "Don't know. All I do know is that her thighs are as thin as my wrists."

Libby fanned herself. "I don't even know her and I hate her."

Bernie laughed and headed the van in the direction of the Longely Elementary School.

Chapter 17

During the school year, at two o'clock in the afternoon, the Longely Elementary School would be in a state of controlled chaos. Children would be pouring out of the building, police officers would be directing traffic, and minivans and school buses would be lining up to take the children home. But it was the beginning of July and day camp had let out for the day so the building was quiet. Just a few people, mostly mothers, lingered in the area talking to each other while their kids played quietly on the grass or ran beneath the sprinklers watering the lawn.

The school had been built in the fifties when land was cheap and plentiful. Surrounded by forsythia bushes and laurel hedges, the school presented a picture of a prosperous, well-tended place, the kind parents felt confident sending their children to.

Constructed of brick, the building sprawled across the lawn angling first this way and that. It boasted a gym, an auditorium, a library, a media room, an Olympic-sized pool, and a large outdoor play area. The last two features were situated in the rear of the school, which was where, for obvious reasons, the summer camp was located. Bernie followed the road around back and parked the van next to the two other cars that remained in the lot. She and Libby had just gotten out of the van and were heading inside when Samuel Cotton came out of the building. He was a tall, skinny, balding guy with a slight stoop to his shoulders and an unfriendly expression on his face.

Even though he was in his mid-thirties, Bernie could discern the seeds of the grumpy old man he was going to morph into in his sixties. Samuel Cotton, she decided, was one of those guys who had been born in a bad mood and had stayed that way.

He was wearing khaki cargo shorts and a bright yellow camp T-shirt that had the catch phrase LONGELY NOW printed across its middle. The clothes were not flattering to him, not that they'd be flattering to anyone above the age of six.

The yellow T-shirt brought out the greenish tinge in his skin, while his shorts emphasized his knobby knees. Of course, the fact that he was wearing black socks and white sneakers didn't help in the appearance department. Samuel looked tired and harassed, although to give him his due, anyone dealing with small children would probably feel that way.

Bernie knew she was stereotyping him, but he didn't fit her image of someone who hunted. In her mind, those guys were big and burly and expansive, not tall, skinny, and nerdy-looking.

"Yes?" he said as Bernie and Libby came toward him.

"We'd like to chat with you for a moment," Libby said.

"Chat?" His voice rose. "I don't chat. We're not in England. We're not sitting down to a nice, cozy cup of tea."

"All right, talk then. My sister and I would like to *talk* to you."

Samuel wiped a bead of sweat off his forehead with the back of his hand. "Can't it wait?" he asked plaintively. "I really need to go home and take a shower."

"This will just take a minute," Bernie reassured him.

"I don't care how little time it will take. I can't talk to you right now," he whined. "It's been a long day and I need to get home."

"This is about—"

He held up his hand and cut her off. "I know why you're here and you could have saved yourself the trouble of coming. I don't know anything about Jack Devlin."

"Why do you assume that's what we wanted to talk to you about?" Libby asked.

"You are investigating the Jack Devlin incident, aren't you?"

"Yes," she admitted.

"So there you are. This is a small town. People talk."

169

"Which people?"

"People." He ran his hand through his hair. His scalp was glistening with sweat. "The air-conditioning broke in the building today." He gestured toward the school. "Do you know what it was like in there?"

"I'm sure it was horrible."

"Horrible," Cotton cried. "I thought I was going to pass out in there! And now I'm told that the repairman won't be able to come until Friday. That's two days away! Two days in this heat! We're going to have to close the camp. It's a health hazard. It's amazing someone didn't faint."

"So you were here the entire day?" Bernie asked him, trying to pin down his whereabouts vis-à-vis Marvin's shooting.

He snorted. "Where else would I be?"

"I don't know. You could have had a doctor's appointment."

"Well, I didn't. I'm here when the little darlings come and I'm here when the little darlings go. That's why they pay me the big bucks." He drew his lips back in a mirthless smile.

"Surely you must get lunch off," Bernie said, thinking that it wouldn't take long to drive from the school to Cotton's house, fire off a shot, and come back again.

"Ha. Lunch off? Now that's a joke. The council is so cheap that they aren't paying the camp counselors anything. They're interns. They work for free. You know what that means, don't you? That means they don't care. That means I have to watch everything, oversee every single detail. No. I bring my lunch with me and we all eat together. Except on Fridays. Fridays is pizza day. We still eat together, but we have pizza and ice cream. The kids love it."

"Listen—" Libby began when Cotton stopped to draw a breath.

"No. You listen." He cut her off once again. His rant seemed to have taken the last bit of energy he had out of him, not that there had been that much to begin with. "I can't think." He put his hand to his forehead then put it back down. "I bet I'm suffering from heat stroke. The last thing I need to do is answer some silly questions about Jack Devlin. I should probably be going to the hospital to get rehydrated."

"We can drive you if you want," Libby offered. "Right, Bernie?"

Bernie nodded. "Absolutely, Libby."

Cotton looked from one sister to another then took a step back. "No no. That's very kind I'm sure, but now that I think about it, I'm positive that a cold shower and a long drink will do the trick."

"This is not about Jack Devlin," Bernie said in an attempt to clarify the conversation.

"I'm not talking about his girlfriends either," Cotton announced. "I believe that everyone is entitled to their private lives, even if they are pathetic and degrading. And I don't gossip. Ever. About anyone. So there's no point in asking me any questions. I've already made my statement to the police and that's what I'm sticking with. Ask them if you want."

Bernie took a swig from her water bottle and replaced it in her bag. "So I take it you talked to them about Elise Montague?" Her tone was conversational.

Cotton didn't reply.

"Because David Nancy says that you and Elise had something going on then Jack Devlin came along and poof." Bernie made an exploding gesture with her hands. "All gone."

"I don't know what you're speaking about," Cotton said stiffly.

"If we talk to Elise, will she tell us the same thing?" Libby asked. "Will she tell us David Nancy was lying?"

It looked to Libby as if Samuel Cotton was swaying slightly on his feet, but maybe that was just a trick of the light.

"I have no idea what she'll tell you," he said after a slight hesitation. "None at all. You'll have to speak to her."

"We intend to," Libby said.

"Because some people would consider that a motive for killing Jack Devlin," Bernie observed.

"She isn't worth killing for," Cotton blurted out.

"You give your sex too much credit. Actually, no woman is, and that's all I'm going to say on the subject."

"Fine," Bernie replied. "Here's another question for you then. Maybe you can answer this one for me. Do you shoot guns?"

Cotton stared at her. "What do you mean?" he asked after a minute had gone by.

"It's a simple question requiring a simple answer. Do you know how to shoot a gun?"

"Why are you asking?"

"Do you always answer a question with another question?" Libby said.

Cotton wiped his forehead with the back of his hand again. "Only if they're stupid."

"Actually, I don't know why my sister is asking you that question," Bernie said, "since we already know the answer."

"We do indeed," Libby said doing a good television game host show imitation.

"And that would be?" Bernie asked.

"That would be yes. Samuel Cotton knows how to shoot," Libby replied in a bright, cheery voice. "So come on down Samuel Cotton and claim your prize."

Cotton peered at her through his sunglasses. "Has the heat claimed your senses? I hear it does that to people."

"Obviously you don't watch a lot of game shows," Bernie told him.

He frowned. "I don't watch any. Now, what are you babbling about?"

"I'm talking about the fact that David Nancy said that you and Rick Evans go hunting."

Cotton humphed. "That's not exactly a secret. We go deer hunting around Syracuse every year."

"With what?" Libby asked.

"With rolling pins," Samuel Cotton replied.

Libby frowned. She could feel a headache coming on. "Seriously."

"We use guns. What did you think we used?"

"Well, it could have been bow and arrow," Bernie countered.

"But it's not."

"What kind of gun do you use?" she asked.

"A Remington Model 870 twelve gauge pump action shotgun that is equipped with a twenty-inch rifled slug barrel. Does that help?"

Bernie didn't say anything.

"No. I thought not. I bet you can't tell one gun from another."

"This is true. But I bet the members of your gun club, the Musket and Flintlock Club, can," Libby said.

"And your point is?" Cotton asked.

Bernie jumped in. "I think the point my sister is trying to make is that you most likely have the expertise to rig a musket."

Cotton snorted. "Anyone with a lick of sense can do it. All you have to do is look on the

Internet to find instructions. Ask anyone in the gun club and they'll tell you the same thing."

"That was my next question," Libby said.

Cotton's voice rose. "Are you suggesting that someone from the gun club did this?"

"Did they?" Bernie countered.

Cotton made a disgusted noise. "You really are nuts. For your information, everyone, except Marvin, in the reenactment belongs to that club and we are all law-abiding citizens. We pay our taxes. We sponsor safe gun classes. We hold charity benefits. We give back to the community."

"So by definition you wouldn't have taken a shot at Marvin?" Bernie asked.

Cotton took a step back. "Someone took a shot at Marvin?"

"That's what my sister just said," Libby told him.

"When?"

"Not too long ago."

"You think because I know how to handle a firearm I shot at Marvin?" Cotton asked incredulously.

"That thought had occurred to us," Bernie told him.

He started to laugh and ended up wheezing. "Allergies," he explained between gasps. "That's beyond absurd," he told Bernie when he could talk again. "Why would I do that?"

"Because you're mad at Marvin," Libby said.

"Why would I be mad at him?"

"Because he killed Jack Devlin," she replied.

He shook his finger at her. "According to you, I wanted Jack Devlin dead, so why would I be angry at Marvin for killing him? He would have done me a favor."

"Maybe you wanted to kill him yourself," Libby hazarded.

Cotton shook his head in disgust. "You ladies have not a clue. You should leave things like this to the authorities."

"You don't like us, do you?" Libby asked.

"I don't like people who overstep their boundaries. Something you two ladies are doing in spades. That's how people get hurt, you know, doing what they don't know anything about, going where they have no business going."

"Is that a warning?" Bernie asked him.

Cotton held his hand up to his chest. "Good heavens, no. It's an observation. I'm just stating a fact. I mean, look at what happened to poor Marvin. He sure isn't having a good week, is he?"

"No, he's not," Libby agreed.

"I'm glad I'm not him. Now if you ladies will excuse me, I'm going to depart. My shower awaits."

"One more question," Bernie said.

"I think not," Cotton responded. With that, he walked over to his vehicle, unlocked it, got in, and drove off.

"So what do you think?" Bernie asked Libby as they watched his vehicle disappear around the bend in the road.

"I think that he knows a lot more than he's telling," Libby said. "I think he was warning us to stay away."

"I think so too. We should have a chat with Elise."

"And Rick," Libby added.

"Definitely Rick." Bernie looked at her watch. "But not right now."

They had to get back to the shop and get to work prepping tomorrow's food.

Chapter 18

By nine o'clock that evening, the heat of the past days had broken. Within a matter of hours, the temperature had dropped twenty degrees to the low seventies. A breeze was coming out of the west, bringing with it the smell of honeysuckle, which lingered in the night air. The wind had kicked up, and Bernie could tell from the way it was blowing, it wouldn't be long before the rain the weather forecaster had been promising would arrive. It was a good thing since the trees and the plants could definitely use it.

After she and Libby had closed the shop at eight, they'd gone upstairs, turned off the air-conditioners, and opened all the windows so that the evening breeze could come in. It had felt good to air out the house.

Bernie, Libby, Sean, and Brandon were sitting around in the living room sipping iced coffee and eating the wild black raspberries that Sean had picked when she and Bernie had gotten back from talking to Samuel Cotton. The plants had self-seeded in the small patch of land in the rear of A Little Taste of Heaven three years ago.

At first, the bushes had yielded just a few berries, but they must have liked it in that spot because they'd taken over the entire patch of land. This year, the bushes had yielded a bumper crop. The berries were so good, sweet and tart, that the girls couldn't bear to let them go to waste, even though picking them could be a painful affair. The bushes were armored with large thorns.

"Worth every scratch," Brandon said as he picked a berry out of the bowl, dunked it in cream, and then in sugar before putting it in his mouth. "God, these are good." He reached over and ate another one.

"Agreed," Sean said as he took a sip of his iced coffee. Before he took a bite of the challah Libby had baked the other day, he slathered the bread with sweet butter that Bernie had gotten from a farm on the outskirts of the town. "I could live on this stuff forever," he commented.

Bernie didn't say anything. It had been a long frustrating day and she was enjoying sitting on the sofa next to Brandon with her feet tucked under her. She watched the curtains dance in the swirls of breeze that eddied in and out of the flat and listened to the silence broken only by the sound of the occasional car driving by.

She sighed and snuggled up against her sweetie. Brandon rarely had an evening off but RJ's was closed for a private party and the people who were giving it had brought their own staff along. That being the case, she was determined to enjoy his time off to the fullest extent possible.

Looking at Bernie and Brandon sitting on the sofa together made Libby feel sad. She wanted Marvin there, too. She'd invited him. After all, the discussion they were about to have centered around his situation. But he'd begged off, telling her he was too tired. She sighed.

"Are you okay?" Bernie asked her.

"Why?"

"You don't seem happy."

"I'm not."

"Thinking about Marvin?"

Libby nodded. "He's so depressed. All he wants to do is sleep. I'm worried about him."

"Don't be," Bernie reassured her. "We'll figure this out."

"Getting shot at put him right over the edge," Libby observed.

"He'll be fine," Brandon said. "He just needs a few days."

"God, I hope so." Libby snagged a chocolate kiss out of the bowl in the center of the table, unwrapped it, and let it dissolve in her mouth. Then she sat back in the armchair and waited to hear the story Brandon had to tell.

"You're going to enjoy this," Brandon had told Bernie when he'd called.

"So tell us what you heard," Sean urged him, before taking another sip of iced coffee.

Unlike the kind that was hot brewed and refrigerated, this coffee was cold brewed, and Sean liked it a tad better than the iced coffee done by more traditional brewing methods. It was a tiny bit smoother, although he couldn't taste the notes of chocolate and cinnamon Bernie claimed she could. Probably all those years of drinking police station coffee had ruined his palate, he reflected.

"It may be nothing," Brandon said.

Bernie sat up and stretched her legs out. "Or it may be something. We won't know if we don't hear it."

Brandon bowed his head in acknowledgment of what Bernie had said and began his tale. "Do you remember Monica Lewis?"

Sean, Libby, and Bernie shook their heads.

"Nope," Bernie said. "Should I?"

"She used to hang out at RJ's. I think you played darts with her once or twice."

Bernie shook her head again. "I've played darts with lots of people."

180

"She won."

Bernie shrugged. "Most do." She was a lousy dart player. "I'm sorry. The name still doesn't ring any bells."

Brandon ate another berry. He found the combination of berry, sugar, and cream irresistible. "What I'm talking about happened almost two years ago."

"What does Monica look like?" Bernie asked.

Brandon thought for a moment. "Back then she had dyed red hair on the orangey side. She was kind of heavyset. Given to wearing lots of bracelets and rings. Had a tat of a butterfly on her right shoulder."

"Sorry. I still can't place her."

"She usually came in on Mondays and Thursdays around eight, had three or four beers, an order of super hot chicken wings, played a couple games of darts, and left the same way she'd come in. By herself."

"I don't remember her, either," Libby said. "Maybe if I saw her."

Brandon popped another black raspberry into his mouth. "Last night, Sanford Aiken came in and about twenty minutes later Monica Lewis sauntered in and they downed a couple beers. Monica left and Sanford started telling me her story. It's an interesting story. I figured you might want to hear it."

"Why?" Bernie asked.

"Because it's relevant."

Chapter 19

Bernie wrinkled her nose. She didn't see where Brandon's story was leading, but knew better than to interrupt him. He enjoyed talking. Eventually, he would get to the point he wanted to make.

"She's living with her brother right now, David Nancy," Brandon said.

"I didn't know he had a sister," Libby said. *But then, why should I know?* David Nancy was a relative newcomer and neither he nor his wife patronized their shop.

"Same mother, different fathers," Brandon explained.

Bernie took a sip of her coffee and put the glass down on the table. One of the window curtains billowed out and she watched it for a moment. Then she spoke. "When you were describing Monica's appearance you said, 'back then.' Has she changed her look?"

"Good guess," Brandon told her.

Bernie grinned. "That's what makes me a detective extraordinaire."

Libby snorted. "So you say."

Sean leaned forward. "Let the man speak," he ordered.

Brandon nodded his gratitude. "I almost didn't

recognize her. In fact, I wouldn't have if she hadn't said hello to me."

"Is she very skinny now?" Bernie asked, thinking of the woman she and Libby had seen getting out of the Miata and going into David Nancy's house. "Does she have long blonde hair?"

"That's the one. Correct on both counts."

Bernie tapped her fingers on her leg. "You know, I saw a green Miata when I was coming back from Rick Evans's house. Now I'm wondering if that was Monica's."

"Can't tell you," Brandon said.

"Go on with what you can tell us," Sean said, urging Brandon along.

"Like I said Sanford and I got to talking. I don't think he would have been so chatty if he hadn't had so much to drink and if he wasn't so upset about what happened to Devlin."

"He was?" Bernie asked.

"Well, he certainly seemed that way to me. Or maybe it was the fact that I asked him about what had happened to Monica. One moment she's a regular, the next minute I don't see her anymore. I figured she'd joined AA or something like that."

"But she hadn't," Sean said.

"Nope. She's just come back from living in some ashram in India." Brandon leaned forward and rested his elbows on his knees.

"So what did Sanford say?" Bernie asked.

They could hear the rumble of thunder off in the distance.

"For openers, Sanford said Monica was really upset that Jack Devlin is dead."

"Interesting." Bernie reached over, took a piece of challah, and buttered it. "Did she want to go out with him?"

Brandon laughed. "Hardly. Actually, she wanted to talk to him. Or maybe *talk* isn't the right word," he mused.

A flash of lightning illuminated the sky.

"The storm's coming," Libby noted.

"About time," Sean observed. "Hopefully the lawns will stop looking as if it's the end of August."

"That would be nice." Bernie took a bite of her challah. "So if Monica didn't want to speak to Jack Devlin, what did she want to do?"

"From the way she was talking, Sanford said he got the impression that she wanted to hurt him. Hurt him real bad."

"I guess she wasn't at the head of the line for that one. Or maybe she was," Bernie commented.

"Did Sanford say why?" Sean asked.

"Yes, he did." Brandon ate another berry. "Okay. Monica Lewis got involved with Jack Devlin two years ago."

"Now there's a shocker," Libby observed. "Who in this town hasn't been?"

"Us," Bernie said.

"True," Libby replied.

"Yes," Brandon said. "But he and Monica got secretly engaged."

Bernie raised an eyebrow. "Obviously a woman who was not clear on the tomcat concept."

"He gave her a ring, but told her she couldn't show it to anyone until the time was right."

"And why was that?" Libby asked. "Did Sanford tell you?"

"Yeah. He did. Because Devlin told Monica he wanted to break his relationship off with Gail Evans first. He didn't want to create undo psychic angst. He was afraid that unless he did it just right, Gail might kill herself and he didn't want that on his conscience."

Bernie snorted. "Very noble. Somehow Gail doesn't strike me as the going-to-pieces-over-a-guy type. What do you think, Libby?"

"Not even remotely," Libby replied. "But it's nice to know that Devlin was such a kind considerate soul."

It was Bernie's turn to lean forward. "Was the ring real?" If she had to bet, she'd have bet that it wasn't.

"Surprisingly, it was. After the whole Devlin thing blew up, Monica took the ring to a jeweler and had it appraised. It was real, but not worth nearly as much as he had said it was."

"So where did Devlin get the ring?" Sean asked. "Did he go out and buy it?"

"Sanford didn't know," Brandon told him, "but my best guess is from Juno Grisham. If I remember right, her ring turned up missing around that time. Or so she said. She told me she lost it. And maybe she did, but now I'm wondering."

"She told me the same thing she told you. Interesting. The rumor I heard didn't have anything to do with her ring. I heard Juno and Devlin had a little thing going when her husband went off to Thailand on a business trip." Bernie thought for a moment. "The timing would be right."

"Maybe Devlin told her he needed money really bad," Libby reflected. "You know, like the loan sharks were after him and if he didn't pay them, they'd kill him so she gave him her ring. Or maybe, he stole it."

Brandon shook his head. "I don't think so, Libby. I think he was more of a con man than a thief. In fact, I'm willing to bet if he wanted to buy a ring for Monica he could have. He had that boat that he docked in Alex Bay and he drove an Audi."

"Then why didn't he?" Libby asked.

"Maybe he did," Bernie said. "We don't know."

"Or maybe he was just cash poor," Brandon suggested.

Sean interrupted. "For the moment, let's just assume Devlin did what Aiken said he did and go on from there."

"All I can say," Bernie told Brandon, "is that if you did something like that I'd be beyond livid."

"If you found out," Brandon said.

"Oh, I'd find out all right," Bernie retorted.

Libby turned toward her. "Would you be livid enough to kill?"

"Wounded pride can be a powerful motive," Sean observed.

Brandon took a sip of his iced coffee. "We don't even know that any of this happened," he protested. "I just said I had an inkling that's what occurred."

"Well, we do know one thing," Libby noted. "We know that Devlin's definitely a busy boy."

"*Was* a busy boy," Bernie corrected. "There are going to be a lot of very unhappy ladies in this town."

"And a lot of happy husbands and boyfriends," Brandon observed as he leaned over, snagged another couple berries, and popped them in his mouth.

"Go on," Sean instructed.

Brandon nodded and continued. "Here comes the part that's really interesting. According to Sanford, right before Devlin and Monica got engaged"—he bracketed the word *engaged* with his fingers—"she came into some money."

"What a coincidence," Sean said dryly.

"Isn't it, though," Brandon replied.

"Let me guess," Sean said. "She lent this money to Jack Devlin."

Brandon clapped. "The man wins the prize."

"I've always been known for my psychic abilities," Sean told him. "Get on with it."

"What did he do with the money, you ask?" said Brandon.

"I do," Sean said.

"He put it into some cockamamie business scheme. If I understood Sanford correctly—he was a little bit loaded at the time—Devlin invested it in a gold mine."

"Salted, no doubt," Sean muttered, shaking his head. How people could be so gullible was beyond him. But one thing his tenure as chief of police in Longely had taught him was that they were.

Brandon buttered another slab of challah and ate it. Pretty soon the entire loaf would be gone. "Anyway, the investment tanked and Devlin lost the one hundred thousand dollars. No big surprise there."

"Nice chunk of change," Sean noted. "I know that I wouldn't be happy if that had happened to me."

"I wouldn't either," Brandon agreed. "It turns out that part of that money belonged to David Nancy. He had been counting on it for a real estate deal he was involved in. So when the money wasn't there, he lost his shirt."

"Fascinating," Bernie murmured. "So he can't have liked Jack Devlin on several different levels."

"That's understating it by quite a lot," Brandon agreed.

"Sounds like a motive to me," Libby said.

"Me, too," Sean said.

"There's more. According to Sanford, right after the deal went south, Devlin told Monica that he'd had a change of heart, the engagement was off, and he asked for the ring back."

"Talk about chutzpa," Libby said. "Did he get it?"

"Yes, he did," Brandon answered. "She went to her jewelry box and threw it at him, at which point, he left." Brandon paused for a moment to build up the suspense. "Then she went nutso."

Sean interrupted. "Such a scientific term."

"Well, she tried to kill herself. She swallowed some pills. David Nancy was the one who found her."

"That can't have made him like Jack Devlin any better," Libby noted.

Brandon nodded. "That's what I figured. According to Sanford, Nancy dropped Monica at the hospital, went back to his house, got his shotgun, and went looking for Devlin."

"He has a shotgun?" Bernie asked, remembering what Nancy's wife had said about him not liking guns, much less having one. Maybe she didn't know. Or maybe she was lying.

Bernie wondered what else Cora was lying about.

"According to Sanford, Nancy has his dad's," Brandon replied. "The thing is old, but it shoots pretty good. Fortunately, he didn't find Devlin. He went home a couple hours later. He picked Monica up from the hospital the next day. She told Sanford they probably would have kept her for a couple weeks if she'd had insurance, but she didn't so they released her with a prescription for some heavy duty tranqs."

"And Devlin?" Sean asked. "What about him?"

Brandon shook his head. "I don't know, but I'm guessing that eventually Nancy and Devlin reached some kind of agreement."

"And you know this, how?" Sean asked Brandon.

"Because Devlin was still walking around."

"Okay, I have a problem," Bernie said. "Brandon, let's say you're right about everything. Let's say Devlin and Nancy had gotten around what he did to Nancy's sister. Would you take a musket from Nancy if you were Devlin?" she asked, thinking of the reenactment.

"He might," Libby interjected. "After all, Devlin thought they were going to be props."

Sean rubbed his chin with his thumb while he took in everything that Brandon was telling them. "What happened to Monica? Get back to the story." He raised his voice slightly so he could be heard over the thunder and the rain drumming on the roof.

"Well, she told Sanford that the tranqs weren't working well for her. At that point, to use her own words, she 'saw the light' and went off to India to meditate in an ashram. She's been gone for a little over a year. She just got back."

"So her year in the ashram made her want to forgive Jack Devlin?" Bernie asked. "She was sorry he'd died, because she wanted to tell him she forgave him?"

Brandon laughed. "Not exactly," he said. "According to Sanford, she said she wanted to kill the son of a bitch and was sorry she'd missed her chance."

"Maybe she didn't miss her chance," Libby said. "Maybe she was the one responsible for the over-primed musket."

"I don't think she was there," Bernie said. "At least, I didn't see her if she was."

"Even if she wasn't, it doesn't mean she didn't do it," Libby said. "Monica could have booby-trapped the musket and her brother could have handed it to Devlin."

"But then why didn't he do anything before?" Brandon objected. "Why would he wait till now to try and kill Devlin?"

"Maybe he didn't get a chance to before," Bernie said. "Or maybe he didn't feel the need to. Then his sister comes back and does a Lady Macbeth number on him. Wakes up all the guilt and the anger that's been festering, and

191

Bob's your uncle. Plus, it's an easy thing to do."

"I can see that," Sean allowed. "It's a definite possibility. The timing is certainly right. The only thing I can't see is Monica doing it. This is more of a guy crime."

"I think we've had this discussion before about it being a guy or a gal kind of crime," Libby said.

"And what did we decide?" Brandon asked.

"I don't think we did," Bernie answered.

"We didn't," Sean said.

"Maybe you should just call it a gender neutral kind of crime," Brandon suggested.

"Maybe we should just call it a violent crime," Sean replied. The phrase *gender neutral* stuck in his craw.

"Yeah," chimed in Bernie. "For all we know, Monica Lewis might have belonged to a gun club. She might be an excellent shot."

Chapter 20

It had started to rain in earnest—the kind of summer storm that flooded the catch drains and pummeled the flowers down to the ground.

"It wouldn't surprise me if she were," Bernie said as she rushed to close the windows. "In fact, we should check out the Musket and Flintlock Club. It's just a fifteen minute drive from here."

Libby nodded and went to shut the bedroom windows. "Works for me. We'll do it tomorrow," she said over her shoulder.

"Definitely." Bernie turned to face everyone. "Okay, let's assume Libby's correct about Monica. It still doesn't answer another question."

"Which is?" Libby asked, coming back in the room.

"Why should David Nancy or his sister shoot at Marvin? That makes no sense, no sense at all."

Sean watched the droplets illuminated under the streetlight. They reminded him of little pinpoints of light. "For that matter," he said, "why should Samuel Cotton or Rick Evans or Sanford Aiken shoot at Marvin?"

"I know," Libby said. "I can't come up with an explanation."

Bernie reached over, got another black raspberry, and sat down on the sofa next to Brandon. "That is the question, isn't it?"

The lights flickered.

"I hope the power doesn't go off," Libby said. It had a tendency to do that during a storm, especially a bad storm.

"Me too," Bernie said, thinking about the contents of their coolers. She decided that tomorrow she and Libby would go down to The Home Depot and get a generator. They really couldn't afford not to, especially since storms were becoming more frequent.

"Maybe it's an outlier," Brandon suggested, breaking the silence.

Sean, Bernie, and Libby turned and looked at him.

"Reading self-improvement books again, are we?" Bernie teased.

Brandon flushed. "I simply meant maybe Marvin's shooting has nothing to do with what happened to Jack Devlin."

"How could it not?" Libby asked.

"No. He may be right," Sean said excitedly. He shook his finger at Libby. "Brandon may be on to something here."

Brandon grinned. "I am?"

"Quite possibly." Sean ran his thumb over his lip while he organized his thoughts. "Well, we've been treating Marvin's event as part of a pattern. We've been trying to find a pattern that would explain both Jack Devlin's death and Marvin's shooting. At least, I have."

"So have we," Bernie and Libby said together.

"But what if it isn't that at all," Sean went on. "What if Marvin's shooting was just meant to distract us from the main point, which is who shot Jack Devlin and why?"

"But if it isn't about Marvin, then why did whoever shot Devlin frame him?" Libby asked.

"He," Sean said, "might not have meant to. There's no reason why suspicion should have fallen on Marvin. I know that if I were investigating, I would consider him an unlikely suspect. Maybe the person who engineered this wanted to make what happened look like an accident. No. I think Marvin might just be collateral damage."

"Charming," Libby opined.

"But true," Sean replied.

"But why take a shot at him now?" Libby asked. "That makes no sense whatsoever."

"Maybe it's a way to muddy the waters," Sean suggested.

Bernie cocked her head. "Explain."

"Well, we're running around looking for an explanation for the two events. Maybe that was the whole idea. Maybe whoever shot at Marvin didn't mean to hit him. Maybe it was a diversion."

"It seems like an awful lot of trouble to go to for a diversion," Libby said.

"This is true, but it's the only thing that makes sense. Hey, if anyone has another hypothesis, I'd be more than willing to listen to it." Sean looked around.

No one said anything.

"So what do we do now?" Bernie asked.

"We go back to concentrating on Jack Devlin's death," Sean said. "I have a feeling that if we find the perpetrator of that crime, we'll find out who took a potshot at Marvin."

"Makes sense. We should talk to Rick Evans,"

Libby said, thinking of Bernie's find in the basement of his house.

Bernie nodded. "He's first on my list, but let's not forget about Elise Montague and Tony Gerard."

"Or Monica Lewis," Libby added. "She certainly has a compelling reason to want Devlin out of the picture."

"At least, according to Sanford Aiken, she does." Sean turned to Brandon. "Why do you think he told you that story?"

"I think he thinks that Monica Lewis and David Nancy might have something to do with Devlin's death, but he didn't want to go to the police with the story so he told me."

"Because he knew that you would tell me," Bernie said.

"Exactly," Brandon said.

"Either that or he wanted to shift the blame to someone else," Sean said.

"Also true," Brandon conceded.

"Which do you think it is?" Sean asked him.

Brandon thought for a minute. "I think Aiken was telling the truth or to rephrase it, I think he believes what he was telling me."

Sean sat back in his chair. "At least we've made a start."

Brandon moved a crumb of challah around on his plate. "What I don't get is why these people talk to you. They don't have to."

Sean explained. "Primarily, I think they'll talk to Libby or Bernie or me because they want to explain their view of what happened. They want to be heard."

"But why should they say anything, especially if they're guilty? Isn't it better to just keep quiet?" Brandon asked. "I know I'd just keep my mouth shut."

Sean chuckled. "It is better. But most people think that they're smarter than anyone else—which is a big mistake. It's all a question of ego."

"So when everyone gets talked to, then what?" Brandon asked.

"Then we compare notes and see what's what," Sean replied.

"Maybe we need to go shopping for some plumbing supplies and a vacuum cleaner," Bernie said, looking at Brandon.

"The stores are closed tomorrow," Sean reminded his daughter.

"Then we can go the day after, if we don't get to Aiken and Gerard before."

"Count me out. I'm working," Brandon told her.

"Not in the morning, you're not," Bernie replied. "Anyway, what's the big deal? I'm just asking you to come along."

"The big deal," Brandon answered, "is that whenever I help you with an investigation bad things happen."

"Like what?" Bernie demanded.

"Like a house blowing up."

"It wasn't the whole house!" Bernie said indignantly.

"You're right," Brandon told her. "It was the bottom two rooms."

"It was just that one time."

"Or almost getting arrested. What about that?"

"But you didn't," Bernie reminded him.

"But I could have."

"Brandon, all I'm talking about is helping Marvin out, but if you don't want to, hey, that's okay by me."

Brandon shook a finger at Bernie. "Now that is a low blow."

"It's the truth," Bernie retorted.

"Excuse me." Sean clapped his hands.

Brandon and Bernie stopped bickering and turned to him.

"I hate to interrupt this love fest, but what about Juno?" Sean asked.

"What about her?"

"She was on the hill. She had a good view of things, right?"

"Right," Libby said, seeing where her dad was going.

"We should talk to Holly and Whitney, too," Bernie suggested.

"You can't," Brandon said. "They're in the Hamptons."

"Fine," Sean said. "We'll speak to them when they get back. In the meantime, Marvin and I will go talk to Juno."

"Good," Bernie said. "Then you can meet Hilda."

"She's really cute, Dad. You'll like her," Libby told him. "While you do that, Bernie and I will go visit the gun club and see if we can find out who belongs there. It might help clarify some things."

They'd already tried looking the Musket and Flintlock Club up on the Web. It didn't have a presence there.

"Happy shooting," Brandon said.

"Ha-ha," Libby replied. "Like that's going to happen."

Chapter 21

Libby looked at Bernie as they drove down County Road 92. They were going to be late for their meeting since they'd missed the turnoff and had to double back.

"You don't look like someone who wants to join a gun club," Libby commented.

Her sister was wearing a pale pink T-shirt, an A-line skirt in a flowered print that featured cabbage roses, and strappy vintage coral-colored wedges.

"And you do, I suppose." Bernie was referring

to Libby's Bermuda shorts, pale blue, button-down, short sleeved blouse, and Docksiders. "Actually, I take that back. You do."

Libby grinned. "Yes. For once I am sartorially correct."

Bernie didn't reply. She was too busy looking for the turnoff.

There was a moment of silence.

Libby thought about Brandon's comment last night when he'd left. She turned to Bernie. "I don't want to shoot. I really don't. I don't like guns. They give me the creeps."

"Since when?" Bernie asked.

"Since the reenactment. I've never been a big fan, but ever since the musket exploded"—Libby shivered—"I can't get Devlin's face out of my mind. I'm still having nightmares about it."

Bernie gave her a sideways look. "Chill. We're just asking for a tour of their facilities."

Libby nibbled on the inside of her cheek. "I know, but what if the guy showing us around asks us if we want to shoot?"

"To quote Nancy Reagan, 'Just say no.'"

"It'll look strange if I don't," Libby protested.

"Not really. We'll tell him we're just thinking of taking target shooting up as a hobby."

"How are we going to get the membership list?" Libby asked as she kept her eyes peeled for the turnoff. It had to be around there somewhere.

Bernie shrugged. "We'll think of something. We always do. But first we have to get there."

Libby spotted the sign. "There," she yelled. "Turn there."

"Where?"

"You just went past it."

Bernie slammed on the brakes and backed up. When she had gone a little over a foot, she saw the sign Libby had been yelling about. Tacked to a tree was a small piece of cardboard with the words GUN CLUB written on it with Magic Marker. An arrow pointed down a narrow dirt road.

"Wow." Bernie stopped the van.

"Wow what?"

"The sign looks like something third graders made and the road doesn't look too great either," Bernie said, thinking of the shocks on their van.

"No, it doesn't," Libby agreed.

The women sat there for a moment watching a hawk riding the thermals.

"If we get stuck, we'll be in trouble," Bernie observed.

"On the other hand," Libby rejoined, "we need the information."

Bernie nodded. "There is that."

She started the van and carefully maneuvered it onto the rutted track, dropping her speed down to five miles an hour as the van negotiated the bumps and dips in the road. The fields on either side were full of clover, tall grass, and dried corn stalks. A crumbling barn, vines growing out of its walls, stood off to the left.

Bernie concentrated on keeping the van on the path. A mile later, the road angled right. "Where is this place?" she complained as they entered a copse of trees.

Libby bit her lower lip. "I've got to say, this seems like a strange way to get to the club. Maybe we made a mistake. Maybe we should go back."

"We can't. We can't turn around."

"Great," Libby muttered as her sister steered the van around a tree root. Suddenly she saw something white between the trees. "What's that?" she asked, pointing.

"Hopefully, the Musket and Flintlock Club."

A few minutes later, they were through the trees and greeted by a shellacked piece of wood with the name of the gun club burned into it. Bernie heaved a sigh of relief. A few feet after that was a white picket fence and another sign that read MEMBERS ONLY.

"You have to really want to come here," Bernie noted as she parked in front of the building.

"I'll say." Libby eyed the place.

It was not what she had expected. The club was housed in a small, shabby blue-trimmed, white colonial. The paint was peeling around the windows and under the roof eaves. Libby thought that the building must have been someone's home once upon a time, but it was evident that no one had loved or cared for the place for a long time.

The same held true for the landscaping, which consisted of a couple of stunted laurel bushes and a lawn that was mostly speedwell and crabgrass. The window boxes on the ground floor were planted with red geraniums barely clinging to life. A sign prominently displayed on the front door instructed people to come on in, so they did.

The sisters found themselves in a wide entrance-way. A man sat at an oversized desk. On either side of the hallway were two rooms furnished with a variety of sofas and armchairs. The pink striped wallpaper in the rooms reminded Bernie of the stuff on the walls of her first apartment before she'd stripped it off and repainted. Somehow she had expected something more upscale. A lot more upscale.

The man looked up from his computer. "I see you made it. I'm guessing you're Bernie and Libby Simmons."

Bernie nodded. "And you're Tim." She put him at about sixty years old. He had a weather-beaten face, a fighter's nose, and gray hair in a braid that hung below his shoulders.

"Good guess." He glanced at the clock on the wall. "You're twenty minutes late."

"We had a little trouble finding the place," Bernie explained.

"Really?" He had a smirk on his face that neither woman fancied.

"The road is pretty bad," Libby added.

"We figure it weeds out the people who don't really want to come."

"I can see that," Bernie said.

Tim rested both hands on the desk and leaned forward. "So what can I do for you ladies?"

"Like I told you on the phone, we're interested in joining your club," Bernie said.

"So you have an abiding love for old weaponry?" Tim asked.

"We'd like to learn," Libby said.

He raised an eyebrow. "And what brought about this sudden passion?"

"Watching the reenactment," Bernie said, not looking at Libby. "The old weapons seemed so interesting."

"Do tell." He cocked his head. "Somehow you and your sister don't seem the weapons type, let alone the old weapons type."

Bernie leaned forward. "Truth?"

Tim crossed his arms over his chest. "By all means."

Bernie favored him with a big smile. "Well, everyone who is anyone in town seems to be a member here."

He grunted. "Go on."

"I mean there's Rick and Gail Evans and Samuel Cotton, not to mention David Nancy and his wife—"

"What's your point?" Tim interrupted.

Bernie did her best smile. "Well, we just thought it would be a good place to join . . . for business and social reasons."

"We're not the Rotary Club," he snapped. "People who belong here have to be sponsored."

"Rick Evans said he would sponsor us," Bernie lied. "Isn't that right, Libby?"

"Absolutely," Libby agreed.

"Is that a fact?" Tim's tone was incredulous.

"Indeed it is," Bernie said, looking him in the eye.

They stared at each other for a minute.

Then Tim picked a speck of something white off his black Harley-Davidson T-shirt. "Interesting. You should also know that all the other members have to vote on you as well. It has to be unanimous."

"That won't be a problem," Bernie told him. "Everyone loves us."

He raised an eyebrow.

Libby decided things were not going well information retrieval-wise. "You should come down to our shop and try some of our muffins."

"I'm gluten-free," Tim replied.

"Is that like being smoke-free?" Bernie asked.

"No one loves a smart-ass," Tim told her.

"That's what people tell me," Bernie replied.

Libby decided to try a more direct route. "So Tim, how many members are there?"

"Enough."

"More than fifty? Less than ten?" Libby inquired.

"Like I said, there are enough."

"Can we get a list of the members?" Bernie asked.

"Why would you want to do that?" Tim asked.

"So we can ask them what they think of the club," Libby said. "Why else?"

"I'm not authorized to give that list out. Now, do you want me to show you around or don't you?"

"Definitely," Bernie said. "After all, that's what we came here for."

"There really isn't much to see." Tim waved his hand around to indicate the rooms on either side of the desk. "We have these two rooms, each of which has a TV. Plus, there's a kitchen in the back, and two rooms upstairs where members can stay."

"And the gun area?" Bernie asked.

"We have our shooting range and gun room out back."

"I wonder if Libby and I could take a quick peek?" Bernie asked.

"Don't see why not." Tim came out from behind the desk and gestured for the sisters to follow him. They headed down the hall, went through a nondescript kitchen that looked as if it was stuck in the 1950s, pushed open a scratched up wooden door, and entered a smaller room.

Boxes of cartridges, gunpowder, and shot were stacked on the table by the wall and five muskets were mounted on a wall rack.

Muskets, Bernie thought, *that look exactly like the ones used in the reenactment. That's interesting. Maybe someone took a gun from here and substituted it for one of the fake ones.* She indicated the wall rack with a nod of her head. "I'm surprised that people still use guns like those."

"Well, not those. Those particular ones are two hundred years old, but you can get new ones that are pretty similar." Tim shrugged. "Some people like shooting with them. They claim it makes the hunt more sporting."

"So if I wanted to try one out?" Bernie asked him.

"We have some we rent out to guests and such, but our members prefer to bring their own firearms."

"Where do you keep the ones you have?" Libby asked.

"In a gun safe," Tim told her.

"And if someone wanted to take one?" Bernie asked.

"As in steal? We'd shoot them."

Bernie laughed.

"Actually, we have a security system." Tim led the women outside. "This is the gun range." He indicated the area in front of him.

Libby estimated it was half a football field in length. There were lines marked out and targets placed at various intervals.

"A lot of people come here?" Bernie asked, looking around.

"A fair number," Tim said.

"I understand this place puts on a reenactment each year," she said.

"A small one, but I'm not involved with that. If you want to know anything, you'll have to talk to the president of the club."

"And who would that be?" Libby asked.

"That would be me," a voice behind them said.

Chapter 22

B ernie and Libby turned. Elise Montague was standing behind them.

"I'll be going then." Tim wandered off, obviously relieved to be quit of his hosting duties.

"You're the president?" Bernie asked her as she heard the sound of a lawn mower starting. She presumed it was Tim doing the mowing.

Elise grinned. "Surprised, huh?"

"Very," Bernie admitted.

"Well, it's better than doing volunteer work at the historical society. I like to shoot. I've been doing it since I was sixteen. And they needed someone." Elise paused for a moment, then said, "So what are you doing here?"

Bernie explained that they were interested in joining the club.

Elise's eyebrows went up. "I didn't know you two were interested in shooting."

"We're interested in exploring that possibility," Libby told her.

Bernie smiled. "Samuel Cotton told us we'd like it here." She watched for Elise's reaction.

Elise's eyebrows went up even higher.

"He said we'd enjoy all the *activities* you guys engage in," Bernie continued.

Elise flushed.

"I thought he was talking about cookouts, but maybe not," Bernie said, managing not to leer.

"The man is an idiot," Elise muttered.

Bernie looked sympathetic. "It must have been hard being here when Devlin was alive."

"Why would that be?" Elise asked.

"You know . . . you and Devlin . . . and Cotton . . ." Bernie let her voice trail off.

"So you know?" Elise asked.

"I think everyone does," Bernie said.

Elise sighed. "I suppose they do."

"It must have been awkward," Bernie said, being sympathetic.

"It was," Elise admitted after a minute went by. "But that's because Samuel Cotton is a very jealous, possessive man. We were never that serious, but he made this whole relationship thing up in his head. It was scary for a while." She lowered her voice. "I really think he might have had something to do with Devlin getting shot."

"Did you tell the police that?" Libby asked.

"No," Elise admitted. "I just didn't want to get involved."

"I can understand that," Libby said even though she didn't.

Elise took a deep breath and let it out. "But things are better now. So, are either one of you interested in shooting? Seeing how it feels? Libby, you said you were."

"I said I was interested in exploring the possibility," Libby clarified.

"No time like the present, I always say," Elise trilled.

At which point, Libby remembered why she'd never liked her in high school.

"What a good idea," Bernie gushed, having just realized that no one was at the front desk, meaning it would be the perfect time to try and acquire the club's membership list. "Yes, Libby," she enthused. "Why don't you go along with Elise? I just have to use the restroom and I'll be with you shortly."

Libby managed to get out a strangled, "Yes."

"See you in a few," Bernie said as her sister and Elise headed for the gun room.

She waited until Elise and Libby were out of sight. Then she scurried toward the entrance hall. The coast was clear and Bernie quickly walked around to the other side of the desk and began going through the two file cabinets opposite the computer. After a couple minutes she had to concede they held nothing of interest. One of the cabinets contained bills, while the other one was empty except for a box of Kleenex and a flashlight.

Hopefully, everything that she needed would be on the computer. It probably was. Actually, she was a little surprised by that since the club wasn't on the Web. Evidently there was no correlation between the two things. Bernie sighed and turned her attention to the desktop. She wasn't great with computers, but fortunately she wasn't a complete Luddite, either.

The screen saver featured a picture of a dead deer and a grinning hunter. *Lovely,* Bernie thought as she pressed the ESCAPE button. A moment later, the desktop jumped into view. That was a picture of a large musk ox. *Slightly better,* she decided as she quickly scanned the icons and clicked on the one labeled MEMBERSHIP INFORMATION.

A moment later, the membership list popped into view. *Thank God the computer wasn't password protected,* she thought as she scanned it. The list definitely had more people on it than she thought it would have. The most notable fact, however, was that everyone who had been in the reenactment at the park except for Marvin was a member. Bernie opened her e-mail account and forwarded the list to herself as an attachment. She grinned. Easy as pie. Even easier. For once, things were working out better than she'd hoped.

She closed the list and returned to the desktop, studying the icons some more. At first glance, there wasn't anything there labeled GUN RENTALS. She was trying to figure out where it would be hidden when she heard a shot and a shriek. *That's Libby,* Bernie thought. She clicked CLOSE and hurried out from behind the desk. By the time she was in the hallway, her sister and Elise were there, too.

"She wasn't expecting the recoil," Elise explained as Libby rubbed her shoulder. "You might want to ice it when you get home. Otherwise, you're going to have a nasty bruise."

Libby nodded. Bernie figured she was saving what she had to say for when they got back in the van.

"Which way did you come up?" Elise asked.

Bernie told her.

Elise shook her head. "You might want to take the main road going back to town. You'll find it's quicker."

"So what did I take to get up here?" Bernie asked.

"The back way. Tim has a strange sense of humor."

"I'll say," Bernie replied as they started out the door. "Does he do this a lot?"

"Only to people he doesn't know," Elise replied.

With that Bernie and Libby went outside. The wind had picked up and the sisters could see the leaves fluttering on the birch trees.

"Don't say anything," Bernie told Libby as they walked to their van.

"That'll be easy since I'm not speaking to you."

"Even though I got the membership list?" Bernie said.

"You could have let me know what you were up to."

Bernie stopped, turned to Libby, and put her hands on her hips. "How, pray tell, was I supposed to do that?" she demanded.

"I guess you couldn't," Libby said grudgingly. She reached up and rubbed her shoulder. "Who's on it?"

"Everyone in the reenactment except Marvin," Bernie said.

Libby frowned. "But if everyone is on it, that means we can't use it to eliminate anyone, which means we're right back where we started."

"Except that now we know Elise and Samuel

Cotton had a really good motive for killing Devlin."

"Nothing like expanding the pool of suspects instead of narrowing it," Libby observed. Despite her throbbing shoulder, she closed her eyes and slept all the way home.

Chapter 23

The rain left behind a crystalline blue sky and seventy-degree temperatures. Sean was marveling at how green and crisp everything looked after the deluge as he and Marvin drove over to Juno Grisham's house to learn what, if anything, she and Hilda had seen during the reenactment.

"I think this is going to be a total waste of time," Marvin whined as he sped through a puddle, splashing the sidewalk. He just missed dousing a dog walker, who stopped and shook her fist at him. He didn't see the woman, and sped on. He was driving the hearse since the police had impounded the Taurus.

Sean couldn't help thinking that almost splashing someone with the company car, especially when one's company car was a hearse, didn't demonstrate the proper solemnity one expected in people allied with the funeral business. But he didn't say anything. He rolled his window down and lit a cigarette. It had been three days since he'd had a chance to sneak in a smoke and he'd been looking forward to this moment ever since he'd badgered Marvin into taking this ride.

"You know you shouldn't smoke in here," Marvin groused once he realized what Sean was doing.

"Somehow I don't think your passengers are going to complain."

"No. But my father will," Marvin replied.

Sean lifted the can of Febreze he'd liberated from the house. "That's what this is for. He won't know."

Stymied on that front, Marvin launched into another line of objection. "Why do you have to smoke anyway? It's not healthy."

Sean snorted. "To paraphrase Clark Gable in *Gone with The Wind*, frankly Marvin, I don't give a damn."

"You should," Marvin objected.

"Listen, I have very few pleasures left in my old age and I intend to take advantage of the ones I can indulge in."

"But what about me?" Marvin cried, turning and looking at Sean. "What about my health?"

"Red light," Sean yelled.

Marvin slammed on the brakes. "Sorry."

Sean pointed at the Lexus they'd just avoided T-boning. "Given the way you drive, I don't think that inhaling one or two cigarettes worth of secondhand smoke should be at the top of your list of concerns. If I were you, I'd try and concentrate on the road. Call me crazy, but your driving seems like a more immediate health risk to me."

"That's unfair," Marvin protested.

"But true," Sean replied.

"I've been getting better."

"Also true, but the object here isn't to get better. The object is to not take your eyes off the road at all."

"I only do that when you're in the car," Marvin told him, trying to explain. "It's because you make me nervous."

"So you've said."

"It's true."

"I'll try not to do that." Sean had no idea how he was going to accomplish that task. According to his daughter, everything he did seemed to make Marvin nervous.

But he didn't know what else to say to the kid. Conversations dealing with emotions eluded him. One thing he did know for sure. In his day, he would never have admitted to an adult male, much less his possible father-in-law, that he made him nervous. Oh well, it was definitely a new time. He sighed. All this talk about being sensitive to each other's feelings just gave him an upset stomach. He took another puff of his cigarette and looked out the window.

"We need to take a left on Wycroff," he

instructed as they approached the intersection.

"I don't know why we're doing this," Marvin said, repeating himself as he made the turn.

Sean kept looking out the window. "I thought we went over this already." He admired a blue jay perched on the branch of a fir tree.

"I still don't get it."

Sean snorted. "What's there not to get?"

"I mean if Juno Grisham knew something she would have told the police." Marvin stopped for the stop sign on the next block without being prompted.

Sean nodded his approval. He felt pleased with himself. He'd remembered to apply positive reinforcement per Libby's instructions. "I hate to tell you this, but people don't come right out and tell the police the truth. That's what makes policing such a fun job. People lie. They lie all the time. Sometimes there's a reason and sometimes there isn't."

"But why would she?" Marvin persisted as he slowed down to drive through a large puddle on the side of the road.

Sean laughed. "Let's see. Maybe she doesn't want to talk about how she got played for a sucker by Devlin. Maybe she's hoping that everyone's forgotten about that. Maybe she actually did it. Maybe she saw something and doesn't realize the importance of what she saw. Memory is funny that way."

"If she does speak to us—" Marvin began, but Sean cut him off.

"She will. You can trust me on that." After all, he hadn't gotten to be chief of police by taking no for an answer. Anyway, he'd already talked to her on the phone. She knew they were coming.

"If she does," Marvin continued.

Sean corrected him. "*When* she does."

"Okay. But if you don't mind, I'll stay in the hearse and wait for you."

"I do mind."

"Why?" Marvin asked, managing to keep his eyes on the road.

"Because I want you there."

"Why?"

"Because you were at the reenactment and I wasn't. You'll be able to spot any inconsistencies in Juno's statement."

Marvin licked his lips. "What happens if I don't want to be there?"

"For heaven's sake, why not?" Sean snapped.

Marvin didn't answer.

"Why not?" Sean repeated.

Marvin's shoulders sagged. "I don't want to talk about it."

Sean looked at him. He took one last puff of his cigarette and flicked it out the window. He wanted to say *Man up. Don't be such a wuss,* but he didn't. First of all, he knew intellectually that that really wouldn't help the situation. Second and most important, he knew that Libby would find out what he'd said to Marvin and not speak to him for days. So he steeled himself, extended his arm, patted Marvin on the shoulder, and did the right thing . . . or at least the right thing according to his daughter.

"You need to go into Juno Grisham's house and help me talk to her and I'm going to tell you why. I know this is rough on you. I know it sucks when people believe you've done something you haven't. Believe me, I really do." Sean was referring to the incident that had cost him his job as chief of police. "But you can't hide. You can't stay in your house and wait for things to cool down, because you know what?"

"What?" Marvin asked.

"Because if you do, you'll never get out of the house again."

"Sure I will. I'm out now."

Sean took a deep breath and let it out. "I'm talking metaphorically."

"Oh."

"You have to get out and take some action. You have to ignore what people are saying behind your back. Ninety-nine percent of the people who are doing that don't have a clue." Sean clapped him on the shoulder. "Trust me, you'll feel better if you confront this thing head-on."

"You think?" Marvin said doubtfully.

"I know," Sean replied.

Marvin chewed on the inside of his cheek. "Because my dad said that I should lie low."

"Well, your dad is wrong. In fact, I'll tell him that if you want."

"No no," Marvin said quickly. "That's okay."

Sean was secretly relieved. He was not a big fan of Marvin's father nor was Marvin's father a big fan of him. "So are you coming in or not?"

"Do I have a choice?" Marvin asked.

"No."

"Then I'm coming."

"Excellent." Sean leaned back, lit another cigarette, and watched the scenery go by.

Chapter 24

Marvin and Sean arrived at Juno Grisham's house ten minutes later. The residence straddled the border between the towns of Jericho and Longely, but for practical purposes, the house was listed as belonging in the town of Longely. The house itself, a two-story brick colonial bordered by a white picket fence, would have looked at home in any town square in Vermont or Massachusetts.

Set in a one-quarter acre lot, large shade-bearing trees, mostly oaks, beeches, and maples, surrounded the house. The lawn looked like velvet, which meant it got expensive, professional care.

In fact, Sean decided, everything about the house screamed money; not in an unrestrained way, but in a tasteful, buttoned-up, old-school conservative kind of way.

"Nice," Marvin said appreciatively as he pulled into the driveway.

"Very," Sean agreed.

"What does the husband do?"

Sean took a last puff of his cigarette. "Libby tells me he's a high-powered exec in one of the pharma companies. I've never met the guy myself."

"So he makes a lot of money," Marvin said, looking at the house.

"Well, he doesn't take home a policeman's salary, that's for certain," Sean replied as he calculated the house's worth.

He was just about to make a comment about what it must cost to keep a place like this running when the door opened and Juno Grisham floated out onto the top step. She was wearing a caftan with some sort of golden thread shot through it. Her hair was piled on top of her head and her wrists and ankles were covered with gold bangles, while her fingers and toes were adorned with a variety of rings. She wasn't wearing shoes.

Sean realized that some of her bracelets had bells on them because she tinkled as she descended the three steps and delicately picked her way through the grass toward Marvin's hearse. She stopped and waited for Marvin and Sean to alight from their ride.

Not typical garb for the wife of a CEO, Sean thought as he hastily put out his cigarette and got out of the vehicle.

"Cool ride," Juno said, nodding in the direction of the hearse.

Sean wasn't sure if she was being sarcastic or not so he decided ignore the comment. "Thank you for seeing us."

She inclined her head graciously. "Anything I can do to help. Anything." She approached Marvin. A look of concern crossed her face as she gazed into his eyes. "I feel your pain," she murmured.

"Ah, g-gee, thanks," Marvin stammered. He didn't know what else to say.

"I feel it in my heart. Right here." Juno clutched her breasts to illustrate her point.

Marvin opened his mouth and closed it again. Words had failed him. Literally.

"You're the reason I agreed to talk about what happened at the reenactment," she continued. She closed her eyes for a minute as if the memory was too great for her to bear. "I wasn't going to at first, but then I said to myself, 'Juno. You must be strong. You must be resolute. Marvin needs you.'"

"I do?" he squeaked.

"You do." She looked at him gravely. "That's what brought you here."

"It is?" Marvin gave Sean a desperate glance.

"I did not know this," Sean said to Juno. "I thought it was me."

"You're the instrument," she replied. Her tone was somber. "I foresaw this visit in my dreams. You may have thought you were coming here to gather information, but your trip has a far deeper meaning."

Marvin forced a smile. "It does?" he managed to get out. After all, he had to say something.

Juno inclined her head. "Indeed it does."

Marvin started backing away, but before he'd taken two steps she grabbed his hands in hers and pulled him toward her. "We must have a cleansing ceremony." She pressed his hands into her breasts.

"No no." Marvin panicked as he struggled to free his hands from her grasp without appearing rude, but she held fast.

Sean came to Marvin's rescue. He tapped Juno on her shoulder.

Momentarily distracted, she loosened her grip on Marvin's hands a little and Marvin managed to slip away.

"Oh, but we must," she earnestly told Sean. "It is of paramount importance." She pointed to Marvin. "He is surrounded by negative energy. Bad things will continue to happen to him if we do not take the matter in hand."

"Well, that's one of the reasons we're here,"

Sean said, hoping to insinuate a note of sanity into the conversation. "We're hoping to stop more bad things from happening. There's been enough already." Seeing the look on her face, he added, "Perhaps we can work together. You can tell us what you saw and then we can talk about this cleansing ceremony."

Marvin shot Sean a panicked look, but Sean ignored it. "I-I don't have time," Marvin stammered.

Juno waved her hand in the air. "Time is a temporal thing. . . ."

"But . . ."

"You do not have to be here if you do not want to," Juno told him, "even though it would be more effective if you were. The sisters can do the ceremony with or without you. We just have to fix the date of the waxing moon."

"Oh, that's fine then," Marvin said quickly. "That's really great. Absolutely great. Fantastic even. It's very nice of you to take the trouble to do this. " He realized he was starting to babble and shut up.

"Good then," Juno said. "I will call the sisters."

Sean stepped into the shade a maple tree was throwing off. Since he'd gotten older, he found he had less tolerance for the heat. "Given that you were at the reenactment, we were hoping you could shed light on what was happening before Jack Devlin's death."

"Poor Jack," Juno murmured. "He will be missed."

"Mostly by the female half of the town," Marvin cracked.

Sean threw him a dirty look and he shut up.

"I was not really paying attention," Juno told them as she twirled the rings on her right hand. "I was communing with my sisters in the fairy circle, but perhaps Hilda can tell us something."

"Excellent," Sean said with a warning glance, cutting off any further comment Marvin might have been thinking of making. "What made you get Hilda?" Sean asked as Juno led them around the house to the backyard. "A pig is an unusual pet."

Juno smiled and moved her hands to her sides. "It was fate," she explained. "I was out at the dog shelter when someone brought Hilda in. Or surrendered her, as they like to say there. When I saw her, I knew we were meant to be."

"What did your husband say?" Sean was curious. He couldn't imagine what he would have said if Rose had walked through the door carrying a piglet under her arm.

Juno stopped and turned toward Sean. Her features had hardened and she was clutching the edge of her caftan with her right hand. "He lost the right to tell me what to do awhile ago," she informed in a stony voice.

"I learned that my first year of marriage," Sean

quipped. "That's when Rose and I started getting along."

Juno's face relaxed a little.

"So I take it he wasn't happy about the pig," Sean continued.

"He's not happy about a lot of things." Juno caught herself and changed the subject. "Wicca has taught me that in order to be happy, it is to ourselves that we must look. It is in ourselves that the power resides."

Marvin jumped back into the conversation. "So Hilda is your familiar?"

"Whatever gave you that idea?" Juno said.

Marvin retreated under her gaze. "I . . . just . . . I . . ." His voice trailed off.

She drew herself up. "I don't have a familiar. You've been watching too much TV."

"I just thought—" Marvin began, but before he could get very far Juno shook her finger in front of his nose.

"Wicca is an old religion," she informed him. "One of the oldest, if not *the* oldest. We utilize the principles of the creation. All creatures exist on the same plane. All creatures are made of the same materials. That is the reason I can understand Hilda and she can understand me. We are one."

"Sorry," Marvin mumbled, although if you had asked him what he was sorry for, he couldn't have told you.

They had reached the backyard. Most of it consisted of a green rolling lawn that could have doubled as a golf course, as well as several flowerbeds that had been planted to resemble an English garden.

"Nice," Sean said, taking it in.

"My husband's pride and joy," Juno replied.

He looked to the left-hand corner where there was a long chain link fence connected to a door that went into the house. Hilda was there waiting for them, her body vibrating with excitement. "He can't be happy about that," Sean said, pointing to churned up dirt and dandelions growing in the pen.

Juno shrugged. "Weeds are nature's flowers. I believe in giving them a chance and as for the dirt, pigs like to root. It helps them get in touch with their primal nature."

"I thought they rooted because they liked grubs," Marvin said.

Juno glared at him.

Again with the glare, he thought as he endeavored to look contrite and failed. He was hot, tired, and weirded out by Juno. He wished he'd stayed in the hearse like he'd wanted to.

Juno ignored Marvin, walked over to the fence, and unlatched the gate. A minute later, Hilda scooted out of the pen and started running in frantic circles around the backyard.

"Hilda," Juno called.

The pig ignored her.

"Hilda," Juno said, raising her voice.

Hilda kept running.

Juno frowned. "I don't understand. Normally, she comes right over."

"Maybe she doesn't have anything to say," Marvin suggested.

Juno compressed her lips and folded her arms across her chest.

Looking at her, Sean knew that if he wanted to get any information out of Juno he was going to have go through the pig. That was the game Juno was playing and he didn't see any alternative except to play along. He turned to Marvin and told him to go get the pig. After all, he certainly couldn't.

"Me? Why me?" Marvin pointed to Juno. "It's her pig. She should go get her."

"That's true," Juno replied. "But you're the one who wants to speak to her."

"A valid point," Sean said.

"We could wait," Marvin suggested. "She'll get tired soon. How long can she do this?"

"A long time," Juno said. "And I have to leave in half an hour."

Since Marvin couldn't think of a good answer to that, he reluctantly started after the pig. "Hilda," he cooed. "Good Hilda. Nice Hilda."

The pig stopped, cocked her head, and listened. Marvin, taking heart, slowly approached her.

Hilda waited until he was a foot away and took off again.

He took a deep breath to keep himself from uttering some very impolite phrases and tried again. "Pretty Hilda," he cooed. "Cute Hilda."

Hilda sat down and waited. She allowed Marvin to get within six inches of her before she bolted. Sensing what she was about to do, he took a flying leap. Hilda slipped away and Marvin landed belly first on the ground.

"Nice try," Sean shouted, trying not to laugh and not succeeding very well.

Marvin got up and brushed himself off. His knees hurt as did his wrists, which had taken the weight of the fall, but he wasn't about to admit that, especially to Libby's dad.

"Keep going," Sean called encouragingly. "You almost had her."

For the next fifteen minutes, Hilda continued her game of chase. By the end, Marvin was so exhausted he could barely walk. He finally collapsed under the shade of a large oak tree, at which point Hilda came over and sat in his lap. She pushed her bristled snout under his hand. He was torn between killing her and petting her so he compromised.

"Bad Hilda," he said in as stern a voice as he could manage while he scratched her underneath her chin.

She let out a contented oink.

Juno came over. "Poor Hilda," she cooed as she knelt down beside her. "You must be thirsty."

"Poor *Hilda!*" Marvin protested indignantly. "What about me?"

"What about you?" She scooped Hilda up in her arms and rubbed her tummy. "Were you scared of the big, bad man?"

"Big, bad man?" Marvin squeaked. "Are you nuts?"

Juno ignored him and continued on. "Do you want to have a talk with Mommy?" she asked Hilda.

Hilda oinked. Twice.

Juno cocked her head to one side. "Really? You don't say? You want to tell Mommy the rest of that in private?"

Marvin would have rolled his eyes if he'd had the energy. He watched her walking away. She had Hilda firmly clasped in her arms. He wanted to go after her, but he couldn't. His legs felt like logs. He didn't think he had the strength to get up. In fact, he didn't think he'd ever felt so tired in his life.

He wondered if he had heat stroke; perhaps he was dehydrated. He should probably go to the hospital and get checked out, but he was too tired to move. He just leaned against the tree trunk, feeling the sweat run down his back, and watched Juno as she stood in the shade of a copper beech, murmuring in Hilda's ear.

After ten minutes, she came back and stopped in front of Sean. "Hilda wants to tell you something," she said to him in a grave voice. "Something important."

Sean waited. Nothing.

"Well?"

"She needs a little more time," Juno said.

After another minute went by, Sean lost his patience. "I bet I know what she wants to tell me. She wants to tell me about Devlin taking your diamond ring and giving it to Monica Lewis."

Juno's jaw dropped then she got hold of herself. "That old chestnut?" she scoffed. "Who told you that?"

Sean smiled. "It came to me in a dream."

"It was Monica Lewis, wasn't it?"

"What if it was?"

"She's a pathological liar," Juno spit out. "You can't believe anything she tells you."

"So it's not true?"

"Absolutely not," Juno declared. "I found the ring a couple weeks later in my washing machine. It had slipped off my finger and I hadn't noticed."

"You must have been glad to get it back," Sean said gravely.

"Oh yes." Juno touched the base of her throat lightly then brought her hand down.

"But you're not wearing it," Sean observed.

"Now I only wear it on special occasions," she

explained. "I wouldn't want something like that to happen again."

"Understandable. Though I have to say, my wife always found it inconvenient to have to go to the bank every time she needed a piece of jewelry." A lie, since the only piece of jewelry Rose had ever worn was her wedding band, which she'd never taken off.

"Fortunately, we have a safe in the house," Juno told him.

Sean nodded. "I'm puzzled though."

She cocked her head and waited.

"Why would Monica say something like that?"

Juno ran her fingers through her hair. "Because she's jealous of me. She's always been jealous of me."

"And why was that?"

"Simple. I got all the boys and she never did."

"You both got Jack Devlin," Sean pointed out.

"What an infelicitous phrase," Juno remarked.

"Killing him would be even more infelicitous," Sean said.

"What are you implying?"

"What do you think I'm implying?"

"You're accusing me?" Juno's voice rose in disbelief.

Sean nodded.

She clutched her breasts. "What a terrible, terrible thing to say. I would never do something like that. Ever."

"And why is that?"

Her eyes widened. "Because I believe that when someone does something bad it comes back to them sevenfold."

"Fair enough," Sean said. "In that case, did you happen to see anything that could help me out?"

She shook her head. "I was in the rose garden along with everyone else helping manifest an Aga."

"The stove?"

"That's right."

"The stove that costs twenty thousand dollars?"

"Yes. That one."

"What happened to the spiritual side of things?"

Juno drew herself up. "Everyone is entitled to both."

Sean managed not to laugh. "Perhaps Hilda saw something?"

"Perhaps that's what she wants to speak to you about."

Chapter 25

So let me get this straight," Bernie said to Libby as she swatted a mosquito away. They were waiting for the 7:15 Metro North to get in from New York so they could talk to Rick Evans. "According to Hilda the pig, either Tony Gerard or Rick Evans handed Jack Devlin the musket, but she's not quite sure which one it was."

"That's what Dad said that Juno said that Hilda said." Libby leaned back against the van. She decided she liked this time of day. Everything became softer in the waning light.

"I know what he said. I was there when he said it."

"I know you were. I was there, too."

Bernie shook her head. "You know, I always thought Juno was nuts, but now I'm sure of it." She bent down and removed a pebble from her sandal. "I've heard the expression *when pigs fly,* but *when pigs talk?*" She straightened up. "I don't get why Juno can't come out and just say what she has to say."

"Maybe she's afraid to, like Dad suggested."

"Afraid of who?"

"Either Rick Evans or Tony Gerard or both."

Libby pictured both men in her mind. Neither seemed particularly threatening to her. Rick Evans was annoying, pompous, egotistical, and ambitious. But scary? Hardly. As for Tony Gerard, the adjective that came to mind when she thought of him was *nondescript*. He was average height, average weight, brown eyes, brown hair. The only thing that distinguished him was that he was a diehard 49ers fan.

"I wonder what Tony Gerard will say?" Bernie mused. She was planning on talking to him tomorrow morning with or without Brandon.

"About vacuum cleaner bags?"

"Ha-ha. No. About what Hilda said." Bernie grinned. "I'll be interested to see his reaction."

"And Rick's," Libby said.

"Yes. Rick's too," Bernie agreed.

Libby watched two teenage boys doing ollies on the platform with their skateboards. "I don't think I could ever have done that." She nodded in their direction. "Not even in high school."

"You definitely take after Mother's side of the family when it comes to klutziness."

"I know. But, at least I didn't get her cankles."

"Thank God for that."

A moment later, the stationmaster came out and chased the boys away. They were laughing and catcalling as they skated down the road. Libby stretched. It had been a long day and she was tired.

Bernie hitched up her bra strap. "You know—" she began then stopped.

Libby turned to her. "What?"

"I'm worried about Marvin," Bernie blurted out.

"Me too." Libby's lips started to tremble. "But we're not going to let anything happen to him, right?"

"Right," Bernie said. "One way or another we will get to the bottom of this. This whole thing is just weird."

"Are you referring to Hilda?" Libby asked.

"Yes. Who has a pig for a pet?"

"They're supposed to be very smart."

"I think I'd prefer a golden retriever." Bernie waved away another mosquito. The smell of newly cut grass perfumed the air. "What does Marvin think?"

Libby laughed. "He thinks Juno is nuts."

"Nobody is going to argue about that. But what does he think about her accusations? Did they jog his memory?"

Libby shook her head. "No. He still says he can't remember who handed Devlin the musket. If anyone did."

"Well, someone had to have handed it to Devlin. You don't rig a musket to explode and just let anyone take it."

"Unless you're a sociopath."

"A theory we're not pursuing at the moment." Bernie closed her eyes and pictured the scene. "Whoever handed Devlin the gun had to have primed it with shot."

"That's the assumption we're going on," Libby said.

"So whoever did this must have had the musket with them so they could hand it to Devlin, or they marked the musket so they could pick it out of the pile and hand it to him when the time was right."

"That is the more logical hypothesis. Too bad we can't look at the muskets to see if that's the case." Libby took a drink of lemonade from her water bottle.

"I bet the muskets are still in the evidence room."

"Maybe Craig could take a peek at them."

"He might if Dad asks him to." Bernie shook her head. "I should have tried harder to see them after Devlin was killed."

"You did try, but Rick Evans wasn't having it."

"I should have been more forceful." Bernie flicked a gnat away.

"You were in shock."

"We all were, but that's no excuse." Bernie watched a blue jay fly by.

Libby took another sip of her lemonade while Bernie consulted her watch. Five more minutes to go.

"Did you know that Juno was a bond trader?" Bernie said suddenly. "A good one."

"Bond trader to Wiccan. That's a big switch," Libby observed.

"Maybe she got bored. Maybe she had a vision."

"It must have been quite a vision."

Chapter 26

The Metro-North was fifteen minutes late, pulling into the Longely Station at seven-thirty. Libby and Bernie watched the commuters descend from the train and walk past the station house, which had recently been renovated at a fairly substantial cost to resemble the original one from the early 1900s.

Men and women stepped off the platform, briefcases in hand, and slowly trudged toward the cars they'd left in the parking lot earlier in the day. They all looked tired and rumpled from their long day at work.

Watching them, Libby was glad that she worked and lived in the same place. She felt a rush of gratitude that she worked with her sister instead of sitting behind a desk in some big impersonal office in the city, and that best of all, she did something she loved.

Rick Evans turned out to be one of the last people to walk off the platform and into the parking lot. He was walking slowly, seemingly on auto-pilot, with his eyes to the ground. A ring of sweat beaded his hairline, his white shirt was creased, and he was carrying his suit jacket in the crook in his arm. Libby and Bernie moved away from their van and went toward him.

"Fancy seeing you here," Libby said.

Rick Evans startled and looked up.

"We'd like to speak to you for a moment," she said.

A bead of perspiration ran down Rick's cheek. He wiped it away with the back of his hand. "This is about Devlin, isn't it?"

Libby nodded.

"I've already told the police everything I know."

"We would just like you to comment on something that Hilda the Pig said," Bernie replied.

"Hilda?" Rick started laughing. "You want me to comment on something a pig said?"

"Yeah, we do," Bernie replied.

"Juno is a lunatic. She should be medicated."

"That seems a little harsh," Bernie told him.

"So what would you call someone who pretends a pig is talking to her?" Rick challenged.

"Eccentric."

"You know, it really doesn't matter what you call that nut job. I've had a long day and I'm anxious to get home."

"To your loving wife?" Libby asked.

"No. To my basset hound. Of course, to my wife. The last thing I want to do right now is have a conversation about something that Juno—"

"Hilda," Libby corrected.

Rick groaned. "That moron said about me. She hates me. She hates everyone. She spreads lies."

"Why does she hate you?" Libby asked.

"Because she wanted to use the old Hinkleman House as a Wiccan Institute and I voted no on a zoning code variance." He shook his head. "First of all, it's in a residential area and people were worried about the parking; second of all, we don't need more crazies running around, conducting ceremonies in the middle of the night."

Bernie cocked her head. "When was this? I don't remember reading about it."

"A couple years ago." Rick shifted his weight from one leg to the other. "Juno's never forgiven me for that. She'll do anything to block my becoming mayor, but that's not going to happen." He shook his head. "She was nice before she got into this Wiccan stuff. Unlike her husband. But now she's off on another planet."

"What's wrong with her husband?" Libby asked.

"Three words. *Possessive, controlling,* and *jealous.*"

"So he wasn't relaxed with the Juno-Devlin situation?" Bernie asked.

"To say the least," Rick replied.

"Like you were with your wife and Devlin?" Bernie asked.

Rick shrugged. "Believe what you want. My wife and I have an open marriage. We've had one for years."

"What about Juno's marriage?" Libby asked.

He shrugged again. "It isn't my business."

"But if you had to say," Bernie pressed.

"It's good if you like blood sports," Rick replied.

"Do you?" Libby asked, changing the topic.

"I hunt, if that's what you mean. But then you already know that."

Bernie leaned forward. "Are you a good shot?"

He preened. "As a matter of fact I am. I shoot competitively."

"We've heard you also know a lot about guns."

He glanced at his watch. "It's no big secret. I'm a collector."

"We've heard that too," Bernie put in. "What does your wife think of your hobby?"

"Not much. She doesn't like weapons. Sees no reason to have firearms in the house. Mine are in the basement. It's easier that way."

So that explains it, Bernie thought. "My dad always says marriage is the art of compromise."

"But she's a member of the Musket and Flintlock Club," Libby pointed out.

"She goes when they're having a potluck, but that's about it. It's strictly a social thing with her."

"I'm with her," Libby said, thinking of her one and only experience with a firearm. Her shoulder still hurt like hell.

"Most women are," Rick said. "Except Elise, of course."

"You know what I find odd," Libby said, changing the subject. "What I find odd is that you gave Bernie and me the distinct impression that you didn't know anything about firearms."

Rick looked at Libby blankly. "Whatever gave you that idea?"

"The way you acted when Jack Devlin was killed," Libby answered.

"What should I have said?"

"I'm not sure," Libby admitted. "Why did you put Marvin in charge of the muskets, anyway?"

"He volunteered to take care of the costumes, and the muskets were part of the costumes. After all, we're talking about props here."

"True," Libby conceded. She took a sip of her lemonade. "Did you take a shot at Marvin?" she blurted out.

Rick shook his head in disbelief. "Why would I do something like that?"

"If I knew, I wouldn't be asking," Libby replied.

"Well, I didn't," Rick asserted.

"Then who did?" Libby challenged.

"How the hell should I know?" Rick cried. "I'm not the Magic Answer Machine." He shifted his jacket to his other arm. "If you want to talk to someone who had a reason to kill Devlin, talk to Juno's husband."

"He wasn't there," Libby pointed out.

"Yes, he was."

Bernie perked up. "Where? I didn't see him."

"Neither did I," Libby added.

"He came late. He was behind the big oak tree in back of the gazebo."

"What the hell was he doing there?" Libby demanded.

"I'm guessing he was watching Juno. You get a clear view of the rose garden from there."

"Why would he being doing that?" Bernie asked.

"Why do you think? I already told you. He's

pathologically jealous of her. And by the way, FYI, Chuck is a reenactor. He knows all about muskets. He did a couple stints at Gettysburg."

Libby started to bite her cuticle, realized what she was doing, and stopped.

"You want answers, go talk to him." Having said that, Rick turned on his heel, marched over to his BMW, and got in. It was one of the only cars left on the lot.

"I wouldn't mind having a car like that." Bernie sighed as he roared out of the parking lot, leaving a fine cloud of dust in his wake.

"Maybe in your next life," Libby said.

"Well, it sure ain't gonna be in this one."

Chapter 27

So what do you think about what Rick said?" Libby asked Bernie as they walked toward their van. The station was all but deserted until the next train came in at 11:10. Overhead, crows were flying in to roost in the big copper beech trees that bordered the parking lot.

Bernie stopped to pick another pebble out of her sandal. "About Juno's husband?"

Libby nodded.

"As in should we talk to him?"

Libby nodded again.

"I don't remember seeing him, do you?"

Libby shook her head. "He must have left before the police came."

"So," Bernie mused, "while everyone else ran toward Jack Devlin, Juno's husband ran away."

"That's what Rick Evans implied."

"Suggestive, isn't it?"

"Very," Libby agreed.

Bernie checked the time on her cell. It was a little after eight. "No time like the present. Especially since we're close to their house."

"If he's home," Libby said.

"I guess we're going to find that out."

"Maybe we should call," she suggested.

"And give him a heads-up?" Bernie shook her head. "I think not. Let's surprise him, see what happens. More fun that way."

"Your definition of fun, not mine."

Bernie grinned and got in the van. "Exactly."

It was eight-fifteen when Bernie and Libby pulled up in front of the Grishams's house. The sun was setting and the sky was an array of soft pinks, oranges, and gray-blues. A jet streaked high overhead, leaving an arching white plume behind it. The air smelled of freshly mown grass and roses.

"This is a perfect summer evening," Bernie noted.

Libby sighed. "We should be having a barbecue."

"We will as soon as we get this figured out," Bernie assured her.

As the sisters got out of the van, they could hear yelling going on inside the house. The noise spilled out, cutting through the evening's tranquility.

"It could be the TV," Libby said in a hopeful tone. The yelling got louder.

"You wish."

"It probably is," Libby persisted.

"Because folks in this zip code don't have domestic disputes?" Bernie asked.

Libby was framing her reply when she heard a scream followed by a crash.

"Definitely a domestic dispute," Bernie said.

Libby frowned. "The smart thing to do would be to call the police, domestic disputes being unpredictable."

"But we're not smart," Bernie noted.

"If Dad were here, he would tell us not to go in," Libby pointed out.

"He's not. Anyway Libby, we're not going in. We're ringing the bell."

"True, Bernie. And the cops could take a while to get here."

"We wouldn't want someone to get hurt in the meantime."

"No, Bernie. We certainly wouldn't."

They headed for the front door. Bernie rang the bell. When no one answered, she rang it again. She was just about to press the button for the third time when the door swung open.

A tall, tanned man wearing khakis, a white polo shirt, and loafers without socks peered out at them. He had regular features, including a nose that was a little too perfect to be real, dark hair that was graying slightly at the temples, and a snarl of an expression on his face.

Now that they saw him, Libby and Bernie realized they'd spotted him at the reenactment walking to the park lot.

Except for the expression, Bernie felt as if she was looking at a Ralph Lauren ad. Of course, the smell of whiskey floating off him wasn't something you'd smell in the perfect WASP world the ads evoked. But then again, maybe you would. Perfect worlds tended to have dark undersides.

"Chuck Grisham?" she asked.

"Yes."

Bernie introduced themselves. "We'd like to speak to you for a second."

"We're busy at the moment," he growled. "Go away."

"We could hear," Bernie said.

Chuck leaned forward. "What's that supposed to mean?" he demanded, breathing on her.

She wanted to take a step back against the onslaught, but pride demanded she stay put.

"We just wanted to make sure everything was all right." Libby summoned up her most ingratiating smile. "We heard a crash. We thought maybe someone got hurt. You know, like the television falling on someone . . . or something like that. . . ." Her voice trailed off as her sister shot her a look.

Chuck narrowed his eyes as he tried to process what Libby was saying. "Why would our television fall?"

"It happens," Bernie told him as she strained to get a peek inside the house. "In fact, it's one of the most common causes of household deaths."

"Really?"

"Yes, really." Bernie couldn't see any blood on the hallway floor or the entrance to the living room, so that was good.

"Well, the television hasn't fallen and we're fine," Chuck told them as he folded his arms across his chest.

"How's your refrigerator? Maybe we should come in and take a look. Make sure it's okay," Libby chirped, picking up on Bernie's cue. "We do know about that kind of thing."

"Thanks, but everything is just dandy. So now you can leave. In fact, I insist on it," he told them.

"Actually—" Libby began.

Chuck snapped his fingers, cutting her off before she could say anything else. A look of recognition passed over his face. He raised his hand and shook his finger at her. "I know you. You were at the reenactment. So was your . . ."

Bernie supplied the word. "Sister."

"You're the caterers, aren't you? The ones who have that fancy-pants shop on Main Street."

"I wouldn't call it fancy-pants," Bernie told him.

"Well, I would." Chuck pitched forward, then recovered and rocked back on his heels. The smell of whiskey coming off him seemed even stronger than it had before.

Bernie decided he had the smell of someone who'd been drinking long enough to become one with the alcohol.

"What's it called, again?" There was a slight slur to his words.

"A Little Taste of Heaven," she said.

He scratched his cheek. "Fancy-pants and presumptuous. Not a good combination in my book."

Bernie wrinkled her forehead. "Excuse me?"

"You heard what I said."

"How can you say something like that when you've never been in the store?" Libby demanded.

Chuck sniffed. "I've heard comments."

"From whom?" Bernie asked before she could stop herself.

"Never you mind," Chuck told them.

"You just made that up," she said.

Chuck glowered at her. "What are you two doing here, anyway? Shouldn't you be behind the counter or closing up or washing dishes or something? Aren't you a long way from Main Street?"

"Geographically speaking, about three miles, which isn't really that far," Bernie answered.

"We were just wondering if you saw anything odd or out of place at the reenactment," Libby asked.

He stared at them for a moment, seeming to have trouble focusing, before he turned slightly to the right.

Bernie noticed a bruise on the right side of his chin. It looked new. She thought about the crash she and Libby had just heard. Had Chuck fallen into something? Judging from the alcohol on his breath that was entirely possible. Or had Juno pitched something at him? That was entirely possible, too.

His eyes narrowed. He absentmindedly rubbed his bruise while he studied them. Finally he said, "People have told me about you two."

"Nothing bad I hope," Libby said.

"They said you fancy yourselves as detectives. Or should I say dabblers in detection."

"I would hardly use the word *dabble*," Libby said indignantly.

"Girl detectives," Chuck sneered. "What a charming concept. So Nancy Drew-ish."

Libby was going to say something, but Bernie squeezed her arm. Libby took the hint and remained silent.

"You said you saw us at the reenactment," Bernie said to Chuck. "We saw your wife there."

"Being the laughingstock of the town."

"But we didn't see you," Bernie said, keeping to the subject at hand.

"I was behind the oak tree."

"You were?" Juno had come up behind him. "I thought you said you were too busy to go."

"I changed my mind," Chuck told her.

"What were you doing there?"

"Watching the reenactment."

"He's just being modest," Bernie said. "He just can't let you out of his sight."

"That'll be the day," Juno muttered.

"That's what Rick Evans says," Libby put in.

Chuck tried to stand up straighter. "He doesn't know what he's talking about."

"Rick also said you were a reenactor," Bernie said.

Chuck nodded. "I am indeed."

"So I guess he isn't lying about everything," she noted.

He didn't say anything.

"How come you weren't in the reenactment in the park?" Libby asked.

Chuck swayed, then regained his balance. "Because I knew this one would be a joke. When I was at Gettysburg, we drilled, we rehearsed. This reenactment was a disgrace. It isn't even based on a real incident! You can't play fast and loose with history." His voice rose. "People like Rick Evans have no respect for anything. They should be marched outside and shot."

"He means metaphorically," Juno clarified. "He's very passionate about history."

"I can speak for myself," Chuck told his wife.

"So you didn't want to kill Devlin?" Bernie asked.

Chuck started laughing and ended up having a coughing fit. "Really? Why would I want to do that?"

"Because you were jealous that he was having an affair with your wife," Libby said.

Chuck pointed to Juno. "Her? Don't be ridiculous. I'm not jealous of her."

"He doesn't mean that," Juno said. "He's just a little under the weather."

Chuck snorted. "Just be glad I didn't say something worse," he told Juno. Then he turned back to Libby. "Where did you get that from? Rick Evans?"

"No. Sanford Aiken," Libby answered.

"That jerk," Chuck muttered. "Always sticking his nose in where it doesn't belong."

"Or was it Elise Montague, Libby?" Bernie said. "I forget."

"No. It was definitely Sanford." Libby paused for a moment and then said, "Or maybe it *was* Rick Evans."

"Maybe you two should just shut up," Chuck snarled.

"So," Libby continued. "I take it that you are going to neither confirm nor deny that you were jealous of your wife and killed Jack Devlin?"

"I think you should be more charitable, Libby. I think you should give old Chucky the benefit of the doubt." Bernie turned toward him. "Maybe you just meant to teach Devlin a lesson and things went wrong. I don't know. Which one was it? After all, you are a reenactor. You just said so. You were there. And you do know your way around a musket."

"So what if I do?" Chuck said.

"So that gives you motive and opportunity," Bernie told him.

He gave her a disdainful look. "That gives lots of people motive and opportunity. All I can say is that I hope your cooking is better than your detecting work."

"Really?" Libby said.

Chuck sniffed. "Yes, really. You're missing the point."

"Would you care to enlighten us?"

"Gladly. Jack Devlin's death isn't about love. It isn't about sex. It isn't about jealousy. It's about good old-fashioned money."

"Because everything always is?" Libby asked.

"Exactly," Chuck told them. "Always has been, always will be."

"Could you be a little more specific?" she inquired.

"Not really," Chuck replied. "You two are supposed to be investigating so go investigate.

You come barging in here in the middle of the night—"

"Eight o'clock is hardly the middle of the night," Bernie pointed out.

"And accuse me of killing Jack Devlin." Chuck hiccupped. "You got a lotta nerve. That's all I can say."

Bernie watched his eyelids begin to close.

He opened them again. "I think I need another drink," he mumbled as he turned and stumbled into the house. Juno closed the door after him.

"So much for finding whether he left before or after Jack Devlin was murdered," Libby said.

Chapter 28

"Must be great being married to him," Bernie said to Libby as they walked toward their van.

"I don't think she's any prize package either," Libby noted. "I wonder if she hit him with something?"

"He probably deserved it."

"Possibly." Libby sighed. "I don't think that talking to them has gotten us any closer to solving this mess."

"I hope you're wrong," Bernie told her.

"How do you figure?" Libby asked.

Bernie brushed a fly away. "Maybe we stirred things up. Maybe somebody will do something."

"That's a whole lot of maybes."

"It sure is," Bernie agreed.

The sound of a tugboat horn floated up from the Hudson River. A dog started singing along. Bernie paused and glanced back. The porch light had been turned on. The sisters continued walking to their van. A moment later, the sprinklers came on and Bernie jumped sideways to avoid getting drenched. "I bet they did that on purpose," she muttered.

Libby frowned. "Do you think Chuck was talking about Monica Lewis when he started talking about money being the motive?"

"Who else?"

"Then why didn't Chuck give us her name?" Libby challenged.

"Or her brother's name. Remember we're talking about David Nancy *and* Monica Lewis."

"True."

"Maybe Chuck thought we'd believe him more if he played the reluctant witness instead of giving them up."

"Maybe," Libby said. "But Chuck didn't strike me as a subtle kind of guy. He's more of a bull-in-a-china-shop type of fellow."

"Maybe he was so drunk he blanked on their names."

"Now that I would believe," Libby told her.

Bernie clicked her tongue against her teeth while she organized her thoughts. "Nancy is a strong suspect," she hypothesized. "Unlike Monica, he was near Devlin."

"And Chuck and Juno were not. I think we can cross them off our list. Juno was busy dancing and Chuck was behind the oak tree, a fact verified by Rick Evans."

"Or," Bernie replied. "Maybe Chuck left early because he was bored."

"Or disgusted by the level of amateurism displayed," Libby said.

"Or maybe Chuck did hand Devlin the musket and he didn't want to stick around to see what was going to happen."

Libby made a face. "That's a stretch. The guy whose wife you are boffing comes up and hands you a musket. Would you take it?"

"Well, when you put it that way, it does seem a little unlikely," Bernie conceded. She was silent for a moment then she said, "I know we've already discussed this, but maybe the musket was meant for someone else. Maybe Jack Devlin getting the musket was an accident. Maybe the musket was meant for Marvin."

"Because of the shot someone took at him?"

Bernie nodded.

"Yeah. I've thought about that a lot." Libby's face was grim. "But I can't figure out why anyone would do that. On the other hand . . ."

"Lots of people had reason to want Jack Devlin dead," Bernie said, finishing Libby's sentence for her.

"Too many people. Too many possibilities."

Bernie frowned. "Like Dad says, I guess we'll just keep poking around until something turns up."

Libby sighed. "Hopefully for Marvin's sake that will happen sooner rather than later."

"Yes, indeed," Bernie replied as she started up the van. It came to life with a sputter and a cough. She wondered how much longer it would go before they had to replace it.

"Do you think what Chuck Grisham was saying is true?" Libby asked after another moment of silence had passed.

Bernie pulled out onto the road. "You mean about Jack Devlin's death being about money?"

"Yes."

"You just asked me that."

"I know. I just wondered if you wanted to revise your opinion?"

Bernie thought for another moment. "It's possible," she admitted. "Unlikely, but possible. Though I still vote for sex."

"Me too," Libby said.

"Sex and money. The two big motivators for human behavior."

"And revenge," Libby suggested. "Don't forget that."

"A dish best eaten cold," Bernie mused. "Or so they say. Do you believe that?"

"No, I don't," Libby said as she bounced up and down in her seat. They were going over a stretch of potholed road.

"Me either," Bernie said, stopping for a herd of deer—seven to be exact—that were crossing the road.

Recently, the deer population had exploded and they were all over the place, eating plants and shrubs, dining out of bird feeders, bounding across roads in the middle of the day. There was a lot of talk about shooting them, but the thought made Bernie sad. She didn't care if the deer had become pests. They were elegant and graceful and she liked watching them. Plus, she didn't garden. Eventually, the last of the deer, a doe and her fawn, ambled across the road and Bernie continued driving.

"Too bad Hilda can't really tell us what happened at the reenactment," Bernie noted as they pulled up in front of the shop. "She was probably the only impartial observer out there."

"And she did like Jack Devlin," Libby noted, flashing back to when he had picked up Hilda. "If pigs could coo, she would have."

"That's right," Bernie said, remembering. "Didn't he say something to you and me like, don't worry we're old friends, before he picked her up?"

"Yes, he did," Libby said.

"So that confirms Brandon's story about Devlin and Juno hooking up." Bernie looked around. No one was out. Everyone was in for the night. "Or at least it proves that Devlin was at her house." She began to get out of the van, but Libby put out a hand to stop her.

"Wait a minute," she said. "Let's finish this up before we go inside."

"Works for me," Bernie said and she closed the van door and faced her sister.

"I'll tell you one thing," Libby said, continuing with what she'd been saying, "I bet Devlin wasn't there to fix her toaster."

"Unless *toaster* is a word for a particular part of the female anatomy," Bernie suggested.

"Rick might well be right about Juno and Chuck. Maybe Chuck was jealous because of an affair she'd had with Devlin . . . especially if she was doing what she wasn't supposed to be doing in their bed."

"Maybe Chuck came home and saw them together," Bernie opined. "That would certainly do it."

"On the other hand," Libby said, playing devil's advocate, "we don't know that she did have an affair. Just because he made that comment to Hilda doesn't prove anything."

Bernie gave her sister an *are-you-out-of-your-mind* look.

"Okay," Libby conceded. "So maybe it does."

"Why should she be different from anyone else?"

"He hasn't slept with everyone in town," Libby said.

"No. But he's made pretty good in-roads."

Libby nodded, acknowledging the truth of Bernie's statement. "I'll say one thing for him. He certainly had a lot of energy. Given his extra-curricular activities, it's amazing he had time to work."

The sisters were silent for a moment.

"So maybe Chuck is responsible," Bernie said.

"How did he give Devlin the gun?" Libby asked.

"I don't know," Bernie admitted.

"What's his motive?"

"Jealousy. Revenge."

"Why now?"

"I don't know the answer to that one, either," Bernie confessed. She stifled a yawn. "I feel as if we're just going around in one enormous circle."

"That's because we are," Libby told her.

"Unfortunately," Bernie said. They both got out of the van. Suddenly Bernie felt an overwhelming desire for some ice cream. The question was what kind? Did she want to go with salted caramel or peach? On the other hand, coffee ice cream also sounded good, especially if she put some salted roasted almonds and a small ribbon of chocolate sauce on top.

There was vanilla in all its pristine purity with its flecks of grated Madagascar vanilla bean sprinkled through it, as well as a few grindings of black pepper. Sweet and spicy. The combination always worked. That would certainly be good plain, or with a few slices of Pennsylvania peaches and some raspberries she'd gotten from the farmer's market sprinkled on top. Or she could always have a little bit of each. So many choices. Fortunately, there was enough time to sample them all. A banana split minus the banana was coming to mind.

She was leaning toward that choice as she studied A Little Taste of Heaven's shop window. They changed it six times a year. She and Libby had decided on a historical theme in keeping with the Fourth of July. They'd decorated it with sepia tinted photos of life in Longely in the 1800s, photos they'd borrowed from the Longely Historical Society and hung from the ceiling on strings. Old wooden milk crates they'd gotten at the grist mill had been placed upside down.

They'd taken old tin and toleware—mostly trays and pie plates—put them on the crates and piled them high with sugar cookies and cupcakes iced in red, white, and blue after which they'd put glass milk bottles filled with sparklers in front of them. Their last touch had been draping old-fashioned red, white, and blue bunting around the window. At first, Bernie had been afraid there'd be too many elements, but somehow the whole thing worked.

"It looks nice," Libby said.

"It looks very nice." Bernie bent down, picked up a napkin lying on the sidewalk, and threw it in the garbage can. "I have to say, I think we do a good job."

"With some things," a voice behind them said.

Bernie and Libby spun around as a man stepped out of the alley shadows.

Chapter 29

Oh, it's you," Libby cried, clutching her chest. "You scared me."

"I'm sorry." Lucy, aka Lucas Broadbent, Longely Chief of Police stepped closer.

It was apparent to Libby and Bernie that he was not even remotely repentant.

"What do you want?" Bernie demanded.

"To talk to both of you," he replied.

"Why don't you try calling instead of lurking around in the dark?" Libby demanded.

"I'm hardly lurking, although as chief of police if I wanted to lurk I am fully entitled to do so. As it so happens, I was coming down after talking to your father and heard your voices, so now I'm talking to both of you, as well."

Lucy hitched up his pants. He was five-foot ten inches tall and weighed close to three hundred pounds. Since he'd taken over as the Longely Chief of Police his girth had increased every year. He reminded Bernie of an egg, with his smallish bald head, white skin, big belly, and small feet.

"Wonderful," she muttered. "The perfect end to a perfect day."

Lucy scowled at her. "What was that you said?"

"Nothing. I merely said it was wonderful that you wanted to talk to us."

"Are you being sarcastic?" he demanded suspiciously.

"No, of course not. My sister and I love talking to you, don't we, Libby?"

"Absolutely. In fact, my father often comments on how much he misses the talks you two used to have."

"Does he, now?" Lucy remembered their talks quite well. Enjoying them was not the phrase that came to mind.

"Oh definitely," Bernie said, backing up Libby.

He took another step toward them. "I've had complaints about you."

"Complaints?" Bernie said.

"About us?" Libby put her fingers to her lips. "Oh dear. That's terrible. I'm appalled. Was it something we baked?"

"We did have problems with the blueberry muffins this morning, didn't we, Libby?"

"I'll say, Bernie. The berries kept on sinking to the bottom."

"That's because we put too much milk in the batter."

"It was my fault," Libby confessed. "I wasn't paying attention to what I was doing."

"My sister has a tendency to ditz out."

Lucy put his hands on his hips and glowered at them. "You think you're funny, don't you?"

"I don't know about funny. Maybe moderately amusing," Libby replied.

"Or mildly humorous," Bernie suggested.

He shook a finger in their faces. "You two are going to get yourselves in a lot of trouble if you keep going down this road."

"Which road?" Bernie asked. "You mean like going down Main Street? I don't know how we'd get to our shop otherwise."

"No, Bernie. He means that as a threat."

Bernie widened her eyes. "Wow, Libby. I did not know that." She pressed her hands against her chest. "I'm really scared."

"Me too." Libby turned to Lucy. "Why are you threatening us? That really isn't very nice. We're just trying to make a living."

"I'm not threatening you," he told them, raising his voice in a fit of exasperation.

"It sounded that way to me. Didn't it sound that way to you, Libby?"

Libby nodded her head. "Indisputably."

"I'm warning you." Lucy's words came out through gritted teeth.

"Oh, why didn't you say that?" Libby asked. "Warning's much different than threatening."

"I'm not so sure, Libby."

"Maybe you should look it up on your cell, Bernie."

"And maybe you two can stop talking and pay attention to what I'm saying to you," he gritted out.

"Of course," Bernie said.

"You had but to ask," Libby reiterated. "So is this about the muffins?"

Lucy turned red. "No. It isn't about the muffins. It's about the questions you've been asking around town."

"You should have said that in the first place."

"I did," he snapped. "What the hell do you think you're doing?"

"I didn't know I was doing anything," Libby told him.

"What you're doing is sticking your nose into the Jack Devlin investigation."

"It's true we're ascertaining a few facts," Bernie conceded.

"You're doing a hell of a lot more than that. I just got off the phone with Rick Evans. He and his wife are not pleased."

"They don't look like people who would be pleased. About anything. It's not our fault that his grand plan went bad."

Lucy shook his finger at the girls again. "I want you to keep away from him. I want you to keep away from everyone."

"We would," Libby said, "if you'd do your job and start investigating and stop targeting Marvin."

"You can complain to his lawyer after he's arrested," Lucy said.

"Are you doing this because you don't like my father and Marvin is my boyfriend?"

Lucy sniffed. "I'm doing this because your boyfriend is guilty."

"You have no proof," Libby cried.

Lucy smiled. "The DA seems to think I do and that's all I need."

"You are not going to arrest him," Libby said.

"Yeah. I am. And I'm going to enjoy doing it, too. Now I'm telling you two for the last time, leave this alone."

"And if we don't?" Bernie asked.

"You're likely to find yourself in jail, as well."

Bernie turned to Libby. "He's threatening us again."

"No, Bernie," Libby corrected. "He's *warning* us."

"You're right. They are the same thing."

"If you think you can save him you are very, very wrong," Lucy told them.

"No. You are," Libby said before turning to Bernie. "I think we're done here, don't you?"

Bernie nodded.

"Good. Because so am I." With that Lucy turned, got in his car, and drove away.

Libby and Bernie watched him go.

"He really wants Marvin bad," Libby observed once Lucy had turned the corner.

"We've got to talk to the rest of the people on our list," Bernie said.

"And we have to find out if one of the muskets was marked or not," Libby added.

"Maybe Clyde can do that," Bernie suggested.

As it turned out, he couldn't so Sean decided to do it, instead.

Chapter 30

While Bernie was out with Brandon talking to Sanford Aiken and Tony Gerard and Libby was filling a last-minute order for five coconut cream and four lemon chiffon pies, plus two strawberry shortcakes, Sean and Marvin were on their way to the Longely Police Department.

"I don't think this is a good idea," Marvin said as Sean lit a cigarette and cracked open the hearse's front window.

"You never think anything is a good idea," Sean observed.

"At the very least you should have told Libby where we're going."

Sean inhaled and blew a smoke ring out the

window. "No. I don't think so."

"You don't want to tell her because she wouldn't think it was a good idea, either."

"I don't want to tell her," Sean said, "because she would have wanted to discuss it and we don't have time for that. Clyde said everyone is going into a staff meeting now and he's leaving the back door open for us."

"Us?"

"Me," Sean clarified. "I'll be in and out in five minutes maximum."

"How about if someone goes in the back and sees you?"

"I'll tell them I'm visiting."

"And if they find you in the evidence locker?"

"I'll tell them I got lost."

"I don't know." Marvin was thinking about the time he'd let Libby's father drive his Taurus and Sean had taken off with it. He'd never seen Libby so mad. "You know, you don't have to do this."

"I think I do. Unless you want to go to jail, that is. We need to find out if the musket that blew up was marked or not."

Marvin couldn't think of anything else to say except thanks so that's what he said.

"You're welcome."

Five minutes later, Marvin pulled up into the back lot of the Longely Police Station. The building had been built as an afterthought about thirty years ago and looked it. Law enforcement was not a priority in a community where the police mostly dealt with DWIs, teenage beer parties, and domestic disturbances of a garden variety nature.

"You stay here." Sean indicated the parking lot with a wave of his hand. "I'll be in and out in ten minutes tops."

"You said five," Marvin pointed out.

"I meant ten." Sean started to get out of the hearse and stopped. "But if I'm not out in fifteen minutes, I want you to take off."

"What about you?" Marvin asked.

"I can take care of myself."

"I can't do that," Marvin told him, a pleading tone in his voice. "You know I can't."

Sean sighed and thought of what his eldest daughter would do if Marvin did what he was requesting. "I suppose not," he allowed. He rubbed his chin in thought. "I'll tell you what. If I'm not out of there in fifteen minutes, I want you to come in and ask me if I'm all right."

"I don't get it," Marvin said.

"That's okay. You don't have to. Just say those words." Sean had Marvin repeat them. "Good," he said as he got out of the hearse.

He ground his cigarette out in the dirt and began walking across the parking lot. He reflected that he had made this walk thousands of times before as he headed toward the police station's back door. It had been what? Almost ten years since he'd been forced to resign from the police force. Ten years. Amazing. But everything still looked the same. The parking lot macadam was still pitted, the paint was still peeling from the back wall bricks, the garbage cans stilled smelled of old fast food.

Of course, Sean thought, *I'm walking a little slower now.* But that was okay. He was thankful he was walking at all. Two years ago, he was in a wheelchair half the time and the other half he was hobbling around with a cane. God had granted him a remission. No one knew why. The doctors certainly didn't, but he didn't care. All he knew was that he could get from point A to point B without anyone's help and that was good enough for him.

He pushed on the back door. It swung open. He turned, gave Marvin a brief wave, and went inside. The locker room was empty, although he could hear people talking out front. The place where everyone was gathered was on the other side of the building, but the walls were thin and sounds tended to carry. He smelled the familiar scents of Pine-Sol, Febreze, dirty socks, and sweat as he noted that the walls in the locker room were still a drab shade of tan, half the lockers were still dented, and the floor and benches still had spatters of paint and plaster on them from when the leak in the ceiling had been fixed.

He took a left, walked twelve feet, made a right and found himself in the place where the evidence was kept. Big cities had property rooms that were gated and had metal shelving and filing systems, but Longely was a small town so its evidence room was more like a cubbyhole. Its shelves were from The Home Depot, and its filing system consisted of a log book resting on a table that was supposed to be manned, but usually wasn't. Sean stepped around the table and went inside. He didn't need to consult the book to tell him where the muskets were because he could see them lying on the middle shelf.

He took a quick look around to make sure no one was coming in, even though he was positive he would hear them before they did, then slipped on the rubber gloves he'd brought with him, and walked toward the muskets. There were eight of them altogether and they had been divided into two groups. One group contained seven muskets, while the other one contained the musket that had killed Jack Devlin.

Sean began with the larger group. He picked up each musket and examined it from top to bottom before going on to the next one. They all looked the same to him. If there was a mark on any of them, he didn't see it. Then he got to the musket that had killed Jack Devlin. As soon as he picked it up, he noticed that it was slightly heavier. His eye traveled down the barrel to the stock.

Outside of the difference in weight, he couldn't see anything that might have passed as a mark. Then he held the musket up to the light. There. A thin line circled the bottom half of the gunstock, but it was so faint it was hard to see. Was that a mark or a scratch? It was possible to scratch steel. So maybe that's what happened. On the other hand, the line was straight and it circled the stock. What would have done that? It looked as if someone had etched the line with an etching pen, which was easy to come by.

It was highly probable that the scratch he was looking at had been made on purpose. Someone had marked the musket. If it had indeed been marked, that led to the next question. What purpose did the line serve?

Someone had to have picked out the gun and handed it to Devlin, but exactly how had they done that? From what Sean understood, Marvin had deposited the muskets on the bench and told everyone to take one. So how had the person handing the gun to Devlin picked out the doctored one? The line on the stock was so faint it would have been impossible to see unless it had been held up to the light. Maybe there was some other sort of mark on the barrel, but that had probably—almost definitely—been obliterated by the force of the explosion.

Sean turned the musket to check the barrel anyway. A small *ping* sounded as a piece of shot fell out and landed on the floor. He picked it up, put it in his pocket, and went back to examining the muzzle. The force of the blast had bent the metal outward. If there had been some sort of mark, it was gone now. He was thinking about where else a mark might be when he realized that the quality of the voices he'd been hearing in the background had changed.

More people were talking and the voices seemed closer, especially Lucy's. He could hear Clyde asking Lucy a question and Lucy telling him he'd take care of it—whatever *it* was—after he returned from the restroom. This was not good.

Sean quickly replaced the musket, taking care to put it back exactly as he had found it. He peeled off his gloves, stuffed them in his pants pockets, and hurried out of the property locker. He was almost at the back door when Lucy entered the room. *This will be interesting,* Sean decided as he saw Lucy's eyes widen, then narrow.

The flesh on Lucy's neck began to redden. "What the hell are you doing here?" he growled.

Sean smiled his most benign smile and patted his stomach. "I had to make a pit stop and this was the closest pit I could think of."

Lucy crossed his arms over his chest. "Are you saying this place is a pit?" he demanded.

Sean watched the flush on Lucy's neck rise to

his face. "Heaven forefend," he replied, still smiling. "All I'm saying is when you gotta go, you gotta go."

"And you just happened to be passing by?" Lucy's tone was sarcastic.

Sean's smile got even bigger if that were possible. "As a matter of fact I was."

"Why?"

"I'm running an errand for Libby."

"If I call her up and ask her what errand that would be?" Lucy demanded.

"Go ahead," Sean challenged. "Call her. I don't mind."

"I didn't ask if you minded or not," Lucy retorted.

The two men locked eyes. A minute passed.

Lucy laced his fingers together and cracked his knuckles. His face was a lovely shade of rose. "What's the point?" he finally said. "She'd just lie for you anyway."

Sean didn't say anything.

"How'd you get in?" Lucy asked, changing the subject.

Sean jerked his head in the direction of the back door. "Through there . . . obviously."

"That door is always locked."

"Not this time." Sean shrugged. "I guess someone forgot."

Lucy unlaced his fingers and brought his hands down to his sides. "Amazing."

"Isn't it, though?" Sean replied, his face a mask of innocence. "You sound as if you don't believe me."

"That's because I don't." Lucy took a step toward Sean. "In fact, I have a good mind to arrest you."

"For what? Unauthorized peeing?"

"Ha-ha. You always did think you were funny. I guess that's where your daughters get it from. No. For trespassing," Lucy said just as Marvin came barreling through the door.

"Are you all right?" he asked, repeating the line Sean had given him.

"Better now," Sean said. "Thanks for asking. We'd better get going. Don't want the butter to get rancid."

Lucy's eyes went from Sean to Marvin to Sean again. "You were in the property room, weren't you?"

"I wouldn't call it a room. It's more like a nook, really. But no. I wasn't. Why would I be since you seem to have the matter so well in hand."

Lucy shook a finger at Sean. "Those muskets better be exactly where they're supposed to be."

"I'm sure they are." Sean pushed Marvin through the door and said, "Not that he'd be able to tell." Once they were outside and the door had closed behind them, Sean patted his pockets. He wanted to get out of there before Lucy changed his mind.

Chapter 31

It was a little before nine in the morning. The sun had just come out and was burning through the morning haze. Brandon and Bernie were on their way to Sanford Aiken's shop when Bernie spotted Monica Lewis's green Miata tootling along Main Street on the opposite side of the road.

"Looky, looky who I see," Bernie said, pointing in the Miata's direction.

Brandon squinted. "Ah, Monica out for an early morning spin. Must be something important. If I remember rightly, she's still a night person."

Bernie tapped her fingers on the dashboard.

"What's up?" Brandon asked her.

"I've changed my mind. Let's go talk to Miss Monica now."

"And leave poor Sanford Aiken in the lurch?"

"You know what they say. Gather ye rosebuds while ye may."

"Yeah, but this little rosebud wasn't at the reenactment," Brandon pointed out.

"True, but her brother was."

"You've already talked to him."

"Also true," Bernie replied. "Now I want to speak to her and see if their stories agree."

"Okeydokey." Brandon took one hand off the

wheel and touched it to his head. *"Oui, mon capitaine.* I am here but to serve."

Bernie grinned. "Exactly."

"I was being sarcastic." Brandon executed a quick U-turn on Main Street.

"Really? Fancy that. I would never have known." Bernie watched Monica Lewis glancing in her rearview mirror. The next thing she knew the Miata put on a burst of speed.

"I think she saw us," Brandon said.

"I think she doesn't want to speak to us," Bernie added.

"Good guess, Sherlock."

"That makes me want to speak to her even more."

"I got to admit, her reaction is suggestive."

"But of what?" Bernie mused. "That's the question."

"How about guilt?"

"I suppose she could have rigged the rifle," Bernie said.

"Or maybe she has errands to do and doesn't feel like talking to you now," Brandon suggested, proposing an alternate scenario.

"She doesn't know I want to talk to her," Bernie objected.

"Of course, she knows. How could she not? You talked to her brother and her sister-in-law, didn't you?"

Bernie allowed that she had.

"Or maybe she just doesn't like you."

"She doesn't know me," Bernie shot back. "Anyway, what's there not to love?"

Brandon laughed. "True. You are a paragon of virtue."

"My thoughts exactly," Bernie told him.

The Miata was putting more distance between them.

Bernie groaned. "Go faster. We're going to lose her."

"I'm going as fast as I can," Brandon snapped. The speed limit was twenty miles an hour and they were already going thirty-eight. "Unless you'd like me to hit someone, that is."

Bernie bit her lip, hunched forward, and concentrated on keeping the Miata in sight. The next moment, a minivan switched lanes, pulling out in front of them and blocking the view of the Miata. When the minivan changed lanes again, the Miata was gone.

Bernie cursed. "Where did she go?"

"Well, she's got to be around here someplace," Brandon answered. "There are just two possibilities. She turned off on Ash or Gifford. I'll just circle around and we'll see if we can spot her. At least, she doesn't have a Honda Civic."

Bernie nodded. Brandon went down Gifford while she kept a careful lookout.

"Nothing," she said when they'd come to the end of the street.

Brandon started up Ash next. He'd gone three blocks when Bernie spotted the Miata in the parking lot of Good Eats, a health food store.

"There," she said, pointing to it.

"I know. I see." Brandon pulled into the lot, parked in back of the Miata, and turned off the motor, but left the key in the ignition. "We are here, my lady."

Bernie opened the truck door. "This is going to be an interesting chat."

"If Monica talks to you."

"She will."

"Why should she?"

Bernie smiled. "My innate charm. Coming in?"

Brandon shook his head. "You go ahead. I'm going to sit here and take a little nap." At which point, he put his seat back. "Call me if you need me," he said as he closed his eyes.

"I will," Bernie promised as she got out of the truck. Not that she thought she would. After all, what could happen in a fancy-schmancy grocery store like Good Eats where everyone thought pure and peaceful thoughts and only put healthy, organic foods into their bodies?

Usually the store was crowded, but it was still early enough in the day to be fairly empty. The place was large. It had been a sporting goods store previously, and was laid out with lots of space between the aisles, which were set on a diagonal, making it easy to see between them.

Bernie spotted Monica in the gluten-free aisle studying boxes of gluten-free crackers. She supposed that eventually she and Libby would have to offer some sort of gluten-free cupcake, although she'd been resisting the fad, hoping that it would die down before too long. It's not that she and Libby couldn't make gluten-free stuff, she just thought it was mostly a load of hokum.

"Are you really gluten-intolerant?" she asked Monica when she was about a foot away from her.

Monica spun around. When she saw who it was, she started to say something then caught herself and stopped.

"Were you, by any chance, going to say, 'I thought I lost you'?" Bernie asked as she advanced on her.

"Go away," Monica told her.

"I must say you look very fetching. Your year in India has done wonders for your weight, and I like the hair. You're a good blonde. I almost didn't recognize you. Tell me, do blondes really have more fun?"

"I said go away," Monica repeated as she replaced the box of crackers on the shelf. She turned and started to walk away.

Bernie followed her. "Oh, dear. Did your brother tell you not to talk to me? I bet he did, didn't he?"

Monica kept walking.

Bernie, undeterred, followed. "Hey, my sister and I have a dollar bet. She says Jack Devlin didn't recognize you, but you know what I think? I think he did. I bet he was surprised to see you."

Monica spun around. "I don't care what you think. You're not the police, which means I don't have to talk to you, and I'm not going to."

"Of course you're not," Bernie said in her most soothing voice as she drew closer. "This must be very stressful for you." She pointed to the filigree silver earrings that were dangling from Monica's earlobes. "Nice. Did you get those in India?"

Monica reached up and touched them. "So?"

"So I like them. They frame your face very nicely. How much weight did you lose?"

"About fifty pounds," Monica couldn't prevent herself from saying.

Bernie nodded approvingly. "Good job."

"It was easier there," Monica explained.

"I bet," Bernie replied. "You know, I understand completely why you don't want to speak to me. If I were you, I'd want to protect my brother, too, especially after what he did for me."

Monica furrowed her brow. "Like what?"

"Surely you know."

Monica licked her lips. "No, I don't. What are you talking about?"

"I'm talking about the fact that your brother rigged the rifle that killed Jack Devlin."

"You really are absurd," Monica protested with

a flutter of her hands. "Why would he do that?"

Bernie's smile was compassionate. "Obviously, because of what Jack Devlin did to you. It must be nice to have a sibling that cares that much. I'm not sure that my sister does. She certainly would never do something like that for my sake. I can't even get her to exchange a pair of shoes for me at Barney's when she's going to be in the city."

Monica gave a strangled laugh. "Now that's funny. Do you think my brother actually cares about that?"

"I was under that impression, yes."

"My brother doesn't care about anyone or anything except himself. He certainly never cared about me. He hated me from the moment my mother married his father and that hasn't changed at all. He resented any attention I got."

"But you're staying at his house now," Bernie said.

"No," Monica corrected her. "I'm renting a room in my brother's house for a couple months before I start my job in New York."

"I see."

"No. I don't think you do."

"Then tell me."

Monica shrugged. "There's nothing to tell."

Bernie tried again. "I guess he cared about the money he lost."

"What money?" Monica demanded, folding her arms across her chest.

"The money you loaned Jack Devlin that he lost in a bad business deal."

"So what? I was stupid, but it was my money and it had nothing to do with my brother."

"The way I heard it your brother was supposed to get some of it and he didn't. As a consequence, he lost a great deal of money in a business he was supposed to go into."

Monica started laughing and kept on laughing. Finally she stopped and got her breath back. She put her hand to her chest. "That is the funniest thing I've heard. I bet you got that story from Sanford."

Bernie didn't say anything.

"You did, didn't you?"

Bernie nodded.

"He's lying, you know."

"Why should he do that?"

"Simple. Because he hates my brother and he wants to get him in trouble."

"And the reason for that would be?" Bernie asked.

"Because David's wife Cora was stepping out with Sanford. When my brother found out, he flipped out. Sanford was supposed to do a refi and David made sure that didn't happen."

"How could he do that?"

"Simple," Monica said. "He's good friends with people at the bank."

Bernie clicked her tongue against her teeth and

shook her head. She needed a cheat sheet to keep track of everyone's activities. She wanted to know where these people found the time, let alone the energy, to do what they were doing. "I thought Sanford was going out with Juno for a while too."

"So what if he was? Devlin wasn't the only player in town, you know."

"Obviously," Bernie answered. "But none of the others have ended up dead."

Monica didn't say anything.

Bernie looked her in the eyes. "Then we come back to you. I can see you wanting Devlin dead."

Monica snorted. "After all these years? Give me a break."

"Two years isn't that long. I know people who have held grudges for twenty years," Bernie said, thinking of her dad.

"It's long enough. If I'd wanted to do anything, I would have done it at the time. I would have slit Devlin's throat and watched him bleed out."

Bernie raised an eyebrow. "Charming visual."

Monica took a deep breath and let it out. "You wanted to hear the truth. That's the truth. But I didn't do that then and I certainly haven't done it now."

"How do I know you didn't?" challenged Bernie.

"Simple. For openers, I wasn't at the reenactment. I was looking at a sublet in Williamsburg. Then there's the question of motive. Why would I kill Jack Devlin now? I mean look at me." She indicated herself with her hands. "You said it yourself—I look better than I ever have. I feel fantastic, and I owe it all to Jack Devlin.

"If he hadn't done what he had, I never would have gone to India and found a new life. In retrospect, his doing what he did to me was the best thing that ever happened. No. I wanted to thank him." Monica made a mournful face. "Alas, it was not to be. And you know what? Juno told me she feels the same way. If it wasn't for Devlin, she never would have found her spiritual side. She would have continued along the material path until her soul withered away."

"That's certainly a very generous interpretation of events," Bernie said.

"I'm serious." Monica's tone was fierce. "You want to know who killed Jack Devlin, talk to Sanford Aiken and Gerard. Those guys had a long history with Devlin and it wasn't a good one." Monica paused for a minute then continued, "There's always Elise Montague. I've got to say, she's a real piece of work."

"Meaning?" Bernie happened to share her opinion, but she was curious to hear what Monica was going to say.

"Meaning exactly what I said." Monica looked

at her watch. "I have a massage in half an hour so if you'll excuse me, I have to finish shopping."

"Call me if you think of anything else," Bernie told her even though she was pretty positive the likelihood of that ranged from slim to none.

Chapter 32

Sanford Aiken's plumbing supply store was located at the shabbier end of Main Street. The stores were smaller, the windows dirtier, and the trees were scrawnier. Bernie and Brandon were sitting in his truck drinking coffee and eating bagels with cream cheese while they waited for Aiken to come back. The sign on the shop door read WILL RETURN IN TEN MINUTES. By Bernie's watch that meant they had nine more minutes to go.

"These bagels are too soft on the inside," she complained after she'd taken her third bite.

"Picky, picky, picky." As far as Brandon was concerned, they were fine.

"I'm not being picky," Bernie countered. "I'm just saying that they're not New York City style bagels."

"Maybe that's because we're in Westchester not New York City."

"Yes, but the store is called New York City Bagels, which means that's what they're supposed to be." Bernie tore off a piece of crust and waved it in Brandon's face. "In fact, these bagels suck. They should be denser and the crust should be chewier. And the flavors? Pomegranate bagels? Please. Also, I can taste the agar in the cream cheese. Given the rent these guys are paying and the quality of their merchandise, I'm betting they're not going to be in business long."

Brandon gave a noncommittal grunt. He took another bite and chewed. Okay. So maybe they were a little soft. Maybe peanut butter flavored bagels weren't the best idea in the world, but they weren't horrible. They certainly weren't worth the indignation Bernie was expending on them.

"Do you believe what Monica told you?" he asked after he'd swallowed.

Bernie wrapped up the rest of her bagel and put it back in the bag they'd come in. She was still hungry, but she wasn't that hungry. "Yeah, I think I do."

"So that whole tale that Aiken was telling me at the bar was just bull?"

"Not all of it. Not the Monica and Devlin part. That was apparently accurate, the rest maybe not so much."

Brandon rubbed his chin. "So Aiken has something against David Nancy?"

"According to Monica he does."

Brandon thought about that for a minute. Then

he said, "You realize that that means Aiken couldn't have killed Jack Devlin."

Bernie gave him a puzzled look. "No, I don't realize that at all. Why are you saying that?"

"Well, whoever killed Devlin set Marvin up, right?" Brandon wiped a smidgen of cream cheese off his cheek.

"My dad thinks that might not be the case," Bernie objected.

"*Might* being the operative word here."

Bernie held up her hand. "Let's not debate that. Let's just go back to what you were saying before."

"Fine. If Aiken hated David Nancy that much and he was the one who killed Devlin, why didn't he set up Nancy instead of Marvin?"

"Hypothetically speaking?"

"Yes. Hypothetically speaking."

"I'm not sure," Bernie admitted. She took a sip of her coffee and made a face. It tasted as if someone had dunked a couple coffee beans in it. The word *dishwater* came to mind.

"So you agree with me?" Brandon asked.

"I didn't say that. Anyway, you can't prove a positive with a negative."

Brandon laughed. "Explain."

"Okay. Two things." Bernie raised one finger. "First of all, even if Aiken did shoot at Marvin that doesn't prove that he killed Devlin. The two things might not be related." She raised a second finger. "Secondly, we only have Monica's word that her brother hated Aiken. She could just as easily be lying as not."

"Let's address your first point," Brandon said. "I know what your dad said about the two things not being related, but common sense says otherwise. It just seems to me as if whoever is doing this is determined to get Marvin in trouble one way or the other."

Bernie rolled down her window and dumped out her coffee. It wasn't worth drinking. "Okay. Then answer me this. Who hates Marvin?"

"No one, near as I can tell," Brandon admitted. He didn't have to think about the answer.

"I rest my case," Bernie said. "I think Marvin is collateral damage."

Brandon took another sip of his coffee. "Poor Marvin. That sucks."

"Yes, it does. How can you drink that coffee?" Bernie asked, switching subjects.

"It's not that bad," Brandon protested.

"It's swill."

"When you need caffeine, you need caffeine," Brandon replied, taking another sip in the face of Bernie's disapproval. "Plus, I put eight sugars in it."

Bernie made a face. "So you're drinking sludge."

"Caffeinated sludge."

"You should—"

"I know," Brandon said, interrupting her. "I should be careful of what I eat. I'll start tomorrow."

Bernie sighed. There was no point in pursuing the conversation. They'd been over it too many times before so she changed the subject. "What do you know about Elise Montague?" Bernie had been thinking about her ever since Monica had mentioned her name.

"Aside from the fact that she's an unpleasant lady, is a lousy tipper, and has man hands?" Brandon asked.

"Yes. Aside from that."

"Probably the same amount that you do. She goes into your place, too, doesn't she?" Brandon asked.

"On Mondays and Wednesdays she gets an order of gingered chicken, a green tossed salad, a pint of coleslaw, and a brownie to go. But she never says anything, except to complain if the chicken isn't warm enough or someone forgets to put extra napkins in her order."

"Same with me. She usually comes in to RJ's on Fridays around six-thirty, has two Stellas with a slice of orange, and an order of chicken wings, extra spicy. She stays for a couple hours, and leaves by herself."

"I wonder what she does the other four nights?" Bernie said.

Brandon shook his head. "Not a clue. I don't

know who she hangs with and I never see her out and about."

"Have you ever had a conversation with her?"

"Nope. She just gives me her order and sits at the bar and watches TV."

"Does she come in with anyone?" Bernie asked.

"Not that I've seen. She's not big on talking to people, either . . . unless she's telling them to be quiet. You can guess how well that goes over."

"Does she ever come in with Samuel Cotton?"

Brandon shook his head. "Not when I've been on, but that doesn't mean she hasn't some other time. You want me to ask Jules and Andy?"

Bernie nodded. "Please. I know she had something going on with Jack Devlin."

Brandon laughed. "Who didn't?"

"I didn't. Libby didn't," Bernie replied.

Brandon amended his statement. "I meant aside from you guys. There is one other thing you might find interesting."

Bernie waited.

"I have a friend who worked a party at the Musket and Flintlock Club. He told me a story about Elise behaving badly. There was this Memorial Day party up there and she got really drunk and needed to use the bathroom, but someone was in it so she went out to the front lawn, pulled her dress up and her undies down, and took a piss. I understand it was quite a show. Especially when Devlin started screaming at her and calling her a slut. Then he dragged her out."

Bernie leaned forward. "Nothing like being humiliated in public, I always say."

"I suppose it's as good a reason to kill someone as any," Brandon allowed.

"Public humiliation? I'd say so. And she does know how to use a gun. Did your friend tell you anything else?"

"About Elise?" Brandon asked.

"About Elise and anyone else at the club?"

"No. He told me they have a mouse problem and that the members drink Bud Light, God help me, and that's about it."

"Has he worked there since?"

"Nope. Too much work, too little pay." Brandon finished his bagel and gestured to the bag with Bernie's bagel in it. "Are you going to eat that?"

Bernie handed the bag to him. "Be my guest." She checked her watch. It was almost time. She nodded toward Sanford Aiken's store. "You coming in with me on this one?"

"Nope. You seem to have done so well the last time I think I'll leave you to it." Brandon yawned. "Just think of me as backup." He pointed to Sanford Aiken who was slowly walking down the street. He was wearing a navy polo shirt with a frayed collar and a pair of creased khakis.

"He doesn't look so great," Bernie said,

alluding to the gray pallor visible underneath his tan.

"He drinks too much," Brandon commented. "I wouldn't be surprised if his liver isn't happy." He clapped Bernie on the shoulder. "Looks like you're up, champ. Have fun."

"Always."

Who knew? Maybe if she played this right she could get Aiken to shed some light on why he'd said what he'd said to the police. Or at least what Clyde said he had said to the police.

Chapter 33

Sanford Aiken had opened his shop door and was putting the cup of coffee he'd been carrying down when Bernie entered.

"Yes?" he said, looking up. "Can I help you with anything?"

"As a matter of fact you can," Bernie replied as she approached the counter.

"A leaking faucet at the shop? A blown gasket?"

"No." Bernie smiled her winningest smile. "Problems of a different nature."

"Ah." Aiken drew out the *ah*. "I take it you'd be referring to what happened at the reenactment."

"You would be right." Bernie tried to sound as if he was the smartest guy in the world for figuring out the answer.

He leaned forward, careful not to knock his coffee over. "I've been expecting you."

"Really?" Bernie kept smiling. "Why's that?"

"Well, I heard you and your sister were going around asking questions and generally stirring up trouble."

Bernie pouted. "Is that what people are saying?"

Aiken nodded gravely. "It is indeed."

Bernie tapped her nails on the counter. "Stirring up trouble is an interesting phrase."

Aiken took no notice of the nail tapping and lifted the lid off his coffee, blew on it, and took a sip. "Especially when it applies to you two. You especially. You're never content to leave things alone, are you?"

"It sounds to me as if you're worried," Bernie replied.

"Me?" Aiken pointed at himself. "What would I be worried about?"

"Sounds to me as if you have a guilty conscience."

Aiken made a dismissive noise. "Hardly. All I'm sayin' is that shopkeepers shouldn't go messing around like you're doing. You lose customers that way." He looked up at her. "Frankly, what you're doing is a waste of time. If you ask me, you should be spending your time finding a good lawyer for Marvin because he's going to need it."

"I'm not asking you . . . at least not about that," Bernie told him, forgetting about being charming.

293

Aiken sniffed. "Have it your way. But why bother with this investigation you and your sister are trying to conduct?"

"Trying to conduct," Bernie repeated. "How about *are conducting?*"

"If it makes you feel better to say that, then by all means." Aiken straightened out the collar of his polo shirt. "But a reliable source has told me that the police are going to arrest Marvin soon. After all, he is the obvious suspect, isn't he?" Aiken shook his head. "You can't deny that."

Bernie crossed her arms over her chest. "To me or Libby or my dad, he's not."

"Well, he is to everyone else," Aiken shot back.

"And who, exactly, is everyone?" Bernie demanded.

Aiken harrumphed. "The town."

Bernie raised an eyebrow. "The entire town?"

He corrected himself. "I was speaking metaphorically. I meant the people at the reenactment."

Bernie didn't say anything.

"Well," Aiken continued, "you have to admit the evidence against Marvin is pretty damning."

"It's all circumstantial," Bernie told him.

Aiken shrugged. "If that's what you wish to think. Not that I necessarily agree with the town," he hurriedly added. "I don't want you to think that."

"Then what do you want me to think?" Bernie asked.

Aiken swallowed. "I don't know what you mean."

"It's a simple question, Sanford."

"All I'm trying to say is you're a tad prejudiced what with your sister and all." He pointed to himself. "I was there. I saw what happened."

"That is what I want to talk to you about." Bernie was tired of dancing around. It was time to ask the questions she'd come to ask.

Aiken turned his hands palms upward. "I don't know what I can tell you that you don't already know. After all, you were there, too."

"Yes, but I was in the gazebo setting up for the picnic. You were down near the shed."

"I know where I was," Aiken retorted.

"You were there when the weapons were given out."

"They weren't given out. Marvin put them on the bench and we took our own."

There it was. The statement Bernie had been waiting for. "Then why did you tell the police that you thought you saw Marvin handing a musket to Devlin out of the corner of your eye?"

"I . . . I . . . did think I saw it," Aiken insisted.

Bernie frowned. "So let me get this straight. First, you're telling me Marvin dumped all the muskets on the bench and then you're telling me he gave a musket to Devlin. Which is it?"

"I'm not sure," Aiken confessed. "I saw him handing something to Devlin."

"What?"

"I-I thought it was a musket," Aiken stammered, "but then I started thinking about it and I'm not sure anymore." He hung his head.

"Then why did you tell the police Marvin handed Devlin a weapon?" Bernie demanded.

"But I didn't," Aiken protested. "I told the police I *thought* he did. That's different."

"Evidently not to the police," Bernie told him.

Aiken took a deep breath and squared his shoulders. "Are you saying I'm responsible for the police suspecting Marvin?"

"Yes. That's exactly what I'm saying."

"That's not fair," Aiken wailed. "You wouldn't want me to lie, would you?"

"Not at all. I'd just like you to tell the truth."

"I've already told you," Aiken whined. "I can't be sure. It was all so confusing out there and we were all hot and running around trying to get everything in order for the show to start. It was chaos. No one was paying attention to anyone else. Were you watching?"

"No," Bernie admitted. "I was setting up."

Aiken smiled triumphantly. "See." He shook his head and straightened up the display of flashlights next to the register. "Such a pity how this turned out."

"Yes," Bernie agreed. "I really feel bad for Marvin."

"No. I meant for Rick. Poor guy. He was trying

so hard to make Longely a tourist destination. What is it they say about no good deed going unpunished? I think this is going to affect his chances of running for mayor, don't you?"

"Probably," Bernie said.

Aiken tsk-tsked.

"You sound as if you care."

"I do," Aiken said. "I was going to vote for him."

"Why?"

"Because he's going to help the small business-man. He's going to get us tax credits. He's going to get the sidewalks cleared in the winter. Stuff like that. If you were smart, you'd get behind him, too."

"I'll think about it," Bernie lied.

"Good." Aiken glanced at the clock and back at Bernie.

"Hey," she said. "Did you see Chuck Grisham at the reenactment?"

"Why?"

"He said he was there, but I didn't see him."

"He was there. He just left early."

"Why do you suppose he did that?"

Aiken shrugged. "Maybe he just couldn't stand watching us anymore. We were pretty lame." Aiken glanced at the clock again. "Now if you don't mind, I have a big order to fill."

Bernie nodded. "Well, I'll get out of your way. There's one other thing I'd like to clear up if that's all right with you."

"And what would that be?" Aiken asked in the voice of the long suffering.

"I'm wondering why you told Brandon that story about Monica Lewis?"

Aiken put down his coffee cup hard enough that a little of the brown liquid sloshed over into the top. "Story?"

"Story," Bernie repeated firmly.

"That wasn't a story."

"Monica says it was."

"So you're accusing me of lying?" Aiken demanded.

"How about embellishing?"

"This is the thanks I get for trying to be helpful?" Two blotches of color appeared on his cheeks.

"Now you sound like my mother," Bernie told him.

"It wasn't a story," he insisted. "It was the truth. You of all people should thank me."

"For what?"

"For trying to help Marvin."

"You just told me you told the police that Marvin gave Devlin the musket. How's that helping him?"

"No. I told you that I told the police that I *thought* I saw him doing it. But then I started feeling bad. I mean, what if I was wrong? So I told Brandon about Monica because I knew he would tell you."

"Well Monica says everything you told Brandon is a lie."

"She would say that, which is funny given that she's constitutionally incapable of telling the truth," Aiken responded.

"In fact, she says"—Bernie closed her eyes trying to get it right—"that you had a thing going with David Nancy's wife."

Aiken wet his lips. "That's absolutely rot."

"Monica says that you weren't too fond of Jack Devlin, either. She said that you blamed him for cutting your affair with Cora short. She said you were furious with Devlin."

Aiken leaned forward. "Why should I be furious with that jerk?"

"Because he took Cora away from you," Bernie said.

"Ha. He was welcomed to her as far as I was concerned." Aiken drained the last of his coffee from his cup, crumpled it up, and tossed it in the wastepaper basket below the counter. "All she ever talked about was herself. She was exhausting. David was glad to have her off his hands. Gave him a rest."

"Who gave who a rest?" Tony Gerard asked as he walked in. Then he looked at Aiken and Bernie and said, "I can come back at another time."

"No no," Bernie said. "I was just coming to see you."

"She's investigating Devlin's death," Aiken explained.

"I thought that was all settled," Gerard said.

"Not according to her." Aiken nodded in Bernie's direction.

"I thought they were arresting Marvin."

"She's trying to prevent that," Aiken informed Gerard.

"Do you mind if I talk?" Bernie said to Aiken.

He shrugged. "Not at all. Be my guest."

"Then who do you think is responsible?" Gerard asked Bernie.

"For Devlin's death?" Bernie asked.

Gerard nodded.

"How about you," Bernie said.

"Me?" Gerard yelped. "Are you nuts?"

"You were there. You could have handed Devlin the musket as well as anyone else."

"But I didn't." Gerard raised his hand. "I swear it."

"He didn't," Aiken echoed. "He was helping me get my uniform on straight."

"Then who did?" Bernie demanded.

"I don't know," Gerard said.

"What do you mean, you don't know?" Bernie said.

Gerard looked at Aiken and Aiken looked at Gerard. Neither man replied.

"If you don't know, why did you say what you did to the police?" Bernie asked.

"Marvin kept on yelling at us," Gerard said. "It was very confusing. The whole thing was confusing. First, he wanted us to go here, then he wanted us to go there. He wanted us to take the muskets, then he wanted us to wait, then he told us to take them."

"He couldn't decide what he wanted," Aiken said. "He was very nervous."

"Yeah, but he shouldn't have taken it out on us," Gerard said to Aiken. "It just made things worse."

"Is that why you fingered him?" Bernie asked in as casual a tone as she could manage. "Is it because you were pissed?"

"I didn't finger anyone," Aiken cried. "I wish you'd stop saying that. What I'm trying to tell you is that everything was chaotic. In truth, I'm not really sure what I saw."

"In truth. Now that's an interesting phrase coming from you," Bernie said.

"You have no right to say things like that to me," Aiken snapped.

"I have every right," Bernie retorted.

"I think you should leave," he told her. "I think you should leave *now*."

"I think maybe you're right," Bernie said. This was getting nowhere. But as she turned to go, she had another thought. Granted her idea was far-fetched, but it also explained Aiken's and Gerard's conduct. "Did someone tell you to say what you did about Marvin to the police?" she asked, turning back.

"No," Aiken said.

"Absolutely not," Gerard told Bernie. "Why would you think something like that?"

"Because it's the only thing that makes sense," Bernie answered.

"Not to me," Aiken declared.

Bernie pursed her lips while she studied the two men, not sure if she believed them. "If you want to do the right thing, you know where to find me."

As she walked out the door, she shook her head. She didn't expect to hear from them.

Chapter 34

It was one o'clock and the noonday rush at A Little Taste of Heaven had subsided to the point where the sisters could leave. They were having what Sean was referring to as a working lunch in their flat above the store. He was eating a fried egg, peppered bacon, and avocado sandwich on two slices of toasted multigrain bread, while Libby's sandwich consisted of egg salad with capers, scallions, and black walnuts on lightly toasted challah. Bernie was tucking into a salad composed of arugula, radicchio, baby frisée, shaved Parmigiano, prosciutto, and homemade roasted peppers.

Everyone was drinking minted iced tea out of tall frosted glasses. A bowl of perfectly ripe white Pennsylvania peaches and a plate of chocolate chip blondies and gingersnaps sat on a tray in the middle of the coffee table waiting to be consumed when everyone finished their main course.

"I don't agree," Sean said to Bernie after he'd shoved the piece of bacon sliding out of his sandwich back in with his thumb.

Bernie speared a piece of arugula lightly coated with walnut oil and lemon dressing and conveyed it to her mouth. She loved the arugula's peppery taste coupled with the salad dressing's tang. "Why not?"

"Because there's no reason to think that either Gerard or Aiken were covering for someone else, that's why not. Or at least I don't know of one."

"But," she objected, "it explains why they were acting the way they were."

"I can think of a hundred other reasons," Sean replied before he chomped down on his sandwich.

Looking for support, Bernie turned to her sister. "What do you think, Libby?"

"I don't know. It's hard to say since I wasn't there. What does Brandon say?" she asked, passing the buck.

"He was asleep in his truck when I talked to Aiken and Gerard."

"I see." Libby took a bite of her sandwich. She

liked egg salad. She liked it a lot. It was forthright and pure and lent itself to an infinite number of variations. In fact, it tasted good—no, it tasted great—without any additions, especially if it was made with homemade mayo, freshly ground pepper, Maldon salt, and fresh eggs which had been properly boiled. That meant putting the eggs in the water, bringing the water to a boil, then turning the flame off, and covering the pot. Take them out after ten minutes and you'd have perfect hard-boiled eggs.

"Okay," she said after she'd taken another bite of her sandwich. "If what you say is true, who do you think is responsible for putting Aiken and Gerard up to this?"

"Rick Evans," Bernie promptly said, the name springing from her lips unbidden.

"Why him?" Sean asked.

"For a variety of reasons," she explained. "I figure he would want to distance himself from the reenactment debacle, given that he's into politics. There's the fact that he's jealous of Devlin. Plus Rick was there. He knows about guns, has a major gun collection, and was the one who started the whole get-Marvin thing in the first place."

"Okay, let's suppose you're correct about all the stuff pertaining to Rick Evans," Sean said.

She nodded and took another bite of salad while she listened to him.

"There are certain implications that spring from your assumption."

"Go on," Bernie said.

"For openers, your scenario means that Aiken and Gerard colluded in Devlin's death. In order for what you're saying to work, they had to have known what was happening before the event and agreed to lie for Rick Evans. So we have two men who are not only complicit in Devlin's death, but are also complicit in making false statements to a law enforcement official. That's pretty serious." Sean paused to take a sip of his iced tea. "Do you really think that either Aiken or Gerard is capable of helping plan a murder and carrying their part through?"

"All they had to do was lie," Bernie countered.

"Lie convincingly to law enforcement officials in a time of maximum stress," Sean said. "That's not as simple as it sounds. Most people can't do something like that well. At least not unless they're pathological liars or career criminals."

"Maybe they didn't think the results would be so bad," she hypothesized.

Sean snorted. "First of all, that has nothing to do with what we were just discussing and second of all, both men are members of the gun club. I'm pretty sure they all knew what over-priming a gun would do."

"I guess when you put it like that I see your point," Bernie said.

"Plus," Sean continued, "that means Rick Evans would have had to trust Aiken and Gerard not to chicken out and run to the authorities."

Bernie thought about Aiken and Gerard. They seemed like shopkeepers, not the kind of men who would plan a murder, see the results, and go about their business. On the other hand, as her mother had always said, "appearances could be deceiving."

"Maybe Rick did trust them."

"Why would he take that chance?" Sean asked. "What possible advantage would he gain?"

Bernie ate another couple bites of her salad while she considered what her father had just said. "Okay," she said, thinking out loud. "How about if Aiken and Gerard were the people who planned the murder? How about if they were the ones who went to Rick Evans with a plan to murder Devlin."

"Again, I ask why would they do that?" Sean took a sip of his iced tea.

"They all had a common goal," Bernie promptly replied. "They all hated Devlin."

"But even so, I still don't see it. At least not with those three."

"Bernie," Libby added, "your scenario still doesn't answer what is to my mind the main question here, which is how did Devlin get the musket?"

"Obviously, someone, most probably Rick Evans, handed it to him," Bernie snapped. "It was marked, remember."

"I know the musket was marked," Libby retorted. "I haven't forgotten. I'm not an idiot."

"I never said you were, Libby."

"You implied it, Bernie."

Sean hit the arm of his chair with the flat of his hand. Bernie and Libby turned toward him.

"Focus, people," he said.

"Sorry," Libby muttered. "I'm just worried."

"We all are," Bernie told her.

The sisters were silent for a moment.

Libby was the first one to speak. "I'm sorry, but how Devlin came into possession of the musket is still not obvious to me."

"Why?" Bernie asked.

"Glad you asked," Libby said, warming to her subject. "Marvin took all the muskets out of the shed and put them in a pile, agreed?"

Bernie and Sean nodded.

"That's what everyone said," Bernie replied.

Having finished her sandwich, Libby reached over, grabbed a blondie, and bit into it. *The combination of brown sugar, butter, chocolate chips, and walnuts is divine,* she thought. Sometimes simple was best, in food and in life . . . simple being something that the case they were talking about was definitely not.

"So that being the situation," Libby went on,

"think about this. You have eight muskets. One of them is marked. How do you know that the one you need is on top? Obviously, you don't because you aren't the one who brought them out of the shed. So what do you do in that case? Go through them and bring what you're doing to everyone's attention? I think not."

Libby paused to take another bite of her blondie. "Then we come to the second problem. How do you make sure that someone other than Devlin doesn't grab the booby-trapped musket? Given the circumstances, that would have been really hard to do. In fact, it would have been impossible. What would you say? 'Hey. Use this one because that one is going to blow up in your face'? Probably not a good strategy. At least, not if you don't want to end up in jail."

"Let's say you're right." Bernie finished her salad and set her plate down on the coffee table. "Have you considered the possibility that whoever did this brought the musket with them and handed it to Devlin there?"

"Yes I have, but where would they hide it?" Libby demanded. "It's not like it was winter and everyone was wearing a long coat. People were either wearing redcoat uniforms or blouses and breeches, all of which are formfitting. There was no place to hide anything, especially not some-thing as large as a musket."

"How about in the bushes?" Bernie suggested.

"What bushes?" Libby asked. "There are no bushes there. It's all grass with a couple of benches thrown in."

"So what's your point?" Bernie asked her sister. "Do you have a better solution to offer?"

"No, I don't, and that's exactly my point. We're pretty much in the same place knowledge-wise that we were in when Devlin got shot. We still don't know who handed him the gun, we don't know why he was targeted, and we don't know who took a shot at Marvin, right Dad?"

"You're partially right. We don't know everything." Sean finished his sandwich, reached over, and grabbed a peach. Juice dribbled down his chin when he took a bite. "If we did, the perp would be in custody and we would be celebrating. However, we do know more than we did before in terms of motive."

"Slightly more," Bernie conceded.

"Maybe a lot more." Sean wiped the juice away with a napkin then put the napkin down on the coffee table. "Let's go over what you guys have found out so far."

Bernie had been in the middle of cutting a slice out of a peach and wrapping it with a piece of prosciutto that had been left over from her salad. As her father finished speaking she popped it into her mouth. "Nice summer combination. I think I like this better than prosciutto and melon," she said as she organized her thoughts and licked the juice off of her fingers. A moment later, she was ready to begin.

"Okay. What do we know?" she asked rhetorically. "We know that everyone in the reenactment and their spouses are members of the Musket and Flintlock Club. We know that Elise Montague is president of the organization and that everyone in it not only knows how to shoot a musket, but presumably knows how they work."

"And that they have access to shot and black powder," Sean noted. "Not that they couldn't buy that stuff in any sporting goods or gun store."

"We also know," Libby added, "that Rick Evans' wife Gail had an affair with Jack Devlin, an affair that Rick says doesn't bother him, but which other people say did."

"Not to mention the fact that Devlin broke off the affair with Gail, which she also says doesn't bother her," Bernie told her dad.

"In other words, they're just your average, unhappily married couple," Sean said.

Bernie reached over, broke a blondie in half, and ate it. "According to them, they're soul mates. Peccadilloes of the flesh don't concern them."

Sean raised an eyebrow.

"That's what they say," Libby reiterated.

"So do you think what they're saying is true?" Sean asked.

"I guess I'm not that highly evolved because it would sure bother the hell out of me," Bernie replied. "I think it would piss off Rick Evans, too, even if he didn't admit it. Ego aside, he wants to run for public office. This kind of thing sure doesn't make him look good."

Sean took another bite of his peach. "No, it doesn't. It makes him look like a fool."

"Dad, that's so retro," Libby cried.

Sean grinned. "Well, I am an old man. Okay. Who's next on the list?"

"Well, David Nancy's wife Cora and his stepsister Monica Lewis had affairs with Jack Devlin," Bernie said.

"Monica's affair with Devlin caused David Nancy to lose a great deal of money," Libby added.

"So David Nancy has two reasons to want Devlin dead," Sean summarized.

"That's if Sanford Aiken's story about Monica is to be believed," Bernie said.

"Shouldn't it be?" Sean asked.

Libby and Bernie looked at each other. "Yes. No. I don't know," they both said simultaneously.

"Which is it? Yes, no, or maybe? They can't both be telling the truth."

"I'm not sure," Bernie admitted. "Maybe both. Devlin definitely upset Monica Lewis to the point where she went to India for a year to regroup."

"Why would Aiken lie?" Sean asked.

"Because he was angry at Monica for leaving him for Devlin. Of course, Aiken was also stepping out with David Nancy's wife Cora."

311

"Who was also sleeping with Devlin," Libby noted.

Sean shook his head. "So Devlin took two women away from Aiken. There's a motive right there. You know what they say about hell hath no fury like a woman scorned? That goes double for guys. Never underestimate the power of the male ego." He reached over and took a ginger-snap. "It's a wonder these people have time to make a living. Who knew there was so much hanky-panky going on in Longely?"

"Hanky-panky?" Libby asked.

"An old term for fooling around. Unauthorized sex," Sean explained after he'd taken a bite of the gingersnap. He let the cookie dissolve on his tongue. That way he could savor it longer.

"Let's not forget about Samuel Cotton," Bernie said, getting back to the subject at hand. "He was sleeping with Elise Montague . . ."

"And that ended badly because Elise quit him to go with Devlin," said Libby, finishing Bernie's sentence. "That leaves Samuel Cotton with a motive to kill Devlin, as well."

"Then Devlin broke up with Elise after she left Samuel Cotton to go with him," Bernie added. "That really rubbed her ego the wrong way. Of course, there's always the Grishams. Devlin had an affair with Juno while her husband was away, and then took her diamond ring and presented it to Monica Lewis as an engagement ring."

Libby took another cookie and nibbled on its edge. "Neither one of them were near the bench when the reenactors acquired their muskets. Not that they had to be."

"Also true," Bernie agreed.

"I'm telling you," Libby said. "When we figure out how Devlin got that musket we will have solved the case."

Sean rubbed the sides of his forehead. He wished he could smoke a cigarette. They always helped him focus. "Was there anyone at the reenactment who didn't have a reason to kill Devlin?" he asked plaintively.

"Nope," Bernie said. "Unfortunately not."

"Not that I can think of," Libby agreed.

"That's too bad," Sean said.

"Why?" Bernie asked.

"Because at least then we could eliminate someone," Sean replied.

Libby sighed. "That's why I said we're not much further along than we were before."

"But at least we know why everyone wanted to kill Devlin," Sean pointed out. "Now we just have to figure out how."

"How do we do that?" Libby asked him.

"Go back to the beginning," Sean instructed. "That's what I used to do when I was stuck."

"Go back to the beginning?" Libby repeated. "What do you mean?"

"Exactly what I said. Revisit the scene with

Marvin. See if he can remember anything. Anything at all. Even the smallest detail can lead to something." Sean reached over and took another gingersnap. "I always liked your mother's gingersnaps," he reminisced as he took a bite. "But I think these are even better than hers."

Bernie and Libby grinned. That was high praise indeed.

"It's the fresh ginger I grate into the batter." Libby was about to explain that her mom had used the powdered kind because that's all there was back then when her dad's cell phone rang.

"Yes?" he said when he picked it up. He listened to the person on the other end for a minute then put the phone back on the coffee table.

"What is it?" Libby cried. From the expression on her dad's face she knew that whatever it was couldn't be good.

"That was Clyde. Evidently the DA is swearing out an arrest warrant for Marvin. He has till tomorrow afternoon to report to the police station with his lawyer. After that, they're going to go get him."

Libby gasped and put her hands to her mouth. "Oh my God," she cried.

"Twenty-four hours. That should be enough time to wind this thing up," Sean said, trying to bolster her up even though he wasn't sure that what he had said was true.

Bernie reached over and patted Libby's thigh. "Don't you worry. This is going to be a piece of cake."

"Like it has been?" Libby asked.

Bernie didn't answer. There was nothing she could say.

Chapter 35

Is there anything you can think of, anything at all?" Libby begged Marvin an hour later. She, Bernie, and Marvin were in the park standing by the bench where Marvin had dumped the muskets.

"How about shooting myself?" Marvin said.

"Besides that," Bernie said.

"Ha-ha. Funny lady," Marvin said.

It was a little after two and the sun was out. As Bernie swatted a fly away from her face, she smelled the roses from the rose garden and that got her thinking. "Libby, you know what we haven't done?"

"Besides solve the case?" Libby replied.

"We haven't talked to Whitney Peters and Holly Roget. Amber told me they're back from the Hamptons. Maybe they saw something."

"They were busy dancing around in the rose garden doing their Wiccan thing," Libby pointed out. "How could they have seen anything?"

"You never know," Bernie replied. "It's worth a shot."

"I suppose we have nothing to lose," Libby agreed.

"I do," Marvin said, remembering his encounter with Juno. "I'm not going anywhere near those two." He waved his hands in the air. "Those people are nuts."

"Maybe Bernie's right," Libby told him.

Marvin bit his lip. "They didn't see anything," he insisted.

"How do you know if you don't ask them?" Bernie demanded.

"I know because they were jumping up and down like lunatics and then they were spinning around and chanting," Marvin retorted.

"Fine. Then don't go." Libby was beginning to get annoyed with him. It seemed as if she and Bernie were doing all the heavy lifting. "We will."

Marvin spread his hands wide. "I just don't want to spend the last bit of freedom that I have doing that."

Bernie snorted. "God, you're negative."

"No. I'm realistic," Marvin replied.

"You'll be out on bail in no time, if it comes to that," Bernie told him. "But maybe if we talk to them that won't happen."

"Maybe." To be polite, Marvin agreed.

Libby was inclined to go along with Marvin's assessment of the situation, but she didn't want to say that. Instead, she redirected the conversation, getting back to where they'd been before Bernie had brought up the Wiccans. "You must have seen something when you put the muskets in the shed. Or took them out."

"I already told you I didn't," Marvin said crossly. The waiting was wearing on him. He just wanted the whole thing over with. He was beginning to think that going to jail would be a relief.

"Be that as it may, I want you to close your eyes and picture the scene," Libby told him.

"Why?" Marvin demanded. "What is this going to accomplish?"

"Dad said we should go back to the beginning, so that's what we're doing. Unless you have a better idea?" Bernie asked.

Since Marvin didn't, he did as he was told. "Now what?"

"Tell me what happened," Libby said.

"I already have more times then I can count," Marvin objected.

"Do it again," Libby ordered.

Marvin let out a long sigh. He was tired. He was hot. He could feel a trickle of perspiration snaking its way down his back. Even worse, his mind was a complete jumble. With all due respect to Mr. Simmons, he thought that what he, Libby, and Bernie were doing was ridiculous. He couldn't see anything when he closed his eyes, except these little amoeba like thingies floating in front of his retinas.

To be honest, he couldn't remember what had happened two hours ago, let alone what had happened the week before. Maybe if he could sleep, it would be different. But he couldn't. Every time he put his head down on the pillow all he could see was Devlin's face. And Devlin's scream when the musket misfired kept on echoing in his ears. It just wouldn't go away.

"What do you see?" Libby asked.

Marvin opened his eyes. "Nothing. I don't see anything."

Now it was Libby's turn to sigh.

"Okay, Marvin," Bernie said, deciding that it was time to try another strategy. "Let's just retrace your steps. Maybe that will jog your memory."

"Fine," he replied. *At least,* he thought, *that's better than standing here feeling like a total idiot.* "I parked my car up there." He pointed to the parking lot near the rose garden.

The three of them walked up there.

"And then?" Bernie prompted.

"I took everything out of the trunk of my car, and carried it down to the shed."

"Pretend to do it," Bernie told him.

He did.

"What did you see on your walk down?" Libby asked.

"I didn't see anything," Marvin immediately

answered. "I was too busy trying not to trip as I went down the hill. I was carrying everything in a big pile and I couldn't see in front of me. I should have made two trips, but I was in a hurry and didn't have the time."

"And then what happened?" Libby asked once they'd gotten down to the shed, which was festooned with crime scene tape.

"I put everything down on the ground."

"Do it," Bernie ordered.

"I feel like a moron," Marvin told her.

"Do it anyway. Then what happened next?" Bernie asked after Marvin had pantomimed the action.

"Then I went to open the lock on the shed, but when I grabbed hold of it, it opened by itself." Marvin talked as he reenacted what had happened. "I figured someone had left it that way so I took the lock out of the metal loop it was hanging on and opened the door."

"Did you see anything inside?" Libby asked.

"Like what?" Marvin responded.

"I don't know. Something. Anything." Libby knew she was grasping at straws, but she couldn't help herself.

"No. I didn't see anything. Just dust and cob-webs. I put everything down on the shelves inside and went out and tried to close the lock, but it wouldn't close. I was really annoyed," Marvin remembered. "I had to get back to work. We had

Mrs. Cullen's calling hours in the evening and I had to get back in time to receive the flowers and set up the chairs."

"So you just left the lock the way it was?" Bernie asked.

Marvin paused. "No," he said slowly, remembering. "No, I didn't."

"What did you do?" Libby asked.

Marvin grinned. "I called Rick Evans. I wanted to tell him about the lock."

"On his cell?" Libby asked.

Marvin shook his head. "No. I tried that first, but when I tried to leave a message his voice mail was full so I called his wife. She gave me the number of the office where he was working so I tried that next."

"Did you get him?" Bernie inquired.

"No. I got a receptionist. She said he was in a meeting and that she'd give him the message as soon as he got out."

"After which?"

"After which I hung up."

"Did you ever call him back?" Libby asked.

"No. I didn't." Marvin frowned. "I guess I should have."

"Not necessarily," Libby said, trying to be supportive.

"But things got really busy," Marvin said. "There were two pickups. I guess it went clean out of my head until now."

"Do you remember the number you dialed?" Bernie asked.

Marvin took his cell phone out of his pocket. "It's probably here," he replied as he pressed CONTACTS, pressed RECENTS, and began to scroll down. "There it is," he cried, tapping the screen. "That's it."

"Call," Libby ordered.

Marvin did. As soon as someone came on the line, Libby took the phone and explained what they needed.

Chapter 36

That was a net loss," Libby observed fifteen minutes later.

According to the woman who had finally come on the line after a five-minute wait, it was simple. Given the circumstances and the time frame, no one at the firm of Aberthay and Marks would possibly remember taking a message like that.

"Oh well," Marvin said, sounding dejected. "It was worth a shot."

"At least we have a direction to go in." Bernie was ever the optimist.

"We need to locate Rick Evans," Libby said firmly.

Bernie nodded. "And find out whether or not he ever got the message."

Marvin repositioned his sunglasses. "What difference does that make?"

Libby gave him the look. "Seriously?"

He swatted at a dragonfly buzzing around his head before answering. "Yes, seriously."

"Obviously, if he got the message then he knew that the shack was open," Libby said.

"So?" Marvin said.

"So he could have gone in and over-primed the musket," Libby said.

"Yeah, but we can't prove that he did."

"It's another nail in his circumstantial coffin," Libby told Marvin.

Bernie laughed. "Circumstantial coffin! I like that. Maybe I'll use that when we talk to him."

"He's not going to talk to us," Marvin declared.

"We won't know till we try, now will we?" Bernie said.

"Even if he doesn't, we can go to Clyde with this. It makes you look a little better—" Libby stopped talking. She'd been about to say *if you have to mount a defense,* but she decided not to go there.

"I hope you're right." Marvin glanced at his watch. He could feel his moments of freedom ticking away.

"I am," Libby reassured him. "But first we have to find Evans."

"*Finding him* being the operative phrase here." Bernie took out her phone and called Rick. The call went straight to voice mail. She left a message and hung up. "He's not answering."

"Now what?" Marvin asked.

"Now we start looking for him."

They walked over to the van and climbed in. A minute later, the search was on. Bernie drove to the Evans house first, but no one was home, then she tried the mayor's office, the fire house, the post office, and the police station as well as the diner down by the end of Main Street and the bar in the strip mall by the new Thai restaurant. No one had seen Rick Evans . . . or if they had, they weren't saying.

"Maybe he's working in New York," Marvin suggested.

"Gail might know." Bernie tried phoning her. That call went straight to voice mail, as well.

"Now what?" Marvin asked.

"Good question." Libby looked at Bernie. "How about the gun club?" It was the last place she could think of to look.

Bernie agreed. It wasn't as if they had anything to lose. "This time, we go the front way."

Libby laughed.

"I don't get it," Marvin said.

Libby explained on the way over. The drive took less than fifteen minutes. Except for a Range Rover and an Infiniti, the parking lot was empty when they got there.

"I think those are Rick and Gail's vehicles,"

Bernie said as she parked the van by a barrel full of geraniums.

"Do you think this is going to help?" Marvin asked.

"It can't hurt," Bernie said, opening the door and getting out.

It was gusty up on top of the hill and Bernie could hear the wind whistling. A breeze tugged at her shirt. She looked around as she tucked the hem of her sleeveless white silk shirt back in the waistband of the floral printed cotton skirt she'd gotten at Barney's last week.

The hills on either side were covered with maples, oaks, and beeches interspersed with abandoned farmland. In the fall, the hills would turn shades of gold and red, but now the trees were a tapestry of light and dark and blue and yellow greens. Bernie was thinking that it would be nice to have a cabin out here when she heard the sound of gunfire coming from behind the clubhouse.

"Maybe this isn't such a good idea," Marvin said nervously.

Libby noticed a sheen of sweat on his forehead. "Are you okay?"

"I'm fine," Marvin told her.

"Really?" Libby asked.

"Not really," he allowed. "It's just that ever since . . . you know . . . the sound of gunfire makes me nervous."

"Me too," Libby said. "Do you want to stay outside?"

Marvin shook his head.

Bernie clapped her hands together. "Okay, people. Enough shilly-shallying. Let's go." She opened the clubhouse door and walked inside.

Libby and Marvin followed. No one was sitting at the front desk, and they walked straight through to the back of the building. The door to the target area was open and they could see the Evanses out there. Rick was shooting at targets and Gail was watching.

"I didn't expect her to be here," Libby commented.

"Me either," Bernie agreed, "but I guess the family that shoots together, stays together."

"Only she's not shooting," Libby said.

The three of them stepped outside. Marvin, who was the last one out, let go of the door, and it slammed in back of them. Rick lowered his rifle and spun around. Gail followed his lead.

"What are you doing here?" he demanded.

"We have a question to ask you," Bernie replied, indicating Marvin and Libby with a wave of her hand.

"Come back when we're open and I'm sure Tim will be able to help you out," Rick said. "We're closed till five o'clock."

"Then how come you're here?" Libby asked.

"We're members," he said.

Gail stroked his arm. "Rick is practicing for a competition and I'm his cheering squad."

"At this rate, I need all the practice time I can get," Rick said.

"This will just take a minute," Bernie said.

He was about to say something, but Gail laid a hand on his arm. "Let them ask. It'll be quicker that way." She flashed a smile at Bernie. "What do you want to know?"

"We want to know whether or not Rick received a message from a receptionist at Aberthay and Marks telling him that the lock on the shed near the rose garden was broken," Bernie replied.

"Unfortunately, I didn't," Rick replied.

"Why unfortunately?" Libby asked.

"Because if I had, I would have fixed the lock, and poor Marvin here," Rick inclined his head in Marvin's direction, "would have been spared what he is going through now."

"What if I told you that the receptionist we spoke to said otherwise?" Bernie asked.

"Then I would say she's a liar," Rick replied pleasantly.

"Why would she lie?" Libby asked.

He shrugged. "Not being gifted with ESP, I couldn't tell you. Your guess is as good as mine."

Gail pointed to the clock. "If you don't mind, my husband would like to get back to practicing. He's facing stiff competition tomorrow night and I know he doesn't want to make a fool of himself."

"My lovely wife is correct."

Bernie and Libby watched as he put down his musket, came over, and clapped Marvin on the shoulder. "I just want you to know that I wish you good luck and I'm sorry for what happened to you. If I could do anything about it, I would."

"He definitely would," Gail echoed.

"That's not what you sounded like when it happened," Marvin replied.

Rick Evans glanced down at the ground, then back up at Marvin. "I know. If it's any consolation, I feel terrible about that. I was . . . I was hysterical. I didn't know what I was saying."

"It's true," Gail put in. "When he got home, he told me he felt dreadful the way he'd acted. He even tried to call and tell the police, but by then it was too late."

Rick nodded. "I did. Hopefully after you're cleared, you'll be able to look at this as a blip on your radar of life."

"That goes double for me." Gail lifted her eyes up to the heavens. "I have you in my prayers."

Bernie, Libby, and Marvin turned as one and headed to the door.

"Great," Marvin muttered as they walked back through the club. "Is that supposed to make me feel better?"

"Well, at least Rick apologized," Bernie pointed out.

Libby frowned. "Small consolation."

"Maybe he'll be willing to testify on Marvin's behalf," Bernie said, thinking ahead.

"Testify?" Marvin repeated. "Did you say testify? I thought things weren't supposed to get that far."

"It's always good to have a backup plan," Bernie explained. "Just in case."

"Just in case what?" Marvin demanded.

Libby stepped in before Bernie could answer. "You're not helping anything," she told her.

"Why?" Bernie asked. "Would lying be better?"

The sisters were still bickering when they got outside. They were all walking toward the van when Marvin came to a complete standstill.

"What's the matter?" Libby asked him.

"I think I just remembered something." He was staring at the Range Rover.

"What?" Libby inquired.

"Oh my God." Marvin put his hand up to his mouth. "I remember this car. It was parked about two feet away when I came back up the hill. Rick Evans must have been there all the time. He must have followed me from the costume store. All that stuff about being sorry." Marvin's voice rose. "He lied to my face."

"Calm down, Marvin," Libby told him.

"I am calm, Libby."

"Why didn't you say anything before?" Libby demanded.

"Because I didn't think that car was Rick Evans's. I thought he drove a BMW."

"He drives both. Let's find out what he has to say about this." Bernie turned around and went back inside the gun club.

Libby and Marvin followed close behind.

"Hey, Rick," Bernie yelled when she got to the gun range. "Marvin says he saw your Range Rover by the rose garden the day he put the stuff for the reenactment in the shed. He says you were watching the whole time."

Rick and Gail turned around. Rick looked ready to bite someone's head off. "What are you babbling about?"

"I saw your Rover at the rose garden," Marvin said.

"You most certainly did not," Rick snapped.

"I did." Marvin shook a finger at him. "You lied to me."

"About what?" Rick seemed genuinely bewildered.

Marvin took a step toward him. "I was right. You set me up. Don't even think of denying it."

Rick was about to reply to Marvin's accusation when Gail tapped him on the shoulder. "Er, darling."

"What?" he spat out, annoyed at being interrupted.

"I, er . . . I loaned the Rover to . . . to . . . Tony."

329

Rick's eyes narrowed. "Tony Gerard? The Tony Gerard that smashed my car into a wall when he was backing into a parking space? That Tony?"

"Well, yes," Gail replied.

Rick's eyes widened. "You loaned *my* Range Rover to Tony Gerard?" His tone was incredulous.

Gail gave a nervous little cough. "It was just for a little while."

"Why would you possibly do that, Gail? That vehicle cost me $75,000. No one drives that but me. You know that."

Gail fingered the edge of her polo shirt. "Tony's car was being fixed and he needed to do an errand," she replied in such a low voice that Bernie had to strain to hear it.

"So you loaned him my car?" Rick's voice got louder.

"It was just for half an hour."

"What were you thinking?" he demanded.

Gail licked her lips. "I didn't think it would be such a big deal."

He shook a finger at his wife. "No. You knew it would be. You just didn't care."

Gail straightened up and put her hands on her hips. "You would never have noticed if I hadn't told you."

"So, that makes it right?"

Bernie cleared her throat. "Excuse me."

Rick and Gail didn't turn around to look at her,

much less answer. They were too busy glaring at each other.

"I guess we'll say good-bye now," Bernie said.

Neither Rick nor Gail answered.

"Don't worry, we'll close the door on the way out," Libby told them.

Chapter 37

Twenty minutes later, Bernie, Libby, and Marvin were back in Longely heading toward Tony Gerard's shop. Located down the block from Sanford Aiken's place, Gerard's Vacuums was sandwiched in between a cleaners and a place that sold bad Chinese take-out. Even though the primary stock in trade was vacuum cleaners, over the years Gerard had broadened out. His was as close to an old-fashioned variety store as you could get. As he'd once said to Bernie, how often do people buy a new vacuum cleaner?

His merchandise ranged from cleaning products to ashtrays, sewing kits and pinking shears, pink Spalding tennis balls, old-fashioned tops, sun hats, winter gloves, beach pails, small boxes of rock candy, and packages of licorice whips.

Bernie once again noted that this end of Main Street looked shabbier than their end. Random tufts of grass grew out of the cracks in the pavement and some of the stores looked as if they could use a fresh coat of paint.

Tony Gerard was stocking shelves when they walked into his store.

"Yes?" he said, looking up from the row of chargers, headphones, and cell phone cases he was lining up. "What can I do you for? You want a box of licorice? Just got some good stuff in. Or some cleaning supplies? This green stuff is pretty good." He indicated a bottle with a label—GOOD FOR EVERYTHING BUT DRINKING—on it.

"We want to ask you something," Bernie said, taking a step forward.

Gerard put down the box he was holding, wiped his hands on a paper towel he was carrying in his pocket, and walked toward her.

"And that would be?" he said in a wary tone.

Libby stepped forward. "We just spoke with Gail Evans."

"And?" Gerard asked.

"She said she loaned you her husband's Range Rover."

"Did she now?" Gerard said.

Libby thought he sounded surprised. "Yup, she did. Her husband didn't seem very happy about it."

Gerard reflexively wiped his hands on his khakis. "Well, it is his baby."

"He was very upset," Bernie said.

"I can imagine." Gerard looked from Libby

332

to Bernie and back again. "So what's your question?"

"Did you borrow the Range Rover?" Libby asked.

He gave a short laugh. "Why do you want to know? How could this possibly concern you?"

Marvin stepped forward and pointed to himself. "It concerns me. You want to know why, I'll tell you why, Tony. Because you followed me from the costume store, you parked in front of the rose garden, and watched me come out of the shed. After I left, you went inside and over-primed the musket."

Gerard put his hands on his hips. "Talk about manufacturing things out of whole cloth."

Watching him, Bernie decided that Gerard seemed genuinely distressed.

"I'm not manufacturing anything," Marvin cried. "I saw you there."

"Maybe you thought you saw me there."

"I did," Marvin insisted.

Gerard pointed to himself. "Did you see *me?*"

"No," Marvin admitted.

"Okay then. Did you get the license plate number of the Rover?"

Marvin shook his head.

"Do you know how many there are in this area?"

"No."

"I agree you saw a Range Rover there," Gerard

replied. "But I wasn't in it. Most likely it wasn't Rick's."

"So what you're saying is that Gail is lying?" Bernie asked. "That she didn't lend it to you?"

Gerard nodded. "That's exactly what I'm saying."

"Why would she do that?" Bernie asked.

"I don't know. You'll have to ask her that yourself."

"I don't believe you," Bernie told him. "I think you're the one who is lying."

Gerard shrugged. "Think what you want. I really don't care."

Libby continued to pursue Bernie's line of questioning. "Why would Gail lie? That makes no sense. No sense at all."

"Like I said," Gerard told Libby, "you'll have to ask her."

"I saw the Range Rover," Marvin insisted. "I know I did."

"Maybe you did," Gerard said, "but I can assure you that I wasn't in it." He turned toward the shelves.

Marvin put a hand on his shoulder and spun him around. "Why are you doing this to me?" he cried. "What have I ever done to you?"

Libby pulled Marvin away. "It's okay."

"It's not okay. It's not okay at all."

"Listen," Gerard said to Marvin. "I'm sorry you feel that way, but there's nothing I can do."

"You can tell the truth," Libby said.

"I am," Gerard flung back.

Before Libby could reply, Bernie stepped in. "Unlike my sister, I believe you. I really do." She smiled. She could see Gerard relaxing. Her smile broadened. "I don't think you were there."

"I told you," Gerard said.

"But what I don't get," Bernie continued, "is why Gail is doing this to you. That's not very nice of her."

"No, it isn't," Gerard said.

"Most definitely not," agreed Bernie. "Why do you think she's doing that? I mean I thought she was nice, but now—"

"She's scared," Gerard blurted out.

Bernie raised an eyebrow. "Scared," she scoffed. "Of what?"

Gerard bit his lip.

"Come on," Bernie wheedled. "It's obvious she's setting you up."

Gerard looked confused. "What do you mean?"

"Well," Bernie explained. "She just told us she loaned you her husband's Rover and Marvin saw it there. It seems to me that's enough to go to the police with."

Gerard didn't answer, but Bernie could see that he was thinking. She decided to give him another nudge. "Why are you protecting her? She certainly isn't protecting you."

"This has nothing to do with what happened to Jack Devlin," he said.

"Then what does it have to do with?" Libby asked.

"It has to do with her husband. She didn't want him to find out."

"About what?" Bernie asked.

"About the fact that she'd taken up with Devlin again."

"Rick Evans told me he didn't care about that kind of stuff. So did Gail for that matter. They both said they were free spirits."

Tony Gerard snorted and slapped his knee. "Now there's a good one. Rick was really, really jealous. In fact, Gail was afraid of him."

"How do you know that?" Bernie leaned against the counter and picked up a bracelet that was on a stand.

"Because she told me, that's how I know," Gerard said. "She told me she was scared that Rick would kill her if he found out that she was seeing Devlin again."

"When did she say that?" Libby asked.

Gerard shrugged his shoulders. "A couple weeks before the reenactment."

"Either she couldn't have been that scared," Bernie noted as she slid the bracelet over her hand and onto her wrist, "or Devlin must have been really good."

Marvin turned to Gerard. "So you're saying—"

"I'm saying that Gail and Devlin started seeing each other again and they were in the Rover when you stowed everything in the shed," Gerard replied.

"How do you know this for a fact?" Libby asked, curious.

"Because she told me," Gerard said.

"Why would she do that?" Libby asked.

"Because I'm her friend. Anyway, would she lie if she wasn't afraid of Rick finding out that she was seeing Devlin again?"

Bernie held up her arm to admire her bracelet. She had to admit she rather liked it. "That's a good question."

"Isn't it though," Libby seconded. "Maybe we should talk to Gail again and find out."

"Maybe we should," Marvin agreed.

Bernie pointed to the bracelet on her wrist. "How much?" she asked Gerard.

"Twenty dollars."

"I'll take it." She gave him her credit card. Then she took out her cell and called Gail.

After a few minutes of pointed conversation, Gail agreed to meet them at the Six O'Clock Diner in half an hour.

Gerard handed Bernie her credit card and receipt, and the three investigators left his store.

On the way to the diner, they dropped Marvin off at the funeral home because he had paperwork he needed to clear up.

"Just in case," he said, looking as mournful as it was possible for a man to look.

"It'll be fine," Libby assured him for the hundredth time.

"I don't think so," Marvin replied, but Libby didn't hear him because Bernie had already taken off.

The diner was one town over, so even with Bernie going faster than she should have, they were five minutes late. Gail Evans had already arrived and was sitting in the last booth as they walked in. She was facing the door, nursing a cup of coffee, and eating an English muffin topped with peanut butter.

Bernie and Libby slid into the seat across from her and ordered the same when the waitress came over.

"I haven't been in this place in years," Bernie noted, looking around. It was a classic diner with chrome fixtures, red leather booths, and a huge menu, of which the hamburgers and BLTs weren't half bad. Maybe it was why most of the people in the place were eating those.

Libby rubbed her arms to warm them up. "They could raise the air-conditioning a few notches. I feel as if I'm in a freezer."

Gail took another sip of her coffee and put the mug down. "I like it. It's refreshing. Now what do you two want?"

The waitress plunked two mugs down on the Formica tabletop and filled them up.

Bernie waited till she was gone. "We spoke to Tony Gerard."

"So?" Gail asked.

Libby added a packet of sugar to her coffee and stirred. "So, he said you were lying. He said you never loaned him your husband's Range Rover. He said you and Devlin were up on the hill . . . ah . . . having a conversation."

Gail swallowed.

A moment later, the waitress returned with two English muffins with peanut butter melting on top and placed them on the table.

Bernie reached down and took a bite of hers. She guessed Peter Pan peanut butter. She couldn't deny it tasted really good. Maybe they should do something with peanut butter at their place. She took another bite as she watched Gail start chewing on her inner lip.

"Why did you lie?" Bernie asked, though she had a pretty good idea.

"I didn't," Gail said.

"So then Tony Gerard was lying?" Libby took a bite of her English muffin and peanut butter. She, too, decided she'd forgotten how good it tasted.

Gail nodded.

"Why would he do that?" Bernie asked.

Gail took another sip of coffee and put her mug down. "I don't know."

Libby noticed that Gail's hand shook slightly.

"I see," Bernie said.

The three women sat in silence for a moment.

"You know"—Bernie took another bite of her

muffin and licked the peanut butter off her fingers—"I had a boyfriend once who scared the hell out of me. I thought he was going to kill me, but when the police came to ask about him, I lied. I told them we were fine."

"Why did you do that?" Gail asked.

Bernie finished off the first half of her English muffin while she considered the answer. Finally she said, "I think for two reasons. One, I thought in some twisted way his acting the way he did was proof that he really loved me, that he felt an I-can't-live-without-her kind of love."

"And the second reason?" Gail asked.

"I was scared. That if I reported him, he'd become worse. And I was embarrassed. That I had allowed myself to get into that situation. I saw it as a reflection on myself."

"Did he hit you?" asked Gail.

"No." Bernie's face grew long as she remembered. "But he used to threaten me if I wasn't there when he wanted me to be. He was very explicit about what he'd do to me." She shivered at the memory and fell silent.

"So what happened?" Gail asked.

Bernie gave a half smile. "He was arrested on an assault charge and I moved away and that was the end of that. I vowed I'd never be in that kind of relationship again and I haven't been."

"I see." Gail bit her lips, then her face crumbled. "I'm so sorry," she said through her sobs as she buried her face in her hands. After a minute, she told them everything that had happened, then she sobbed some more. "I feel so bad," she moaned. She looked up and beckoned Libby and Bernie closer. "I think he killed Devi," she whispered. "I do. I think he killed him because of me." She started to weep again. "It's so horrible. I don't know what to do."

Libby and Bernie exchanged glances.

"I think we need to let the authorities know," Bernie said gently.

Gail looked up. Her eyes were red and puffy. "I don't know if I can do that."

Libby leaned over and patted her hand. "You're not being fair to yourself or Marvin or Rick if you don't tell them."

Gail hiccupped. "What do you mean about being fair to Rick? I'm turning him in. That can't be fair."

Libby explained. "Maybe Rick didn't do this. But if you don't give him a chance to clear himself, you're never going to know. You're always going to suspect him."

Gail blinked. "But if I do, and he's not guilty, he's never going to forgive me," she wailed.

"Maybe we can work it so he doesn't have to know," Bernie suggested as she called Clyde.

Gail brightened. "You think so?"

"I don't see why not," Libby fibbed.

She and Bernie waited with Gail until Clyde

arrived to drive her to the police station to take her statement.

"Why can't she drive herself?" Libby asked as they walked past Gail's Infiniti.

Bernie shrugged. "I guess you'll have to ask Clyde that."

"Nice car," Libby commented as she peeked inside. Except for a couple glittery things in the backseat half hidden by a white cloth, the car was immaculate. *Unlike our van,* she couldn't help thinking.

"I think I'd rather have a MINI Cooper," Bernie said.

"I'd like to have anything that doesn't eat gas," Libby replied. They were almost at their van when she turned and asked, "Did that really happen?"

Bernie glanced up. She'd been fishing around in her bag for the keys. "What are you talking about?"

"The boyfriend thing."

Bernie looked puzzled.

"The story you told to Gail. Is that true?"

Bernie laughed. "God no. Don't be ridiculous. I made that up."

"But it sounded so real," Libby exclaimed.

"That's because I'm a good liar."

"Frighteningly good." Libby didn't know whether to be impressed or scared. She decided she was a little of both.

Chapter 38

The next morning, A Little Taste of Heaven was jammed with people wanting to hear all the details of Rick Evans's arrest served up with their coffee and muffins. Even though the story hadn't made it into the local newspaper, that paper being a weekly, the gossip grapevine had gone into full activation mode and cell phones had been ringing all over town. The story promised to be the scandal of the week, maybe even the year, especially since everyone in town knew the players or knew someone who knew the players.

"I can't believe it," everyone who came into the shop kept on saying to one another, as well as to Libby and Bernie. "Rick Evans is such a nice man, so responsible, so civic-minded." *As opposed to Jack Devlin* remained largely unsaid.

Well, Libby and Bernie didn't think that Rick Evans was nice or civic-minded, not that they would say that to any of their customers. When one was in retail one learned to keep one's opinions to one's self. Although they were certainly glad that Marvin was off the hook, there were still things that worried them, things that Rick Evans's guilt did nothing to explain.

Things like how Devlin had gotten the musket

in the first place. That was a niggling issue. It was something they pushed to the back of their minds, something they told themselves would no doubt be explained in the weeks to come. They told themselves their job was done and they should be happy with the result. Marvin certainly was.

By the time Whitney Peters and Holly Roget walked into the shop at ten-thirty, Libby and Bernie were heartily tired of discussing the particulars of the case. Not that they would ever say that, being extremely mindful of the fact that the new faces in the shop were there to hear all the details, details that they would then repeat to their nearest and dearest. Instead, both women smiled at Holly and Whitney and prepared themselves for another recital of the facts as they knew them.

"I heard about Rick," Holly said as she ordered a coffee with cream, two sugars, and a chocolate raspberry muffin. "Unbelievable. It shows you never know a person."

"But you must be happy," Whitney said to Libby after she'd ordered a mint tea and a toasted corn muffin with store-made strawberry jam and butter fresh from Blueberry Hill Farm.

"I am," Libby replied.

"I never thought Marvin did it in the first place," Whitney replied.

"No one did. People are too quick to judge," Holly said as she handed Libby her credit card.

"My treat," she said to Whitney. To Libby she said, "Gail must be devastated. It's true we didn't have a good view from the rose garden. But still."

"We saw enough," Whitney replied, taking the tea that Bernie was holding out to her. She watched as Bernie took a corn muffin out of the display case, sliced it, and put it through the toaster. "I love those muffins. I think it's the corn and cheddar you put in it. And something else?"

"Fresh ground black pepper," Bernie replied while she took the corn muffin out of the toaster, slathered it with butter, wrapped it up, and handed it to Whitney.

"What do you mean, you saw enough?" Libby asked her.

"Well, we heard the scream and we saw all the people running to poor Jack," Whitney replied.

"It was very disruptive. We were trying to invoke the Great Mother to manifest an Aga and then that happened." Holly shook her head. "We couldn't concentrate after that. We all tried, but it wasn't any good. Maybe that's why Juno hasn't gotten her stove yet. "

"No," Whitney corrected. "She hasn't gotten her stove yet, because she wasn't there."

"That is not true. Marie says you don't have to be as long as you have a substitute."

"Obviously, she's wrong, Holly. I told Juno from the beginning that this would happen. I said I guess you don't want the Aga that badly then."

"Excuse me," Bernie said as she handed Holly her coffee and muffin. "But I thought Juno was there."

"She was in the beginning. Then she left." Holly furrowed her brow. "She came back a little later."

Libby leaned forward. "How much later?"

Holly turned to Whitney. "Did she come back before that thing with Devlin happened or after? I don't remember."

Whitney shook her head. "I think right before, but I can't be certain. Things were so confusing."

"Why did she leave?" Bernie asked.

"She said she was worried about the pig," Whitney recalled. "That she'd be too hot or something so she went to check on her."

Bernie wiped a drop of spilled cream off the counter while she processed what she was hearing. "But Hilda was under the Rose of Sharon bush. Samuel Cotton put her there. I know because I saw him, but I definitely didn't see Juno . . . and she'd be hard to miss."

Whitney shrugged. "What can I tell you? I'm just repeating what Juno told me."

Libby raised another objection. "But there were nine people in the circle." What Whitney was saying made no sense to her. "I remember counting them. If Juno wasn't there, there would have been eight."

Holly took a sip of her coffee. "Well, Gail took

over for a little while so the circle wasn't broken if that's what you mean. The number isn't as important as the fact that once you start the chant you keep it going."

Libby leaned forward. "You mean Gail took Juno's place?" she asked incredulously.

"Exactly." Whitney rolled her eyes. "That's what I've been saying."

"She just walked in?" Bernie asked. "Just like that? What was it? Some sort of happy coincidence?"

Whitney shook her head. "No. Of course not. Don't be ridiculous. Gail was there so the circle wasn't broken. At least, I assume it was."

Holly took a sip of her tea. "Although Juno's choice surprised me."

"Gail?" Libby inquired.

Holly nodded.

"How so?" Bernie asked.

Holly nibbled on her muffin while she thought of how to frame her answer. Finally she said, "Because she's so . . . so . . . not like us. I mean, I think she is one of the most unspiritual people I've met."

"Besides," Whitney said, "Gail and Juno aren't exactly best friends. But maybe she couldn't get anyone else."

"So," Bernie reiterated, "this whole thing was set up in advance?"

Whitney took a sip of her coffee. "That's what

I've been saying. Juno came to me a couple days before the ceremony and told me she might need to switch out with someone for a little while. She'd seen the weather forecast and was concerned about Hilda. In fact, she told me she was setting up a bed for Hilda in the shed just to be on the safe side."

The sisters exchanged glances.

"Really?" Bernie said.

"Yes," Holly said. "She's very devoted to Hilda. I mean breaking the circle isn't the best thing, but sometimes one has to make do."

"One certainly does," Bernie replied.

The sisters exchanged another glance. As soon as Holly and Whitney walked out the door, Bernie said, "I have an idea."

"So do I. You first." After Bernie spoke, Libby said, "I'm thinking that, too."

"It's a stretch," Bernie said.

"More like a giant leap," Libby said. "You want to go see anyway?"

"Definitely," Bernie said. "I'll call Clyde and let him know what we're thinking."

"What did he say?" Libby asked after Bernie had finished talking.

"He said he'd meet us there."

"Cool beans." Libby told Amber to hold down the fort and got their dad to man the cash register.

"Cool beans? What does cool beans mean?" Bernie asked as they jumped into the van.

Libby shrugged. "I don't know. I just like the way it sounds." She was quiet for a moment then said, "If the musket is there, why hasn't anyone found it yet?"

"Maybe they weren't looking in the right place," Bernie said, keeping her eyes on the road.

"I can't believe that Juno and Gail switched places," Libby said after another minute had gone by.

"I can't believe that we didn't see that. Okay, they pretty much are the same height and weight, but their builds are different."

"Both of them have brown hair."

"I guess, when it comes down to it, everyone looks the same in a gown and wings."

"We should have talked to Holly and Whitney earlier," Libby said.

"Not our finest hour."

Both sisters were silent for the rest of the trip. There really wasn't any more to say.

Chapter 39

Everything was as it should be when Libby and Bernie pulled into the Deitrich Rose Garden parking lot. The roses sparkled, the bees buzzed, and an occasional butterfly flitted through the air. Groups of people sat on the benches eating early lunches or simply sunbathing. A young woman and her toddler ambled down the paths between the flowers. Every now and then, the woman would hold a flower down for her child to sniff. A little farther on, an elderly lady dressed in a pink sheath, pearls, and yellow high-tops was pruning the roses, while in the next row over, three teenage girls in shorts and tank tops were taking pictures of the flowers.

"We should come here once in a while," Bernie said as she parked the van.

"You're saying we should take time to smell the roses?" Libby asked.

"Yes. That's exactly what I'm saying." Bernie looked around the lot. "Clyde isn't here yet."

"I'm not waiting," Libby uncharacteristically declared.

"I didn't ask you to," Bernie replied, although she didn't think it would be a bad idea.

Libby got out of the van and headed to the shed. It was strung with yellow crime scene tape, which made it look rather festive in an odd sort of way. Bernie was right behind her. Libby hesitated for a moment before pulling the tape away and breaking the seal on the door.

"Lucy is going to have a fit," Bernie noted as she watched her sister at work. Usually Bernie was the one that engaged in questionable activities.

"It's not as if I'm going to tell him I'm responsible." Libby opened the door. It creaked because the hinges needed oiling.

"You're going to tell him you found it this way?"

Libby grinned. "Yup. Coming?" she asked as she stepped inside.

Bernie followed her in. "Wouldn't miss it."

Libby bit her cuticle. "What if we're wrong?"

"Then we're wrong, Not a big deal."

The two women looked around. Nothing had changed since the last time they had been in there. The shed was still dark and musty with cobwebs strewn across the ceiling beams. It vaguely smelled of mouse droppings and old cut grass. The only light came from the opened door and a small dirty window located on the left side of the building. On the right side of the shack were three rows of shelves, empty except for a few boxes of fertilizer and assorted gardening tools. That was where Marvin had stored the cartons filled with muskets and Revolutionary War costumes.

A rusted push mower stood under the window as did a wooden ladder, a couple blue plastic tarps, some peat pots, and a bag of rose food. The far end of the shed had a built-in cabinet bisecting its wall. Libby approached it, opened the top, and looked inside. The first thing she saw was a muddle of torn white sheets and bundles of newspapers.

She leaned in, grasped one of the sheets with the tips of her fingers and pulled it back. Nothing was there except a column of small black ants carrying a dead mosquito back to their nest. She let out a gasp of disappointment. "I was positive it would be here."

Bernie sighed. "So was I."

Libby frowned. "Maybe I'm wrong."

Bernie shook her head. "No, you're not. It's here. It has to be. It's the only thing that makes sense."

Libby made a gesture that took in the entire room. "But where?"

Bernie set her jaw. "Good question. Let's find out, shall we?"

While Libby watched, Bernie began looking on the shelves and in the cabinet. She lifted the tarps and peered in the corners. When she was done with that, she began tapping on the walls and the floorboards.

"You don't honestly expect to find anything doing what you're doing, do you?" Libby asked.

"Yeah I do. Otherwise, I wouldn't be doing it."

"It's not as if there's a secret compartment in here," Libby observed. "It's not a castle or anything. It's a friggin' garden shed."

"I know what it is." Bernie heard a car outside and came to a standstill. "Jeez, I hope that's not Clyde, because I'm going to feel like a fool if it is."

Libby popped her head out to take a look.

"Nope. It's a family. But he should be along any minute."

Bernie brushed a cobweb off her cheek. "Maybe the musket is outside."

"That doesn't make any sense," Libby objected. "Of course, nothing about this thing has made sense." She turned to her sister. "What are we going to tell Clyde?"

"I don't know." Bernie bit her lip and glanced up. Then she grinned. "We're not going to tell him anything. We're going to show him."

"What do you mean?"

Bernie pointed to the ceiling beam.

"I don't see anything," Libby said.

"Look harder," Bernie instructed.

Libby tried again. A moment later, she did see it. The musket they'd been looking for was lying on one of the rafters. In the gloom, the colors blended together making the rifle extremely difficult to spot. The only reason Bernie had seen it was because a ray of sun had reflected off her watch face.

Libby let out a sigh of relief then went over and got the ladder. She steadied it while Bernie climbed up and brought the musket down. It looked exactly like the ones the reenactors had used.

"So we were right," Libby said.

"About what?" Clyde asked as he came through the door.

Bernie showed him the weapon. "This. I'm betting this is the one Devlin was supposed to use."

"And the one that Devlin did use?" Clyde said. "Where did it come from?"

"I'm betting the Musket and Flintlock Club," Bernie said.

"Why do you say that?" Clyde asked.

"Because it looks exactly like the one I used at the club," Libby said.

"You shot a musket?" Clyde asked, surprised.

Libby drew herself up. "You sound as if you don't think I'm capable of doing that."

"Given the way you feel about weapons, I'm just surprised is all," Clyde replied. "Good work." He reached for the musket.

"Not so fast," Bernie told him, taking a step back and bringing the musket down to her side. "We have an idea." She told him what it was.

Clyde shook his head. "I don't know if I can do that. What you're asking is highly irregular."

Bernie gazed up at him and fluttered her eyelashes. "Not even for truth, justice, and the American way . . . not to mention three peach and blueberry pies?"

The corners of Clyde's mouth went up. He could never resist Sean's girls. On the other hand, charm and good baking only went so far. "I could get fired."

"Or you could get rewarded," Libby said.

"Anyway," Bernie said, "do you really want those two running around?"

Clyde's eyes darkened. "No. I most definitely do not. There has to be another way."

"Like what?" Bernie asked.

"The right way. We could drag everyone down to the station."

"And beat them till they confess?" Bernie said. "Probably not."

"They'd be lawyered up in a heartbeat," Libby added. "You know they would be. Do you really think they'd say anything down there?"

"No," Clyde conceded after a moment's thought. "I don't." He pondered the problem for another moment. "How do you know they'll both be there?"

"Because I'm going to call and arrange a meeting," Bernie told him.

Clyde lifted an eyebrow. "How are you going to do that?"

"I'm going to tell them I have something to show them."

"And if they won't come?" Clyde asked.

"Then I'll think of something else. So are we on?"

Clyde nodded. "I'll need at least an hour."

"And I'll need some fancy wrapping paper, a bow, and an oversized gift bag," Bernie said.

Clyde shook his head. "I'm not even going to ask."

Bernie smiled. "It's probably better not to."

Chapter 40

Two hours later, Bernie and Libby pulled into Juno's driveway and parked in back of the Infiniti. "So she can't get out," Bernie explained.

"I figured." Libby looked down at the package by her feet. The gift bag was a plain bright blue bag, while the gift inside, if you could call it that, was covered in Hello Kitty paper and finished off with a big pink bow for reasons she could not discern. "I don't know about this." She'd been having second thoughts about what they were about to do.

"Don't be silly. What could go wrong?"

"You want a list?"

"Not really." Bernie turned and reached for the wicker hamper in which she'd stowed a bottle of champagne and four glasses. "It satisfies my sense of occasion," she'd replied when Libby had asked why they needed it.

"Yeah. But the good stuff?" she had complained. "You could have gotten domestic."

"I don't do domestic," Bernie had replied. "I do French. Otherwise, what's the point?"

Libby was still thinking about her sister's comment as Bernie grabbed the hamper and got out of the van. Libby followed with the present.

A minute later, Clyde's car pulled up in back of

them. Bernie made a V for Victory sign with her left hand, Clyde nodded, turned off his vehicle and got out. He watched the women walk down the path that led to Juno's backyard, as he got himself and Rick situated behind a large blue spruce. Clyde wanted to be sure they were able to hear everything without being seen. In fact, that was the point of the exercise.

"Let's do this," Bernie said to Libby when they got to the gate. She pushed it open and they stepped inside.

Juno and Gail were sitting at the wrought iron table. They turned when Libby and Bernie came into the backyard and set the hamper on the table.

"What's this about?" Juno asked. She was wearing another caftan and even more jewelry than the last time Bernie had seen her.

Bernie smiled brightly. "I thought we'd celebrate." She went over to Hilda and gave the pig a few pats on her head and an apple she'd saved for her.

"Celebrate what?" Gail asked. She was dressed in a raspberry-colored linen shift and three-inch red espadrilles.

Bernie walked back to the table, opened the hamper, and set out the champagne and the glasses. "Only the best for us."

Juno frowned. "I don't get it. What are we celebrating?"

Bernie popped the cork. An arc of champagne

flew out. "We're celebrating your accomplishment, of course." She poured some of the champagne in each glass then lifted her flute. "To taking out the trash."

Libby lifted her glass. "To teamwork."

"What on earth are you talking about?" Gail demanded, although Libby could tell Gail had a pretty good idea of what she meant.

Bernie took a sip of her champagne. "My sister is talking about your and Juno's teamwork. It was very impressive." She watched Juno swallow in fear.

"I think you should leave." Juno's voice was a little shaky.

"Don't you want to know why we're here?" Libby asked.

"Not really." Gail's voice, too, was unsteady.

"If that's the case, why did you come?" Libby challenged.

Gail didn't answer.

"I have to say, that's a very chic ensemble you're wearing. You must be broken up by your husband's arrest. If it were me, I'd be wearing something a little more subdued, but I guess everyone grieves in a different fashion." Libby shook her head.

Gail wet her lips. "Exactly. Different people react to things in different ways. Getting dressed up makes me feel better."

"Really?" Libby said.

"Yes, really," Gail answered.

Bernie smiled an even bigger smile. "Would you like to see the present we brought you?"

Juno tittered. "A present? For us? First the champagne and now a present?"

"Yes. It's a surprise." Bernie put the bag on the table and took the present out. "I'm sorry about the paper, but I was in a hurry. It was either this or Thomas the Tank."

Juno and Gail looked dumbfounded.

"You don't mind if I unwrap this for you, do you? Good," Bernie said before either of the women had time to answer.

As everyone watched, Bernie unwrapped the musket she'd found in the shed. "Look what I found." She brandished the rifle in the air. "Isn't it amazing? You know, this thing is worth a lot of money. How much do you figure, Libby?"

"I don't know, Bernie. I don't want to be greedy."

"But we don't want to shortchange ourselves either, Libby."

"No, we don't, Bernie. A modest amount . . . say a thousand a month . . . would suffice."

"From Juno and Gail each or from them together?"

"Definitely from each. Does that seem fair to you?" Libby asked the women.

Neither replied. They were sitting with their mouths open.

"Here. Have some champagne," Bernie said. "I find a little bubbly always makes things easier."

Juno found her voice first. "Are you trying to blackmail us?" she spluttered.

"She gets it," Bernie told Libby. "Finally."

"You can't do that," Gail cried.

"Of course, we can." Libby indicated her sister. "We are."

"But we haven't done anything," Juno stated.

Bernie widened her eyes. "Really?"

"Yes, really," Juno said.

Gail put her hands on her hips. "Tell us what you think we did," she demanded.

Bernie extended her hand to Libby. "You start."

Libby nodded. "With pleasure. You're both responsible for killing Jack Devlin."

"That's ridiculous," Juno cried.

"Absurd," Gail added. "We weren't even there at the time. Juno was in the rose garden and I was home."

"And then," Libby continued, ignoring Gail's comment for the moment, "to add insult to injury, you framed your husband for it, although you were really sloppy about that."

"No, I didn't."

"Frame him?"

"That's right," Gail said.

"Interesting," Bernie said. "I'm remembering the conversation in which you confided that you thought your husband had killed Jack Devlin. We urged you to go to the police, and you did. Clyde took you down to the police station and you made a statement, which is why they arrested Rick."

"Well, I was scared of him," Gail said. "Anyway, you should be happy. It got your boyfriend off the hook."

"Why was he on the hook in the first place?" Libby asked her.

"I had nothing to do with that," Gail blurted out.

"Oh. So you had something to do with the other thing?" Bernie asked.

"That's not what I meant," Gail spluttered.

"Then what did you mean?" Libby inquired.

At that point, Juno turned to Gail. "Just don't say anything."

"I'm not," Gail said.

"Good," Juno answered.

"Not that it matters," Gail told her. "I don't think they know anything, anyway."

"Yeah, I think we do," Bernie told her.

Juno folded her arms across her chest. "Then tell us," she challenged.

"That's what I'm trying to do," Libby said.

"Go on," Gail goaded.

"Okay. This is what happened. You were both pissed off at Jack Devlin for his generally piggish behavior. That brought you together and

361

you got to talking about revenge. How could you get back at him? That was the question because he certainly deserved it. Then you had an idea. The reenactment was coming up and you saw it as a God-given opportunity to kill him and make it look like an accident. That was plan number one."

Libby turned to Gail. "But what if that didn't work? What if the police decided it was murder? Then what? You decided to let your husband take the fall."

"And why would I do that?" Gail asked.

"Because you really don't like him. Despite what you told me, he's a pretty jealous guy and the whole open marriage thing wasn't working out so well for you."

"That's not true," Gail said.

Bernie took a sip of champagne. "It must have been hard being married to someone like that. Someone who follows your every move." She gestured to Juno. "That's another thing you two have in common."

Gail blinked. "Rick's a control freak, but there are worse things to be."

"I bet he always wanted to watch," Bernie hypothesized.

Gail gasped. "Who told you that?"

"No one," Bernie said.

"Then how do you know?"

Bernie took another sip of her champagne.

"An educated guess. It's kind of like having your cake and eating it, too."

Gail shuddered. "It gave me the willies."

"I can imagine. He didn't approve of your going it alone with Devlin, did he?"

Gail didn't say anything.

"So killing Devlin was an efficient way to take care of both problems," Bernie observed. "A two for one shot, if you'll pardon the bad pun."

"Would you like to hear how you went about it?" Libby asked.

Juno cocked her head. She'd regained her composure. "By all means. I'm fascinated."

"With pleasure. Either you or Gail got a musket from the gun club."

"How did we do that?" Gail demanded. "They're under lock and key and would be missed."

"Simple," Libby said. In the interval between speaking to Clyde and arriving at Juno's, she had rethought her idea and made a few phone calls. "First, you went to the costume store, rented another musket, and substituted it for a real gun at the gun club. Then you took one of the muskets from the shed and swapped it out for the real gun."

"Wouldn't someone at the club have noticed?" Gail asked.

"Not unless a guest came by and tried to use it," Bernie answered. "The chances of that were pretty slim because the club doesn't get many guests. Granted, it was a chance, but it was a chance you were prepared to take."

"And then what?" Juno asked Libby.

"That's where you came into play," Libby told her. "The big question was how to get Devlin to take the musket. That's the question that's been bothering me, but you had it figured out."

"And how did I do that?" Juno taunted. "Magic?"

"Suggestion. It was ingenious really. You spoke to Devlin and warned him that someone was out to get him, probably Elise Montague."

Juno flinched and Libby knew she'd gotten it right.

"But you reassured him and told him not to worry, that you'd take care of everything. You'd mark the musket so he'd know which one was safe."

"Is that it?" Juno asked.

"No. There's more," Libby said. "You got to thinking. How were you going to make sure he got it? The only way that you could see was if you handed it to him yourself. But you were supposed to be up in the rose garden. Then you had another idea. You and Gail would switch places. No one outside the circle would know. To anyone in the distance, all people wearing fairy wings would look pretty much the same."

She turned back to Gail. "You should have gotten rid of those wings in the back of the

Infiniti or at least covered them up all the way. In any case, Juno came down and handed Devlin the real musket from the gun club. She then hid the prop left over after Marvin had set the muskets on the bench. I'm guessing it was in a bag that she had put in a trash can by the shed. When everyone was gone, she got it and put it up in the rafters, after which she went back to the rose garden and you and Juno switched places again. You went home and she waited for Devlin's gun to go off."

"Are you done?" Juno asked.

"Pretty much," Libby said. "Did I cover everything? Is there anything else you want to add?"

"Not really," Juno said. "This whole scheme seems pretty elaborate to me. Why did Gail and I do this together?"

Bernie jumped in with the answer. "Because this way, you supplied each other with alibis." She looked at Juno and Gail. "So do we have it right?"

Gail favored Libby with a *how-stupid-are-you* look. "I didn't set Rick up. Not at all. But once he realized what had happened, he tried to deflect the blame onto Marvin and when that wasn't working, he copped to it. The whole thing was his decision, not mine. He loves me. He'll do anything for me."

"I guess that makes him stupid, considering how you feel about him," Bernie observed.

"I guess it does." Gail had a smug smile on her face.

Juno's eyes narrowed. "Will you shut up," she hissed at Gail.

"No. You shut up," Gail snapped back. "Don't you get it? It doesn't matter what we say. There is no proof."

"We have the rifle," Bernie pointed out.

"So what," Gail said. "We wiped it clean."

Juno dropped her head into her hands and groaned. "I can't believe you said that."

"Neither can I," Rick said as he stepped through the gate with Clyde close behind him.

"You told me Devlin had raped you," Rick said, advancing on Gail. "That's why I did what I did."

Bernie looked at Gail. All the color had drained from her face.

"He d-did," Gail stammered. "I s-swear it."

"You've been lying to me all this time," Rick snarled. "I can't believe that you were the one who turned me in to the police."

"No. No, I haven't. I swear." Gail was breathing fast.

Rick balled up his fists and took another step closer. "You had me cover for you. You had me shoot at poor Marvin. You had me almost put Marvin in jail."

Gail shook her head. "He's crazy," she said to Clyde. "He doesn't know what he's talking about."

"I loved you." A small trickle of spit ran down Rick's chin. "I would have done anything for you. Anything."

Gail held out her arms. "I know baby, I know," she crooned.

"No," Rick said. "It's way too late for that."

"It's not," Gail pleaded. "We can go back to the way it was."

"You bitch," Rick yelled.

Before Bernie knew what was happening, he yanked the musket out of her hands. "Wait," she cried. But it was too late.

Rick raised the musket, released the safety, and fired at his wife.

She screamed and fell down, but there was no blood.

Bernie grabbed the musket from Rick. "Did you really think it was loaded with real shot? It's a prop gun. How stupid do you think I am?"

Juno sighed. "Evidently not as stupid as we are."

Chapter 41

Three days later, after all the hubbub had died down, Bernie, Libby, Marvin, and Hilda were eating a late lunch in the Deitrich Rose Garden. It was two-thirty in the afternoon. Aside from the five volunteer gardeners from the Longely

Garden Association, the quartet had the place to themselves. Bernie and Libby had packed Brie and Black Forest ham sandwiches on multigrain baguettes, spicy fennel slaw, apricots, plums, peaches, and a selection of cookies for everyone.

"Should she be eating that?" Marvin asked, indicating Hilda who was consuming her sandwich with a great deal of pleasure.

"Sure, why not? Pigs eat everything." Bernie stroked Hilda's back. "I wish we could keep her."

"Where?" Libby demanded.

"In the house," Bernie said.

Libby rolled her eyes. "There's barely enough room for us."

Bernie ate a spoonful of slaw. "You can housebreak them, you know."

"That is not the issue," Libby replied.

Marvin broke in. "What is going to happen to her?"

Libby answered. "We found a sanctuary for her, so she'll go there."

"But she's used to people," Marvin objected.

Libby shrugged. "It's the best we can do."

Marvin scratched under Hilda's chin. She oinked her approval. "She is very sweet."

"You have room. You should take her," Libby said.

"My dad would kill me." Marvin broke off a

piece of his sandwich and fed it to Hilda who had already finished her own.

"Maybe you should get your own place," Libby suggested. "Then it wouldn't be a problem."

Hilda leaned into Marvin.

"What about Juno's husband? Can't he keep her?" Marvin asked, conspicuously ignoring Libby's suggestion.

Bernie laughed. "Chuck? Are you kidding? He'd just as soon send Hilda to the slaughterhouse. Seriously, I think you should get a place. I know one that's coming up soon on Apple Street. It would be perfect. They even have a backyard."

"They probably won't take a pig," Marvin said.

"The guy moving out has two Burmese pythons, an anaconda, and a monitor lizard. I don't think Hilda is going to be a problem," Bernie informed him.

Marvin finished the last bite of his sandwich. "I'll think about it."

Libby snorted.

"What does that mean?" Marvin asked.

"It means you won't," Libby answered. "You keep saying you'll move out, but you don't."

Bernie sighed and took a bite of her sandwich. "Poor Hilda. All alone with just other pigs for company. She'll waste away from loneliness. They'll probably give her slop to eat."

Marvin fidgeted with his collar. "I'm sorry I brought Hilda up."

Libby frowned. "Okay."

The silence that followed lasted longer than it should have.

"Are you mad at me?" Marvin finally asked Libby.

"Why should I be?" she asked in a voice that would freeze ice.

There was another moment of silence. Then Marvin said, "This isn't about the pig, is it?"

"Not totally," Libby allowed.

"It's just . . ."

"Just what, Marvin?" Libby snapped.

"Nothing." He reached over, grabbed a plum, and began to eat it. "You really are angry, aren't you?"

"What I am is no concern of yours," Libby told him.

Another moment of silence went by.

"Okay."

"Okay, what?" Libby asked him.

"You know."

"No, I don't."

"I'll do it."

"Do what?"

"I'll get a place."

"Don't do it on my account," Libby said.

"No no. It's time."

"Seriously?" Libby asked.

Marvin nodded. "Seriously."

She beamed and gave him a great big hug and kiss. "That's great."

Bernie looked down at Hilda. "See. You're getting a new home."

Hilda oinked and went back to eating a cookie she'd managed to weasel out of the hamper.

The trio finished their sandwiches and drank the iced Sumatra blend coffee that Libby had brewed earlier in the day.

"It's a good thing that musket wasn't loaded," Marvin said as he wiped his hands on a napkin.

"It certainly was," Bernie replied.

"Did you know it wasn't?" Marvin asked.

"Of course I did," Bernie lied. She'd assumed that it wouldn't be.

Marvin snagged a peach. "So what's happening to everyone?"

"According Clyde, Juno and Gail are going to be tried for Devlin's death. Rick Evans agreed to testify against them so he's copped a plea for obstruction of justice. If he gets six months, it will be a lot."

"Even though he shot at me?" Marvin asked.

"He didn't hit you," Libby pointed out.

"But he could have," Marvin said.

"But he didn't," Bernie replied.

Marvin leaned over, took two French macaroons, gave one to Hilda, and took a bite of the other one. "What I don't understand, is why Rick implicated me in the first place? What did I ever do to him?"

"Nothing," Libby told him. "Absolutely nothing.

But when he saw Devlin, he realized what his wife had done, and he panicked. At that point, he thought she still loved him."

"So he didn't have a clue?" Marvin asked.

Libby shook her head. "Nope. Not an inkling. You were the nearest person so he tried to throw the blame on you. Then he felt guilty and tried to undo what he'd done by shooting at you, but that backfired and had the opposite effect."

"Whose idea was all this?" Marvin asked.

Bernie took a nibble of one of the brownies. "Juno says it was Gail's and Gail says it was Juno's. It doesn't really matter because they're both equally guilty."

Libby took another sip of coffee and watched a beetle alight on the pink petal of a Sweetheart Rose. The beetle's shell, green and blue, shimmered in the summer sun.

"I guess there aren't going to be any more reenactments in Longely for a while," Bernie said.

"I wouldn't suppose so." Libby reached for the last remaining French macaroon.

For the next half an hour, they sat there enjoying the peace and quiet, while Hilda dozed under the bench.

RECIPES

Most of the recipes seem to fall into two distinct groups—salads and desserts, although there's one for chicken marinade, as well.

These first two recipes are from Walter Tono. He's part Bolivian, part Japanese, and a great cook. These recipes don't have exact measurements but they are very forgiving and always seem to come out well no matter what proportions are used.

Bolivian Potato Salad

5 large potatoes
8 carrots
½ pound fresh peas, shelled
4–5 eggs
½ cup fresh parsley
Mayonnaise
Salt and pepper, to taste

Peel the potatoes and boil until done. Then dice.
Peel the carrots and boil until done. Then dice.
Shell the peas. Boil until done. Then strain.
Hard-boil the eggs. Allow to cool and dice.
Finely chop the parsley.
Make sure everything has cooled down. Mix all ingredients and add enough mayonnaise to bind. Season with salt and pepper to taste. Try it. In this case, the whole is definitely better than its parts.

Walter Tono's Chicken Marinade

This makes a great grilled chicken. I should know because I've had it repeatedly.

Two chopped garlic cloves
Vinegar
Oil
Salt and Pepper
Cumin
⅓ bottle lite beer
Yellow chili paste (Aji Amarillo. Goya has it.)

Combine ingredients and marinate chicken for at least two hours. Can be marinated longer if desired.

Maybe My Mother's Carrot-Raisin Salad

This salad is from my daughter-in-law Betsy Baum Block, an ex-Texan who now resides in California.

I grew up with a mother who didn't love cooking, who cooked because she was supposed to, and left behind a legacy of stories of her kitchen failures and unusual and fabulous moments of her kitchen glories (like homemade bread). I've managed to thieve most of my mother's cookbooks from my dad's house since she passed away many years ago, but the carrot-raisin salad that was ubiquitous at my family summer holiday gatherings was nowhere to be found. My dad searched her card catalogue of recipes; then I spoke to my first aunt, who claimed she actually hated carrots; and my other aunt, who reminisced over how she loved the salad and counted on my mother to always make it . . . but no one had the recipe. It couldn't be that difficult—shredded carrots, mayo, and raisins. And it wouldn't take that long, as my mom rarely made things that required more than five minutes of preparation.

Lucky for me, the Internet provided me with Luby's Cafeteria version of the recipe (with crushed pineapple) as well as an updated version (with ginger and cinnamon) by one of my favorite bloggers, The Homesick Texan. I've tested these and offer up my version here. Experiment and enjoy: The only critical ingredients are the three I most remember, combined to your liking and sweetened a bit.

Ingredients

1 10-ounce bag of shredded carrots
1 cup raisins, soaked in warm water to plump. Drain well.
⅓ cup powdered sugar (optional, but I prefer the slight sweetness)
½ cup mayonnaise

Variation 1: Add 1 8-ounce can crushed or diced pineapple, drained well.
Variation 2: Add juice from one orange (or 2 tablespoons orange juice), ½ teaspoon cinnamon, ¼ teaspoon ginger.

Combine all ingredients in a bowl and mix well. Serve.

Now we come to the desserts.

Jim Burtless's Strawberry Sparkle Cake

Jim comes from Aurelius, New York. This recipe has been in his family for seventy years. It's always made on the Fourth of July.

Ingredients

1 package Duncan Hines Angel Food cake mix
1 cup boiling water
1 package (3 oz.) strawberry-flavored gelatin
1 package (1 lb.) frozen sliced strawberries
½ pint (1 cup) whipping cream
2 tablespoon sugar
Red food coloring

Bake angel food cake as directed on back of package and cool.

Dissolve gelatin in water and add frozen block of strawberries. Stir to break up and mix berries.

Place cake, widest side down, on a serving board. Cut one-inch layer from the top and set aside. Cut around cake one inch from inner edge to one inch from bottom. Gently remove the section of cake between cuts, tearing it into small pieces. Fold pieces into strawberry mixture and pour it into cake shell. Place the set-aside cake on top.

Whip cream until thick, stir in sugar, and add a few drops of red food coloring until the whipped cream is pink. Spread sweetened whipped cream over top and sides of cake. Decorate with whole strawberries, if desired.

Refrigerate at least one hour before serving.

Best Blueberry Pie

This recipe is from Barbara Beckos, an excellent cook and good friend.

Crust

1 cup flour
2 tablespoons sugar
Dash salt
5½ tablespoons unsalted chilled butter cut into small pieces
2–3 tablespoons ice water

Filling and Streusel topping

1 cup sour cream (can use light sour cream if desired)
6 tablespoons flour
¾ cup sugar
1 teaspoon vanilla extract
¼ teaspoon salt
1 egg, lightly beaten
3 cups stemmed blueberries
½ cup pecans
¼ cup unsalted butter

To prepare crust

Place flour, sugar, salt, and butter pieces in food processor. Process, pulsing on and off until the mixture resembles flakes.

With machine running add 2 tablespoons ice water through feed tube and process until ball of dough forms. If mixture seems dry, add remaining tablespoon ice water.

Form dough into flat round disk approximately 6 inches wide and wrap in plastic. Refrigerate for 30 minutes or longer.

Roll out dough on floured board into 11-inch circle.

Ease dough into 9-inch tart pan or pie plate. If using tart pan, press dough firmly into fluted sides. If using pie plate, crimp folded dough at top of sides.

Pastry crust can be prepared ahead and refrigerated for one day or frozen. Cover tightly with plastic wrap. If dough is frozen, defrost in refrigerator before using.

To prepare filling and pecan streusel topping

Combine sour cream, 2 tablespoons flour, sugar, vanilla extract, salt, and egg in mixing bowl. When batter is smooth, carefully stir in blueberries.

Spoon filling into pastry shell and smooth top with spatula.

Place 4 tablespoons flour, pecans, and butter in cleaned food processor and pulse into small bits. Set aside.

Place pie in center of oven and bake at 400 degrees for 25 minutes.

Remove from oven and sprinkle topping evenly over top of pie.

Continue baking pie at 400 degrees for another 10 minutes until topping is slightly browned.

Cool pie to room temperature. Chill for 6-8 hours. Remove from fridge a few hours before serving.

Center Point Large Print
600 Brooks Road / PO Box 1
Thorndike ME 04986-0001 USA

(207) 568-3717

US & Canada:
1 800 929-9108
www.centerpointlargeprint.com